PLAYING GAMES

Franklin U #1

Riley Hart

Copyright © 2022 by Riley Hart
Print Edition

All rights reserved.

No part of this book may be used, reproduced, or transmitted in any form or by any means, electronic or mechanical, including photocopying, recording, or by any information storage and retrieval systems, without prior written permission of the author, except where permitted by law.

Published by:
Riley Hart

This book is a work of fiction. Names, characters, places, and incidents are products of the author's imagination or are used fictitiously. Any similarity to actual persons, living or dead, is coincidental and not intended by the author.

All products/brand names/trademarks mentioned are registered trademarks of their respective holders/companies.

Cover Design by Natasha Snow
Cover Image by Michelle Lancaster
Edited by Keren Reed Editing
Proofread by Judy's Proofreading, Karen Meeus, and Lyrical Lines Proofreading

Brax

Tyson Langley thinks the *king* in Franklin University Kings is in reference to him. Star lacrosse player and God's gift to the female *and* male population, there's nothing the spoiled jock can't have.

It's impossible for us to be in the same room without talking crap to each other. But I also have a secret... As much as I despise Ty, I want him too. I revel in our banter and in never knowing what he'll say next.

I've spent too much time on the wrong side of the law for someone like Ty, though, and if I want to make it through college and escape my past, he's a distraction I don't need.

Ty

Braxton Walker needs to learn to lighten up. If you search *brooding* online, his name pops up. He's the bad boy with a leather jacket and a scowl. We couldn't be more different.

Finding ways to annoy him is like the longest foreplay session of my life. And when we end up working together, it gets harder to deny how hot he makes me.

What's a little hooking up between enemies?

We weren't supposed to become friends or share secrets. We weren't supposed to understand each other and all the complicated stuff we're going through.

I'm used to playing games, only the more time I spend with Brax, the less it feels like playing around and the more it becomes something real.

CHAPTER ONE

Braxton

"**H**ELL YEAH, MOTHERFUCKERS!"

My gaze darted toward the door of Shenanigans, the local bar close to the Franklin University campus. I'd known the voice without looking, so I wasn't sure why I had. What kind of person had to announce their arrival so loudly and obnoxiously, like they were a gift to the fucking world?

Tyson Langley, of course.

Nearly everyone's attention snagged on him. I hated that mine did too. Unlike the others, I didn't like the guy, didn't pray to the spoiled little lacrosse god because he was gorgeous, cocky, and had a rich daddy. But I had to admit, he *was* hot, which just pissed me off. I hated sports, hated jocks and the way people worshipped them. Why did I also have to find them so damned sexy?

This wasn't the first time, and I feared it wouldn't be the last.

It was annoying as shit.

"Hey, man. You ready for the season?" a guy asked Ty as he made his way toward the counter. It was January, and they hadn't even played their first game yet. The only reason I knew was because it would be all over campus, and the team often landed at Shenanigans as their place to celebrate. Being within walking distance of campus made it convenient.

When it came to sports, there were two at FU that everyone lost their collective shit over—lacrosse and football. The former, mostly because of Tyson Langley, and the latter, due to Peyton Miller. Apparently, Peyton's two dads had both played in the NFL or something. I didn't pay enough attention to know. I had too much going on to care.

"Bro, can I get a beer?" asked a guy wearing a Franklin University tank.

"Yep," I replied. "What do you want?"

"Cheapest," he answered. *You and me both, man. You and me both.*

I checked his wristband. Shenanigans was an

eighteen-and-older bar—Oscar, the owner, had wanted to make sure he could capitalize on all the FU students—though only those of age could drink. For alcohol you had to have a wristband, which they gave you at the door—different colors for each night. Tonight was light blue with little suns on it. Oscar liked to shake things up. I thought it was dumb, but what did I know?

I grabbed him a bottle, handed it over, and took his payment, wishing I was anywhere but there. I had a shit ton of homework to do. I had to have B's or better to keep my scholarships and not get tossed out of school on my ass.

I made a few drinks as Ty and his friends laughed and talked shit, being loud as hell, like they always were.

I'd just given margaritas to a few girls when I heard, "Braxton Walker...do you ever smile?"

Fuck my life. I looked at him and crossed my arms. "Tyson Langley, do you ever shut up?" I didn't know why he insisted on trying to talk to me. We were both computer science majors and had a lot of classes together, but we weren't friends. We never would be, and as far as I could tell, he was on the same page. He just liked to get under my skin. And like everything else in his life, he got his way with that too.

"Now is that any way to talk to your favorite customer?"

"You're not my favorite shit," I replied. He bit back a laugh, and I rolled my eyes. Of course he would take it that way.

"Did you do your Ethics in Computing homework?"

My brows pulled together. What the fuck was he playing at? "No." I hadn't done it, but I would.

"Oh, I got it finished early." He puffed his chest out smugly.

If I had more time, I'd be done too. But between school, my TA hours for my scholarships, and my job, I was busy. I'd looked into entry-level jobs in my field, but companies paid shit until you had a degree. I made more bartending because of the tips. Next year, I'd have to do a co-op, but I'd cross that bridge when I came to it.

"Unlike you," I told Ty, "some of us have to actually work on top of going to school. They're called jobs, and it's what I'm doing right now."

Was it me, or did he flinch? Ty trained his blue eyes on me again. "Want me to give you the answers?"

"Fuck no. I don't want to fail." *Stop talking to him. Walk away.* I didn't know how he had this power over me. With anyone else I would have told them to suck my dick and left, but with Ty, I kept it going, wanting to see how far we would take it, always needing the last word.

"Aren't guys like you not supposed to care about stuff like grades?" He cocked a brow.

The hairs on the back of my neck stood on end. "Guys like me? Do explain."

He waved his hand, motioning up and down my body. "The black hair…leather jacket…permanent scowl. You're basically the cliché bad boy in every teen show. All you're missing are the tattoos. I heard Remy at Indelible Ink is good."

I couldn't help it; a loud laugh jumped out of my mouth. "First, fuck off. Second, and you're not a cliché? Rich boy jock, check. Blond hair, check." He shook it out of his eyes. It was messy, longer on top but shorter underneath, the strands flying every which way and flopping onto his forehead. "Blue eyes, check. Asshole, check."

"Oh, ouch." Ty grabbed his heart. "And here I thought you liked me."

I leaned over the counter, mouth close to his ear. I breathed in, the scent of his cologne invading my senses. Somehow he *smelled* like a jock. Did jocks have a scent? Ty did, like grass, fresh air, and physical exertion. "You. Wish." And then, because I didn't give a fuck what anyone thought of me, especially him, I swiped my tongue out and licked his earlobe before pulling back.

Ty jerked away, his pupils blown wide in a look I couldn't read. "What the fuck, man? I don't know where your tongue has been."

"And you never will, Lacrosse."

"Thank fuck for that."

"Why don't you go play with your friends and let the adults do grown-up stuff."

"Whatever, Sunshine," he countered.

"Yikes. That one hurt."

"Yo! Ty! Get your ass over here!" one of his jockholes called just as I heard, "Bartender, can I get a drink?"

Ty gave me a smirk and a wink before walking away.

I made drinks as Shenanigans got busier. When my gaze found his, he was touching his earlobe where I'd licked him, and damned if it didn't make me smile.

IT WAS ALMOST three in the morning when I slowed my motorcycle down in front of the house my brother, Asher, and I had lived in on and off with our grandma for most of our life. Dad had lived there too sometimes, but he was always coming and going, in and out of jail, currently incarcerated. Gram had moved into an assisted-living facility a few months earlier. She was one of my favorite people in the world, so I was still getting used to that.

Asher, on the other hand, was taking advantage of it the way he did most things. He was exactly like our dad that way.

The driveway was packed with cars, some spilling down the street. Muffled music from inside drifted on the salty air. Grandpa had bought the house in the eighties. It had been his and Grandma's dream to have a place in San Luco, not far from San Diego. Now, neither of them was around to enjoy it, Grandpa having died fifteen years earlier.

I was still on edge from my run-in with Ty. He'd ended up going home with some chick. It was always a toss-up for him—girl or guy—and tonight it had been a blonde. He'd licked her ear while looking at me, the fucker.

I drove onto the lawn and around back because I didn't trust any of the drunk-ass people inside not to hit my ride when they left. I'd worked my ass off, fixing it up. My Harley Sportster was my baby.

I pushed the kickstand down and turned it off. I was tired as shit and wanted nothing more than to go to bed, but I needed to get some schoolwork done. Either option would likely be impossible. Clearly, the party wasn't dying down anytime soon.

The moment I entered the kitchen through the back door, I saw a few guys holding my brother's legs in the air while he did a keg stand, because of fucking course he was. Asher was two years older than me, but you'd never know it.

The house was packed, some of them chanting

chug, chug, chug as Asher drank. The scent of weed tickled my nostrils, mixed with sweat, alcohol, and maybe puke. Typical night at the Walker house.

When they flipped Asher back onto his feet, he stumbled slightly, hand out to hold on to the wall so he didn't fall, before his gaze caught mine. "Braxton! My little fucking brother is home. Someone get drink him…get him a drink… Did I say that right?"

I cocked a brow. "You're an idiot." I had to speak loudly so he could hear me over the music and the people.

"You're an idiot."

"Shut up."

"Shut up."

"How old are you?"

"How old are—"

"Jesus fucking Christ, Asher." I was surrounded by morons all the time, which immediately made me think of Ty. It made sense because he was a dumbass, but I also wanted him out of my head. He took up entirely too much space there. It sucked wanting to have sex with someone you hated. My dick needed to get with the program, but when it came to jocks, I seemed to lose my head. Well, one other time I had, at least.

Someone shoved a red Solo cup at me, beer sloshing all over my shirt. "Hi, you're hot." The girl who'd gotten me the drink gave me a smile.

"He likes dick," Asher told her. *My brother, ladies and gentlemen.* What a tool. But he was also correct.

"I have a strap-on," she replied.

My fucking life. "It's not quite the same thing. Dick is great, but it's not the body part so much as the fact that I like men."

"Ugh. All the hot ones do." I took the cup from her, and she walked away.

"Drink up, buddy," Asher said. A body slammed into his, making him bump into me, more beer spilling.

"I just worked all night, and I have a shit ton of homework this weekend. You said you wouldn't have a party."

"See…I didn't plan it…but then it happened…and I was drunk, so I forgot… Love you, brother!" With that gem of a parting shot, my brother turned and called out, "Hey, strap-on girl!"

I dropped my head back and sighed, then dumped the beer and went straight for my bedroom. I used my key to unlock it because I sure as shit didn't trust anyone not to come in and fuck with my stuff.

I walked over to my bed, the frame squeaking when I fell onto it. My walls vibrated with the music, punctuated by hoots and hollers.

I could go out there and party with them, find some guy and bring him back to my room so we could spend the rest of the night getting lost in each other's bodies. The thought was tempting, but instead I grabbed my backpack off the floor and pulled my books and laptop out. No way I'd get any sleep, so I might as well do something productive.

CHAPTER TWO

Ty

IT WAS REALLY inconvenient that I wanted to bone Braxton Walker.

I mean, he was hot, yeah, but he also had a stick shoved so far up his ass it sprouted out of his mouth. Typically, I was a fan of things in asses because fuck, it felt good, but he'd almost ruined that for me with his holier-than-thou attitude, all while blaming me for the same thing. I didn't know what he had against me, but from the first time we saw each other, he'd looked at me like I'd kicked his puppy.

And maybe it shouldn't, but the constant back and forth between us made me hotter for him. It was like we'd been engaged in a three-year foreplay session. In one way or another, he'd been edging me since we were freshmen. At first simply because he was so good-looking, and I couldn't help admiring that. Things kicked up a notch at the beginning of our junior year this past August, when he'd started working at Shenanigans. We'd had a shit ton of classes together before, but we didn't start the verbal fucking until he got the job and we saw each other outside of class. I guessed the different atmosphere changed things between us, gave us this space to let loose on each other.

I'd had sex with a beautiful woman last night after leaving the bar, and today I'd just kicked ass at lacrosse practice, and yet when I rubbed one out in the shower, I thought about him licking my ear… And now, while my friends were playing *Madden*, I was *still* thinking about him.

I couldn't imagine what I would do if he knew how frequently he made an appearance in my fantasies.

"What the fuck, Langley? Where's the beer?"

It was my turn to buy it. We had a rotation on who bought what and when. This was the first year three of my teammates and I had managed to get a place in Liberty Court, the shared-house district on campus, where each place was named after past FU deans. We were in Adler House. There was also Freidman, Mundell, and Stormer, the latter known as the stoner house. An adorable twink named Felix lived in Freidman. We hadn't gotten together, and even though I wasn't his type—big—he flirted with me all the time. He'd sometimes give me a playful wave while he sat on the roof of their house, which made me jealous AF because we didn't have a two-story like they did.

"I've been too busy to go shopping," I yelled at Ford, one of our defensemen. This would be the third year the group of us played lacrosse together. They were my boys. My freshman year, I told them I was bisexual, and none of them had batted an eye. We played the game together and partied together. I'd always been told these would be the best years of my life, so I was trying to soak that shit up while I could. One and a half more years, and I'd be doing a job I hated with a man I'd idolized my whole fucking life only to discover he was nothing but a fraud.

I wasn't going to go there today, though. Nope. I was mostly doing well pretending my dad didn't exist and that my new self-imposed money problems wouldn't become an issue. Because I wasn't going to let myself take any more cash from him, wasn't going to use my credit cards or let him pay me off. His money had always been able to get him what he wanted, but it wouldn't with me.

"We have like, no food," Ford said from the kitchen. "What's up with that? We're growing boys. I need some chips or something." Ford came back in and plopped down on the couch. The guy could eat all day, every day. I should probably do some shopping, but I was trying to preserve the cash I had in my account.

I had no idea what the hell I was going to do. My tuition and housing were paid through the year, but what about the next one? What about random shit that popped up along the way? All I knew was, I'd figure it out because I sure wasn't having anything to do with Montgomery Langley, not until I absolutely had to. Not after finding out I had a brother, Perry, a year younger than me. A brother he'd known about but never told us…and that little bombshell leading to the fact that since then, he'd been cheating on my mom, *again*. That he and his new *girlfriend* had a one-year-old daughter. And then he left Mom to be with them.

"Hello? You in there, Langley?" Collins flicked my ear.

"What the fuck?"

"You were spacing out," Collins replied.

Aaand, definitely time to change the subject. I wasn't going to risk them asking what was up, but the truth was, I didn't know that they would anyway. It wasn't something we did. They didn't pay attention to shit like that, and I liked it that way.

"Gimme that." I pulled the controller out of Collins's hand. "Let me show you assholes how it's done."

As I'd hoped, they immediately forgot about me getting lost in my head, instead talking shit while I kicked their asses at the game.

Watty, whose real last name was Watson, said, "Speaking of pricks, was Asshole Bartender giving you shit again?" That was their nickname for Braxton, so clearly, I wasn't the only one who thought he was a dick.

"Yeah, what the fuck is his problem?" Ford added.

I shrugged. "Nothin'. It's just a thing." I wasn't going to tell them I liked it more than I should.

We chilled for a couple of hours. When my phone buzzed on the coffee table, *Dad* lighting up on the screen, I bit back a groan and scooped up my cell. Watty and Collins were currently playing. Ford was looking in the fridge and cabinets again like he expected food to have magically appeared since the last time he looked. "Be right back," I told them.

They didn't pay me much attention as I slipped out the door and into the quad area in Liberty Court. There were barbecue grills, hammocks, picnic tables, and a fountain between the white, Spanish-style houses matching the school building. I eyed the cactus and palm trees in the area.

When I didn't answer soon enough, he called right back. When Montgomery Langley phoned, you picked up. I'd always respected that about him, the way he'd commanded everyone's attention. Now it made my skin crawl.

"Hold on," I said, walking out of the quad and around a building. I didn't want to risk anyone hearing me. It was early evening, the sun already having gone down, the air a cool midfifties, which was basically the coolest it ever got here. I loved that about Southern California. "What?" I asked.

"I don't know who you think you are, Tyson, but it has never been okay to talk to me that way, and it never will be."

"You don't get to do that. You don't get to dictate how I spend my life anymore." Not after twenty-one years of lying to me. Lying to Mom.

"What's going on between me and your mother has nothing to do with you."

"The fuck it doesn't!" I said too loudly, a few people walking by looking my way. "I have a brother and a sister you never told me about! One of them is twenty years old! Hell, for all I know, there could be more. I *respected* you. I thought you loved me, but you were lying the whole time. You threw fake-affection and money at me while paying off my brother's mom so no one would know about him. I'm sure you did the same with your new girlfriend before she made you come clean." His whole life, he'd been able to get away with whatever he wanted by offering to write another check. Hell, even I'd ignored signs that he might not be who I thought he was, and every time he'd distract me with some kind of gift. I wasn't doing that anymore.

"I won't have you talk to me that way."

"Then don't call me."

He sighed. "You do know that if you take money

from your mom, that's also money from me. Let's just…put this behind us. You're still my son. We'll get past this. You'll finish your last year and a half of school, then come home and work with me—"

"No," I cut him off.

"How do you expect to survive? Outside of school and sports, you've never had to work for anything a day in your life." Jesus, what was up with people telling me that? First, Braxton last night, and now my dad. "You have a lifestyle you're used to keeping. Stop playing games, Tyson. What are you going to do when your tuition is due? If you think I'm going to let you treat me like shit and then come through next year, you're wrong. And please tell me you're being discreet about our little issues." His cash and name had solved that problem too.

Because that was all he thought about—money. It was all he expected me to think about too, and…well, I couldn't say I blamed him. I was quite fond of spending it. I *was* used to a certain lifestyle, but… "I don't want your money, and I don't want to talk to you."

I ended the call and tried not to wonder about the brother I'd never met and the sister I'd only seen once. About the pain he'd caused them and my mom.

Loud laughter came from the direction of Adler House, and I looked up to see my friends coming out. "We need some fucking food, Langs," Ford said. "We're heading out to eat."

I wasn't stupid enough to give back the money I already had, but I was determined to stop myself from taking more money from him. If I did, he had me. I'd be stuck depending on him. My dad liked it that way.

I was going to need to get a job...and soon.

Fuck.

WE WALKED TO our favorite taco stand on the pier. It was a popular hangout area, and they had tables and chairs out front and along the promenade. I got three tacos because Ford was right. We were growing boys and all. I had to eat.

We met a few girls from campus and hung out with them until about nine, when everyone decided to hit up Shenanigans again.

An electric current zipped up my spine before I stamped that shit out. There was no reason for me to be excited to possibly see Braxton and talk shit to him again. I had a million other things to be concerned with.

"You guys going to take us to the championship this year?" Krista, I thought her name was, asked. "The football team did, but then, they have Peyton."

"Peyton who?" I joked. Peyton Miller and I had this frenemies-rivals thing going on because we were both the best at our sports. I was way hotter, though.

"Ha-ha," Krista replied.

"Also, fuck yes, we are. Is that really a question when the team has us?"

Watty, Collins, and Ford cheered, ass and back-slapping me as we made our way to the bar.

One thing I loved about the area around campus was that everything was within walking distance. We had the beach across the street, the pier farther down, and Shenanigans between that and the school.

"I'm freezing my balls off," Watty said. "I didn't grab a hoodie."

"It's like fifty," I countered, playfully trying to trip him.

"You East Coasters can handle this weather. I'm a SoCal boy for life, and my ass needs a fucking hoodie if it's under sixty." We all laughed. I pulled mine off and gave it to him, which prompted Watty's, "Aw, are you asking me out? I don't swing that way, but I might be willing for you."

My friends were fucking idiots. "You're not hot enough for me."

"Dude, Langs just called you ugly," Collins teased.

"Why are boys so dumb?" Krista asked.

Moments like this, I could almost forget all the other shit going on in my life, but it was still there, waiting for the perfect time to spring out.

We got to Shenanigans. The building was hella old, aged by the weather, but it had four walls and alcohol, so who cared? Oscar, the owner, did get a new paint job last year, but the white was already slightly dirty.

"What up, man?" I asked the guy at the door.

"What's up?" We showed him our IDs, and he gave us daisy wristbands.

I hated myself for it, but the second I stepped inside, my gaze went straight to the bar to see if Sunshine was there.

It was busy as hell, especially considering how early it was. The counter was surrounded by people, but it didn't take me more than a second to spot him pouring vodka into a glass. He had on a black T-shirt that was tight across his chest. I couldn't see his jeans, but I assumed they were the same color since they typically were. He wore them slightly loose so they hung below the band on his underwear, which I saw and maybe drooled over when he stretched in class. So sue me.

He looked tired tonight, even as he was laughing at something a guy said. Braxton wore rings on more than one finger, a chain bracelet, and a necklace I'd never seen him without. His hair was dark as coal, and though I was sure he would never admit the truth, it was clear he spent quite a bit of time styling it every day so it stuck up in front, just the right way to look sexy as fuck, like he'd run his hands through it one too many times.

As if he sensed me there, Braxton's gaze shot in my direction, the smile sliding off his face, his strong, square jaw hardening.

I grinned.

His scowl deepened.

Fucking with him shouldn't be this fun, but I had a feeling that as much as he fought it, he felt the same.

"What are you looking at, Langs?" Ford grabbed my shoulders and squeezed.

"Nothin'."

"Wanna drink?"

"Nah, I'm good tonight." Everyone headed for a table except Ford, and I pivoted and said, "I'll help you get them."

Ford talked random shit, and I listened as we waited what felt like for-fucking-ever for it to be our turn. While my boys knew I was bi, they wouldn't get my attraction to Braxton. Hell, I didn't even get it. We were complete opposites. He made it obvious he was allergic to jocks. I didn't think he'd been to even one of the lacrosse games, and like...who didn't go to those?

All those truths did, though, was get me more keyed up.

Finally, we made it to the counter, Braxton rolling his eyes when he saw me.

Ford muttered, "Christ, maybe you guys should hire some help in here."

"Well, shit. Why didn't we think of that?" Braxton replied. "You mean, when a business is short-staffed, they should look through applications, call people in for job interviews, then hire and train someone? Do you think that takes more than a day? Asking for my boss."

I had to bite down on my cheeks so I didn't laugh.

"You don't have to be a dick," Ford replied.

"But you make it so easy," Braxton countered. "So what do you want to drink? As you see, we're busy and short-staffed. Our busboy-slash-dishwasher no-showed, so the extra bartender is going back and forth."

"So you're hiring?" I asked, two sets of eyes bearing down on me in confusion.

"Why do you care?" they asked at the same time.

"Just curious. Is there something wrong with that?" And maybe my feelings were slightly hurt because even my friend seemed shocked at the thought of me being interested in a job. I could work. I wasn't completely helpless.

"Figures," Braxton replied.

"What does that mean?"

"Nothing. I don't have time to play your game tonight, Lacrosse. What do you want?"

It was on the tip of my tongue to keep this going, to say something sarcastic, but he really did look tired, and they were busy. I wasn't a total dick, so I just ordered two pitchers of beer.

Braxton didn't make eye contact with me again, and before I knew it, Ford paid and we were walking away.

I was pretty sure I'd just found myself a job.

I had mixed feelings about that. The upsides were having my own cash coming in and more time for foreplay with Sunshine.

The downside…I'd have a *job*. But working at the bar would be better than some entry-level position in tech. I wanted to put off doing what I hated for as long as I could.

"Asshole Bartender really hates you," Ford told me.

"Gee, thanks, man." Being hated had never been so fun.

CHAPTER THREE

Braxton

"WELL, IF IT isn't my favorite person in the world." I gave Grandma my best smile as I walked into her small apartment at the assisted-living facility.

"I taught you to kiss ass better than that." She grinned, sitting in her rocking chair by the window. She was in a decent place—not the worst, but not the best. If she didn't have Grandpa's pension, it would be a whole lot shoddier. Hell, I hadn't known if we'd be able to afford somewhere for her to go at all. Plus, this was Southern California, so everything cost both arms and both legs. Still, she was looking out at palm trees even if it wasn't the beach, and the sun was always shining.

Grandma was the happiest person I'd ever known.

She was good at looking at the bright side of things in a way I'd never been able to. I tried for her, but I was basically shit at it. "I'm shocked you think that's all I have in me." I kissed her cheek before sitting in the chair beside her. "You look lovely today. Is that a new muumuu you're wearing?"

She swatted my arm with a chuckle. "You brat."

"Your favorite brat ever."

"My boy with the best head on his shoulders out of the three of you. You've always reminded me of your grandpa." By all three of us she meant me, my dad, and Asher. Dad had always gotten in trouble, from a young age, and things got even less...lawful the older he got. Once he had kids, while most people wanted better for their offspring, he'd decided he wanted us to go into the family business with him, which was basically anything illegal. Grandma had done her best to keep us from doing that, but it hadn't always worked, not even with me.

"That's where I get my good looks from." It was so much easier to talk about stuff like that than anything deeper. Also, I wasn't sure she saw me in quite a clear light, but I wasn't dumb enough to point out my flaws. I was just better at hiding them than

Dad and Asher.

"Tell me about school."

"Not much to tell. I really like my Ethics in Computing class. The professor is pretty badass. I'm not so sure about Communication for Engineering and Technology." Both of which I had with Ty. And what the fuck had that been last night? I still couldn't figure out why he'd asked if Shenanigans was hiring. He was too perfect to get his hands dirty washing dishes and busing the tables of drunk college kids like himself. How would he have time to go to class, play lacrosse, and fuck his way through the FU population if he had to work too?

"Computers. I can't believe you're going to college to work with computers. Your grandpa would be so proud." She grabbed my hand and squeezed.

"There's nothing to be proud of. It's just what people do." And it also cost a fuckload of money, which she was helping me pay. Scholarships and loans only went so far.

All I knew was, I couldn't let myself become my dad, or hell, even my brother, who vacillated between being fun to be around and being a huge asshole, same as Dad. Asher didn't have any goals outside of, well, keg stands and getting his dick wet.

"Any nice boys?" Grandma asked, making me roll my eyes.

"Nope. Just like there weren't the other times you've asked. I'm surrounded by spoiled rich kids and jocks. Besides, I'd have to like people to want to date them."

"You like people."

I really didn't. Not most of them. "Lies," I countered.

"You'll change your mind one day. You'll meet a nice boy who will drive you crazy in both good and bad ways. That's the way it was with your grandpa and me. Whew, that man could piss me off, but sometimes even the fighting was fun with him, and the making up was my favorite."

"Um…TMI." I was positive I was the only person in the world whose grandma would say that.

"You're no fun." Grandma winked. "And your brother?"

"Good. He's been busy looking for a job," I lied, making an excuse for why he hadn't been in to see her. Asher was rarely ever employed. I needed to kick his fucking ass. The only reason we'd had a seminormal childhood was because of Grandma. We lived in her house, and he couldn't come and visit? Especially when he made visiting hours often at the prison for Dad?

We talked for a little while before playing a game of Monopoly. When I yawned, Grandma said, "You're tired. That's at least the fifth time you've done that. Go home and get some rest before class tomorrow. You work too hard, Brax. You can't make up for your daddy and Asher by putting too much pressure on yourself."

Maybe I couldn't, but I didn't have it in me not to try.

THE NEXT DAY in class, I groaned when Tyson fell into the seat beside me. "Jesus, are you obsessed with me? You're like a bad itch that won't go away."

"You should consider getting that checked," he replied. "Is it…" I glanced over to see him nod toward my crotch. "You know…"

He was so ridiculous. "Fuck you. Stop trying to come up with an excuse to see my junk."

"Nah, you're not my type."

"You one hundred percent want me, Lacrosse. You can't keep your eyes off me. I bet you jerked off thinking about that one second when I licked your ear." I had too, but he wasn't going to find out about that. "I'm really good with my tongue. I can deep throat like a motherfucker, though from what I've heard, that's not hard with you."

"You wish, asshole." He palmed his dick for emphasis, and I shook my head. He was wearing track pants and a long-sleeved FU Kings Lacrosse tee. Yes, we were the FU Kings. If I were into sports, I'd be all over that shit.

"You know I'm not helping you with your work, right?" I told Tyson. "If you're trying to find someone to copy off of, it's not me."

"Have you ever, in your life, been happy?" he countered.

I didn't know what it was about that question that made my pulse stumble, but it did. "Have you ever, in your life, had to work for something instead of having your perfect daddy get it for you?"

Something unfamiliar flashed in Tyson's eyes, like a storm blowing through, making his sky-blue gaze turn dark and thunderous. But just as quickly, the clouds cleared like it had never happened at all. That was…weird, and definitely not a look I'd seen from him before.

Tyson shrugged. "Do you see my dad on the lacrosse field with me?"

"I don't know. I've never been to one of your games. I try not to do boring shit."

He laughed. "You should come. I could give you a jersey with my number on it. You could cheer for me on the sidelines, instead of looking up videos of me on social media to jerk off to afterward. It's okay if you like me, Sunshine."

"Not even if you were the last man on earth."

"Whatever you have to tell yourself."

Unfortunately, when it came to Tyson Langley, my dick wasn't on board with the rest of me. He was very much interested in getting to know Lacrosse up close and personal.

Professor Meyer came in then, so I didn't have to respond. He launched straight into a lecture.

I pulled out my computer for notes.

Tyson did the same.

I started typing.

He did too.

The more I wrote, the more he did. I sped up my fingers, and he did as well.

"Are you really trying to turn this into a competition?" I whispered.

"Oh, I'm sorry. I didn't realize you were still here. Aren't you supposed to not care about school? There should only be nerds in this scenario. Not guys who look like you, ride motorcycles, and have been arrested."

"Who's looking up whom online again?" I didn't care that he knew about my past. I wasn't proud of any of the dumb things I'd done, but I wasn't ashamed of them either. It had all been at my dad's insistence, and I hadn't done anything like that for years. Most of it had been scams Dad had tried to pull, using me and Asher as pawns. Free meals out, faked injuries, he'd made us do it all to help him get the things he wanted. The one and only time I'd been arrested for stealing was something he pushed me into doing too. "Also, what's with you and all this bad boy, nerd, whatever the fuck? You're always mentioning it. I feel like you live in a teen rom-com."

"Mr. Walker, be quiet or get out, please. If you don't want to be here, then don't," Professor Meyer said before slipping right back into his discussion. Because of course it would only be me he mentioned. Not Mr. Star Lacrosse Player. But I was used to the way the world worked.

I got back to taking notes, completely ignoring Tyson. He was a distraction I didn't need. When class was over, I shoved my shit into my bag and went for the door.

"Hey, Sunshine. Wait up," Tyson called, following me.

"Fuck you."

He fell into step with me as we walked outside. "It's not my fault Meyer is a prick."

He wasn't most of the time. I actually really liked him. "No, but it is your fault you're one."

"Takes one to know one. Pricks unite!"

Don't smile. Do not fucking smile. "There's something wrong with you." I didn't have time for this. I had class, my TA responsibilities, then work.

"I guess this isn't the best time to tell you I met up with Oscar yesterday."

I stopped dead in my tracks. No. No, no, no, no. "On a Sunday?"

"He's desperate. Most people are when it comes to me."

"Has anyone ever told you you're a conceited asshole?"

"Just you," Tyson replied. "My new coworker. Who's more than a little bit in love with me."

Fuck. My. Life. Why did he want to screw with me so much? It wasn't like he needed a job. "No matter how many times you tell yourself that, it doesn't make it true."

He looked at me, full of smugness, like he knew my dick was really interested in making his acquaintance. I hated that he could see it, that he always found a way to get me off my game. But then I remembered his reaction to my tongue meeting his earlobe...and the fact that what I had to say was also true.

So I stepped closer, like I had at Shenanigans Friday night. "I might not like you, but if I'm bored enough and you're lucky enough, I might be willing to fuck you. You know, just to do you a favor and all, since you're so obsessed with me."

I stepped back. Tyson's mouth had fallen open,

and damned if I didn't notice how kissable his lips were, if I didn't think about how they'd look stretched around my cock.

When I walked away, he didn't have anything to say. For the first time, I'd left Tyson Langley speechless. The satisfaction didn't last long because I really did want to fuck him…and now I was going to be spending even more time with him at Shenanigans.

I was so screwed.

CHAPTER FOUR

Ty

THIS WHOLE JOB thing already sucked, and I hadn't even had my first shift yet.

Today I'd only had two hours between my last class of the day and practice. Coach was working us like crazy because our first game was coming up. We were expected to be the best as we were the reigning champions from last season. And now I had to work on top of it. The good thing was, Oscar had been ready and willing to give me a job ASAP *and* work around my lacrosse schedule—something that would have been practically impossible if I'd tried for a position in tech. I couldn't pretend that accommodating me wasn't partly because of who I was. San Luco lived and breathed Kings lacrosse and football—well, everyone except Braxton, but I wasn't thinking about him. Nope. Not at all.

When I'd told Oscar my reason for needing a job was personal, he'd just nodded, asked when I could start and told me that I should provide him with my game and practice schedule each week and he'd figure it out.

I was sweaty and exhausted after practice, and now I had to rush home, shower, and get my ass to Shenanigans. Why had I thought this was a good idea again?

Oh, and I had to tell Coach and the guys. Because that wouldn't be weird at all.

"Coach, can I talk to you for a second?" I jogged over to him.

"What's up, Langley? Looking good out there. Your dad will be happy to hear it."

I forced myself not to roll my eyes. My dad was an FU alum and had donated enough money to the school that he could basically do whatever he wanted. He was one to take advantage of that too. "Thanks, sir. I'm feeling good. Ready to bring home that championship again."

"That's what I like to hear."

"Listen…I, um…" My gaze darted to Watty,

Collins, and Ford, who were chillin' close by, waiting for me. Fuck. I'd hoped they would go on without me. "I have some personal things going on, and I had to get a job. It won't get in the way of lacrosse or school. I made sure the schedules don't overlap."

Coach frowned. He had to be wondering what personal things I could have going on where I needed a job and why my dad hadn't mentioned it. "I can't pretend I'm not concerned. Your first responsibility needs to be to this team, but I can't stop you. I think you should consider what's important to you, though."

My first responsibility should be to the team? Not even class or my future? Or hell, what if I *needed* the money? But then, why would I? They all knew who my dad was—well, as much as anyone ever did. I'd thought I'd known who he was too.

"Lacrosse comes first. I know that. It won't interfere. I promise."

"It better not, Langley. The team is counting on you. *I'm* counting on you."

Way to pressure a guy. My shoulders felt like they might fold due to the weight. "You can count on me."

He hesitated. When he spoke again, I wasn't surprised when he asked, "What does your dad have to say about this?"

"It has nothing to do with him." I straightened my spine, hoping he saw I was serious, because I mean, fuck this. I was twenty-one years old. I didn't need my father's permission to work.

Coach gave me a simple nod and walked away. That was it. No worry. No concern over why I might need a job. Not that I would have told him the truth, but still. All I was to him was a way to win.

"Wanna repeat that?" Watty asked.

"I got a job, you fucker." We headed toward the locker room. *Please don't ask why I said this has nothing to do with my dad.*

"Why would you do a dumbass thing like that?" Collins asked.

"My dad...cut me off," I lied. Hopefully they'd think that's why I said it had nothing to do with Dad, and not mention it again. I didn't want Coach to know I said I'd been cut off, especially if he talked to Dad. "He wants me to get a taste of what the real world is like. I don't know. Parents fucking suck." It was a lot easier than telling them the truth. I would die before I admitted how big of an asshole my father was.

"Shit, man. What a prick. I can't believe he's doing this at the beginning of the season your junior year." Ford smacked me on the shoulder.

"I know, right? What a dickhead." *Hello, my name is Ty, and I'm a lying liar who lied.* Well, my dad *was* a dickhead, but the rest of it was bullshit. The thing was, I didn't know if the guys would get it. Even if I did tell them what my dad did, would they understand why I wanted nothing to do with him? Why I didn't want to need or depend on him? Why I wanted to forge my own way? "He played in college and worked or some shit like that, so he thinks I need to do the same."

"Sucks for you," Collins said, and they all laughed.

Way to show support, guys.

"Yeah, I'm not looking forward to it. Plus, I have to work with Braxton."

"Emo Asshole Bartender totally wishes you were dead," Ford taunted.

"He's not emo."

"But he's an asshole who wishes you were dead?" Watty chimed in.

"Yep. That about covers it." I still didn't get why I found that so hot or why I was looking forward to spending more time with him. "Anyway, I gotta bail. Talk to you guys later."

I ran ahead of them to the locker room. I showered quickly, got dressed, then ran back to our house and made a sandwich, which I ate on the way to Shenanigans. Braxton was scowling the second I walked through the door.

"Hey, bestie. Did you miss me?" *Don't think about how he said he might fuck you, don't think about how he said he might fuck you.* Which was exactly what I was doing. I willed my dick not to get too excited about the possibility—which was not a real possibility. I wasn't going to fuck around with Braxton. I'd never let him know how much I wanted him.

"Is it your goal to make my life hell?"

"I mean…basically yes. You do make it too easy, though. A little competition would be nice."

"Fu—"

"Tyson, you're here," Oscar said, cutting off what I was sure was a fuck-you.

"Yes, sir. Ready for my first day." There were about ten or twelve people there, but it was still early.

"That's what I like to hear." He turned to Braxton. "Want to show Tyson how to get clocked in and then give him a brief rundown of how things work?"

I couldn't say I was excited about what I'd be doing. I would be the guy who wiped down the tables, took the dirty dishes to the back, washed them, and shit like that, but hey, it was a job, and I knew my father would hate it. If I was going to be working at all right now, he would expect it to be something to do with computers.

"Yeah, sure. Of course," Braxton replied.

"I'll be in the back. Let me know if things pick up and you need me," Oscar said before disappearing.

Braxton eyed me while I walked behind the counter…at my new job…where I would have to *work*… Jesus, this sucked.

"Why are you really here?" he asked.

"Dad thinks I need more responsibility." I shrugged, lying again.

"I don't believe you."

"You don't have to."

He sighed. "Did you download the app?"

I nodded and pulled my phone out. Braxton was standing next to me as I scrolled.

"Pfft."

"What did I do now, Sunshine? Breathe?"

"That and..." Braxton flipped a page back. "Of course you have a hookup app."

"Well, ya know, I like sex. I'm good at it too. With your awesome personality, I figure that's the only way you can get laid, so don't tell me you don't have one. Unless...oh shit, are you saving yourself for me?"

He ignored that last question. "It's not hard for me to find sex. Believe me."

"Whatever you say."

"I'm serious."

"I agreed with you."

"Yeah, but you said it in that stupid voice where—you know what? Never mind." He ripped my phone out of my hand like he owned the damn thing, opened the work app, and clocked me in.

"Are you two done flirting now so I can get another beer?" a guy asked.

Oops.

"We weren't flirting," Braxton replied.

The dude next to the first guy said, "Seriously, you guys should just bone and get it over with."

"He wishes." Braxton took their glasses and filled them. "Come on, Lacrosse. I saved the tables just for you."

He told Gwen, the head bartender, that he'd be back. She had bright-pink hair, septum and lip piercings, and a wide smile.

Braxton led me through the swinging doors and pointed to the left. "Sink. Dishwasher. Clean dishes there. Dirty there." With each word, he used his finger to show me where he was talking about. "The bins are kept here for you to put the dishes in, clean washcloths in this cabinet." He opened and closed it. "Soap is in this one." He did the same with the next. "I'm assuming you can figure out the washer, but you might not have ever had to run one before, even at home, so if you need me to, I can show you how."

"I know how to wash dishes," I snapped, though it was obviously different from the machines at home.

"Well, you never know. You are the prince of Lacrosse, after all."

"King."

He rolled his eyes before heading to the other side of the kitchen.

"Who's the newbie?" a guy asked. He looked familiar from campus, but I didn't know his name. He was by the grills and fryers.

"Benny, Tyson. Tyson, Benny, a.k.a. SpongeBob."

"Friendly neighborhood fry cook at your service," Benny replied.

"'Sup?" I nodded at him before turning to Braxton. "Since you're so grumpy, does that make you Squidward?"

"Whatever you say, Mr. Krabs," Braxton replied.

Shit. I stepped right into that.

We left the kitchen and continued down a hallway. "Storage rooms are back here. That's not your job, but we all pitch in and help when needed. For now, you can head out there and clean the tables, wipe them down, then run the washer."

"Yes, sir!" I mock-saluted him.

He shook his head, took a couple of steps, and stopped. "I hope you take this seriously. A lot of us are here because we need this job. It's not a joke to us, nor a choice. And there are others out there who need the work more than you."

Guilt swam deep in my gut before turning into frustration. "You don't know shit about me."

Braxton cocked a brow. "Do you?"

Did I know myself? What kind of question was that? Of course I did. "What's that supposed to mean?"

"Nothing." Braxton walked off without another word. I was so pissed I didn't even take advantage of the fact that I could watch his ass as he went.

I took a few deep breaths to calm myself, found my cocky smile, and headed into the kitchen. I grabbed a clean washcloth and a cart and bin for dishes.

There were more people in Shenanigans when I went back out. I really hoped the guys didn't stop in tonight. I hoped they didn't stop in at all. They'd do nothing but give me shit.

I headed to one of the tables and started scraping the food into the trash on the rolling cart, then tossed the dishes into the bin. Fuck, people were gross. There was a pile of ketchup on one of the plates, with salt and pepper poured over it. Another had chewed-up food that the person had clearly decided they didn't like and spit out.

I gagged. Twice. Maybe three times. Okay, four, but that was it.

I looked over my shoulder to make sure Braxton wasn't watching. He was mixing a drink, but his gaze flicked over to mine at just the right time for it to look like I was staring at him.

He smirked.

I blew him a kiss.

He shook his head and, wait... Was he trying not to smile? My pulse danced, which was *not* what it should be doing. Who gave a shit if Braxton Walker liked me or not?

I got back to work, an unexpected need to prove myself to him burning through me. *I'm not grossed out by the food. I'm not grossed out by the food.*

From now on, I would never ever leave a restaurant with my table being anything other than perfectly straightened up. I guessed mixing alcohol and college students made it worse.

I cleaned up the tables, wiped them down, took the dishes to the back, washed everything, and by the time I got back out, there was shit all over the place again. More people filled the booths, tables, and counters as well. A band was playing toward the back. They had open mic nights with all sorts of different music.

It went on like that all night.

All. Fucking. Night.

Didn't people go home? Didn't they have homework to do?

On weeknights, Oscar made sure any of the staff with morning classes were out of there by eleven, which included me and Braxton. He made it to the back before me. I expected him to be gone, but he was lingering in the kitchen, looking at his phone.

He pretended not to see me, not to be paying attention, but somehow, I knew he was.

I walked over to where he leaned against the wall, close to the hallway where the storage room was. At the end was a door that led outside, which we could exit or where employees went out for their breaks if they smoked or wanted fresh air.

"Yes," I said to him.

He frowned. It fit his face like it was used to being there, like maybe it was his natural state of being. "Yes what?"

"You were waiting so you could offer to walk me back to Liberty Court, right? I mean, I'd be fine on my own, but it's sweet of you to offer."

"I didn't offer."

"But you were going to."

"No," he replied. "I... Shut the fuck up. You know I wasn't going to ask."

"It's okay, Sunshine. I won't tell anyone you like me. I'm sorry that I don't feel the same, but we can continue being frenemies."

Braxton shoved off the wall. "What the fuck is a frenemy?" He headed toward the door, and I went with him.

"Us."

"We're not friends. Just enemies."

"Only because it's so hard for you since you like me." God, he was fun. I could do this all night. Five minutes ago I was exhausted and wanted to fall into bed and never get out. Now, a new burst of energy exploded inside me.

"I don't like—Jesus, how do you make me do this? I know exactly what hand you're playing, yet I fall right into your trap." He opened the door, and I walked out. Such a gentleman.

"It's a gift."

"You're annoying, and I hate you."

"There's a thin line between love and hate."

It was quiet behind the bar, nothing but the

sound of the ocean and cars in the distance.

"I think..." He took a step closer to me, then another. I had a feeling the bastard was about to turn the tables on me. He was good at that, and I didn't like it...or maybe I did. "You *want* me to like you." Another step. My back hit the building, so apparently I'd been moving too. He kept coming. "Looking to slum it with a guy you know will make Mommy and Daddy angry?"

Braxton's breath was warm against my face. Fuck, I hated that he could manage this, that I could go from having the upper hand in this little game we played to thinking the guy in the bar was right and we just needed to bone and get it over with.

He leaned in, mouth close to my ear, and I wondered if he'd lick it again. "Remember what I said earlier? If you ask nicely, I might be willing to fuck you."

Mayday! Mayday! Mayday! My dick was throbbing, begging for me to open my mouth and say please. But there was no chance I was letting him do this. He'd gotten the best of me earlier, and now it was my turn. "Oh, Sunshine, when we finally succumb to this, no one said you would get to be the one doing the fucking."

He sucked in a sharp breath.

This round went to me.

CHAPTER FIVE

Braxton

ASHER HAD PEOPLE over again when I got home, but not as many as the other night. Weekend, weekday, it didn't matter to him. If it ended in *day*, it was the perfect time to party.

I stayed up and smoked a bowl with them before heading to my room. Fucking Tyson. I couldn't believe he'd left me speechless. I liked being the one to do that to him, liked leaving him standing there slack-jawed and dick hard, instead of the other way around.

And I had been—hard. Just by being close to him.

I showered. I'd moved into Grandma's room when she'd gone into the home. I hadn't wanted to, but she'd insisted it be me instead of Asher, so I had my own bathroom in there. I kept a small fridge too because there had been too many times I'd bought food and Asher's friends had eaten it all. I fell into bed wearing nothing but my boxer briefs, then did an hour or so of schoolwork before hitting the lights and looking at my phone.

The only social media account I had was an old Instagram page I'd had to start for a school assignment. All that shit was dumb if you asked me. It made people feel bad about themselves looking at everyone's happy life without realizing that behind the scenes, they were dealing with shit too.

Still, I found myself logging in to the account, going to the search screen, and typing in *Tyson Langley*. It was exactly what I knew it would be—lacrosse, parties, his friends, getting drunk and stuff like that. Nothing real, nothing of substance. What the fuck was it about him that twisted me up so much?

But then I saw a photo of the beach at sunrise. It didn't have as many likes or comments as the others. No one said, *Hawt,* or *Fuck yeah, bro!* or any of the other dumb shit I saw on his more popular pictures.

He hadn't captioned it. It was just a quiet photo, the sky full of pinks and oranges, at a time of day I wouldn't have thought Tyson ever woke up.

A few rows down, there was a *Fuck liars* meme. The comments were agreeing with him, backslapping and ass-kissing kind of comments, but he hadn't liked or responded to them the way he had on the party or lacrosse photos.

I scrolled down further. More dude-bro shit, jock stuff...and then a photo of an article headline about a local nurse who'd saved someone's life when they got hit by a car. He'd captioned it *Badass* and hashtagged it *heroes*.

I went through his whole page. Most of it was exactly what I would expect from Tyson, but every once in a while, a post would stand out, something that felt like it belonged to a different person than the one who took the rest of the pictures.

There was a video of a homeless man singing and playing the guitar, and Tyson told people to go listen and give him money. There was random graffiti of a broken heart filled with thousands of names, which he'd captioned *Art*. None of those photos got the same amount of attention the others did, but they felt more real to me. And fuck, I was becoming way too damn obsessed with this guy. I needed to get off social media and get my ass to sleep, but instead, I went through and hearted all the photos that were unique—the sunrise and the nurse and all those things that actually felt like they mattered. He wouldn't know it was me. The account wasn't in my name.

Before I did something stupid like become even more curious about Tyson, I closed the app and went to sleep.

I HAD TWO classes with Tyson on Tuesdays, which was just fucking peachy.

He was following in his dad's footsteps. His father was some tech giant on the East Coast, and I was sure Tyson would have a job waiting for him when he got out of school. I wondered if that was what he wanted, to go back to wherever he came from and work for his family…and then I wanted to remove my own brain, which was clearly defective since it kept coming back to Tyson.

One of his friends, Jeff, was in our Software Engineering class with us. They sat a couple of rows in front of me. Tyson didn't try to talk to me at all, but every once in a while he'd look back. I winked, trying to get under his skin.

He did it back, so I wasn't sure if my plan worked or not.

When our professor dismissed us, I packed my shit, forcing myself not to look down at him. The universe must have been out to get me because as soon as I stepped outside, Tyson and his friend were there.

"Later, man," Jeff said. "I gotta get to class."

"Catch ya later, Watty," Tyson replied as Jeff walked away.

"Pfft."

"What did I do to upset your delicate sensibilities this time?" Tyson asked.

"Watty?"

We started across the campus together, heading in the direction of the café. "Yeah, his last name is Watson. It's called a nickname. Have you never heard of them before?"

"Ha-ha."

"Did you think about me last night?"

Yes. I stalked you on social media. Someone kill me now.

"No." But then this urge to beat him at his own game, to see him tremble and know I was the cause, came over me again. "Maybe," I added.

"I'm listening." His eyes darted around as if he was trying to make sure no one else was. People walked by, but no one too close.

We stopped under a palm tree, with one of the white stucco buildings in the background. I'd always loved the Spanish-style architecture with the orange, terracotta-tiled roofs. "What can I say, I was horny. My dick apparently doesn't have the best taste."

He shrugged that comment off, but his voice was an octave lower when he asked, "What did you do about it?"

This was getting dangerous quickly. I never planned to let it get this far, not with him, but fuck, we'd been dancing around this for three years. There was no denying I wanted him. I still wasn't sure I'd let myself have him, but this? Making him crazed as hell for me? That I could do.

"I was in bed…felt like coming anyway…so I

stripped out of my clothes. Took my dick a little while to get into the game, just because it was you I was thinking about."

"Oh, fuck you. You're a liar."

I ignored that. "But eventually I got hard. That's the first time I've ever had that problem, but then, as I said, it's you."

"Me who you want."

I ignored that too. "By then I was fucking leaking. I had my slick cock in hand, was stroking it while thinking about how much I don't like you. That's what really got my balls full, what made me shoot my load all over my stomach. It was a big fucking load too."

"Shiiiiit." Tyson whimpered, fucking *whimpered*, at me telling him how I got off. My gaze darted down. There was definitely a bigger bulge in his track pants than what he'd had before. "Go somewhere with me. I wanna blow you."

"Excuse me, what?" free-fell from my mouth. I hadn't seen that coming. At. All.

"It's just sex. We've been playing this game for too long now. Sooner or later, we're gonna fuck. You know it. I know it. Why keep fighting it?"

My cock was beginning to swell, the words *fuck yes* on my tongue, but what came out was, "But I hate you."

"Do you hate orgasms? Because I'm not offering to be your boyfriend or even your friend. I'm offering to drain a load out of your balls. Tick-tock. We only have an hour before our next class."

I could say no. We'd keep not liking each other but wanting each other until eventually we cracked and got off together...or I could stop telling myself I would ever be satisfied not hooking up with him, take him somewhere, and watch him get on his knees for me.

It really wasn't much of a choice. You didn't have to get along with someone to have sex with them. We were proof of that, and at least with Tyson, we both knew what it was. No empty promises, no pretending to feel things for each other while we sneaked around, only for one of us to crush the other's world. I'd let that happen with one jock before, and I wouldn't allow it again.

"Let's go." I nodded toward the building we'd just left.

"Where are we going? Where do you live? It can't

be this direction. We can try my place. I don't think anyone's there, but—"

"No," I cut him off.

"No, what? I want to suck your dick. That doesn't mean I'm gonna blindly follow you or do what you say."

"Empty room," I said, opening the door.

"On the third floor. You're a genius, and…fuck, that's kinda hot."

"I know."

"That you're a genius or that it's hot?"

"Both," I replied, and we chuckled as we hurried down the hallway to the other side of the building, where we took the stairs up. There were people here and there, but no one paid us any attention. We acted like we weren't going to find an empty room to fuck around in, and they minded their own business, going to class.

When we got there, we had to hang around for a second until everyone was gone. Walking to the third floor was one thing. Going into a closed classroom was another.

Once the coast was clear, Tyson reached for the handle. "Fuck. It's locked."

That didn't deter me. I pulled a card out of my wallet, along with a tool that had helped me more than once at home. "Keep an eye out, will ya?"

"Holy shit. You're picking the lock."

"What was your first clue?"

"You keep a tool in your wallet for breaking in? How many times have you done that?"

"It's a habit at this point. I don't use it on other people's places. I had to do it when my dad would lock us out." I froze, unable to believe I'd just said that to him. It was clear Tyson was shocked too, because when I risked a glance at him, his eyes were wide…and pitying. Fuck, I hated pity. "Don't—"

"It's right this way," a voice interrupted, getting closer. Whoever they were, we could hear them coming up the stairs. The lock clicked, and I slid the door open, Tyson and I both stumbling inside. I quietly closed and locked it behind us.

"Brax—"

"Don't." I wanted him to forget I'd said that. To forget everything except having my dick in his mouth.

I took his hand and pulled him deeper into the room. We went toward the back, against the wall, on the opposite side of a bookcase, so if anyone came in, hopefully it would help shield us.

Tyson didn't waste any time, immediately dropping to his knees. "I hate that I want you."

"The feeling is completely mutual."

He worked open my jeans with quick, skilled fingers. I watched, wanting to see him, needing to see that it was Tyson who craved me so badly, he'd offered to blow me.

He pushed my pants and underwear down, below my ass, and my dick sprang free, hard and pulsing.

"Jesus, this is a nice cock, Sunshine." He stroked me slowly, and I bit down on my tongue not to cry out already.

"Lick it."

"Say please."

"No," I replied. He winked, started his tongue at my sac, and let it take a journey to the tip of my erection. "Fuck…" My eyes rolled back.

"This is gonna be fun. I've always loved sucking cock, but it's even more fun when I know it's you I'm driving out of his mind, you who will be saying my name over and over again, no matter how much you hate it. That's so sexy."

"Suck my dick, Lacrosse." My words didn't come

out quite the demand I'd gone for. It was more like a plea.

"Gladly," Tyson said, and took me to the back of his throat like my cock belonged in his mouth. He pulled off and licked my balls, then went back to my erection, sucking me down again and swallowing around the head.

I didn't take my eyes off him the whole time, held the back of his head, and guided him even though he didn't need it. Tyson knew his way around a cock. His mouth was hot and wet, the sound of him slurping at me echoing through the room. "Fuck, that's it. Jesus, I can't wait to give you my load."

He kept working me, teasing my crown with his tongue, long laps, short ones, nursing the head, and taking me deep, while shoving down his own pants and underwear.

He had a nice dick too. The hair at his groin was trimmed, a bit darker than the blond on his head but not by much. His balls were tighter than mine, his head swollen and red, precum pearling at the tip.

Tyson licked his hand, lowered it to his erection, and stroked himself while getting me off. My eyes fluttered, but I wouldn't let them close, couldn't look away from Tyson Langley blowing me in an empty classroom. It was one of the most erotic moments of my life.

All too soon, my balls drew up, pleasure shooting up my spine. "I'm gonna come," I warned, but he didn't back off, didn't move away, so I let loose, careened over the cliff, Tyson draining me as promised. He swallowed me down before pulling off and jacking his dick faster, then spurting his load all over the floor and hitting the wall. "Fuck." I dropped my head back.

"Good, right?"

"Until you ruined it by speaking."

Tyson stood up. "I like this…like seeing you blissed out and knowing I'm the one who did it." He took off his hoodie and wiped his hands on it, then his dick, before tucking himself away.

Before I realized what was happening, Ty covered my mouth with his. I opened up for him, tasted myself on his tongue in the quick, demanding kiss.

"Next time it's your turn," he said, then walked away and out of the room, leaving me standing there with my dick out and his load on the wall and floor.

That motherfucker.

I found a roll of paper towels in a cabinet, cleaned up, tugged my clothes into place, and even wiped up Tyson's cum.

When I slipped out of the classroom, I realized I was smiling.

Next time, I'd be the one making him come his brains out.

CHAPTER SIX

Ty

I WATCHED BRAXTON in our next class, wondered if he still felt as keyed up as I did. My body was jittery like I'd had too much caffeine, but there was also this lightning storm inside me, sparking mini fires every time our gazes caught.

It was hot as fuck to see him across the lecture hall, knowing what we just did. It was hot as fuck to *think* about what we did in general. I never thought we'd actually get together. I sure as shit hadn't thought it would happen where it had either, or that I'd just offer to blow him in the first place.

It had given me the upper hand, even if I knew Braxton would eventually get it back. That was how we worked.

Neither of us spoke to each other when class was

over. I would never tell him this—I was embarrassed to even admit it to myself—but I might have offered to get him off again if we'd spoken.

I had practice that afternoon again, and I basically killed it. I mean, I typically did, but maybe Braxton's cum was a superfood or some shit. Coach complimented me afterward.

The electrical storm started up inside me again when I headed into Shenanigans to work that night, only when I got there, Braxton wasn't behind the bar.

"Hey, man. What's up?" I said as Marshall gave me a wave. He was this big-ass teddy bear of a guy everyone on campus loved, and he used those arms of his to keep us stocked with liquor.

"How's it going, Tyson? I didn't know you were the new lacrosse guy working here." He pushed his glasses up his nose.

"Yep." I looked around to make sure no one was listening. "Is Braxton here?"

Marshall frowned as if confused by my question, and he one hundred percent should be. I had zero business asking or caring if Braxton was there or not.

"I think he's off tonight. Someone got a crush?" Marshall waggled his eyebrows playfully.

"Fuck no. Well, not me on him, but I think he's got it bad for me."

Marshall gave a deep belly laugh. "Yeah, okay."

Um...he expected me to like Braxton but not the other way around? What was so wrong with liking me? I was a fucking catch.

"Don't take it personally," Marshall said. "Brax doesn't like anyone. And no offense, but you don't seem like his type. He goes for guys with a little more edge."

Then why had I had his dick in my mouth earlier? "I'm edgy."

Marshall laughed. Hard. I didn't like him anymore.

I got to work, but thoughts of Braxton didn't leave my head all night. I hadn't ever seen him with a guy, but I hadn't seen him with a woman either. I was pretty sure he was gay and not bi. I didn't doubt he had sex, but I had no frame of reference to what he actually liked. He did want me, of that I was certain. That spark between us couldn't be faked and, Jesus fucking Christ, *spark*? I didn't want that with him. I didn't.

Still, I *could* be curious about him, and I was.

Marshall had clearly seen the kind of guys Braxton fucked, and they apparently weren't me. My thoughts circled back to earlier today—how he'd broken into the classroom, and what he'd said about his father.

His own dad used to lock them out of the house? It made me wonder what else he'd been through.

Looked like we had asshole fathers in common.

Aaaaaand, I totally needed to get him out of my head. He'd spent entirely too long there. But…that one blowjob hadn't been enough to sate my curiosity about Braxton Walker.

THAT MOTHERFUCKER.

Braxton wasn't in class the next day. I couldn't remember him ever missing one. I was sure he had. How could he not? But it was a pretty big coincidence that he was gone the day after I'd sucked him off.

I couldn't believe he was avoiding me. I'd never had that happen after I hooked up with someone before. Hell, it was typically the other way around. I couldn't say it was real fun to experience it from this side.

Plus, that didn't really seem like Braxton. Not that I knew him. It wasn't as if the two of us were close. Still, somehow I knew I'd never seen him with a Starbucks, and that he liked to wear his leather jacket when it was cool. He didn't smile all that often, but when he did, it was like you won a prize because you'd been able to make him do it. He knew how to pick locks. He liked cheap beer. And he liked Hershey bars, as I'd seen him eat them more than once.

Huh. Maybe I did know him some.

What I didn't know was his phone number, or if he had social media, or why the hell I cared if he was being a big baby and keeping his distance just because he'd had his dick in my mouth.

Today I had a lighter class load, which meant more time between school and practice. When I got home, Collins was the only one there, and the two of us played video games while I tried to keep my mind off Brax. It shouldn't be this difficult. He was really starting to piss me off.

My cell rang, and I peeked over to where it sat on the coffee table to see *Mom* on the screen. "Hey, I gotta take this." I paused the game, scooped up my phone, and stood.

"Why do you leave when you talk on the phone lately?" Collins asked.

Wow. Who knew he paid attention? "I don't know. Why do you smell like a grandma's house?"

"I smell like an old lady?" He sniffed himself, and I laughed. "Fuck you."

"See ya at practice." As soon as I was out the door, I answered the call. If I talked to Dad, we fought. If I talked to Mom, Dad was always discussed or sometimes argued about. It was easier for me to simply leave so no one heard.

"How's my favorite son?" Mom asked. I didn't mention the fact that I was her only son, though apparently not Dad's.

"I'm good. How are you?" As soon as I asked the question, I wished I could snatch it back and maybe burn it. How well could she be?

"I'm all right. Your dad got the rest of his things out of the house this past weekend. I'm thinking about getting new things. I realized none of this is my style at all. It's his. I don't think I would have chosen one piece of furniture in this house if it wasn't for him."

Anger sat heavy in my gut. I hated him so fucking much. "You should do it."

"I think I will." I knew she was smiling without having to see her. "I hate how everything went down, but I have to admit it's kind of exciting too. I feel like there are so many things about myself I didn't explore because I put your father first. Because I wanted to be the perfect wife, to be exactly who and what he needed. And those aren't even things I can blame on him. I made those choices myself."

The quad was busy, people chillin' at the tables, some with books and some not. I walked around one of the buildings and leaned against the wall to get some privacy. "I hate him."

"He's your father, Ty. I know you're angry and hurt. You have every right to be, but he's still—"

"No. He's not. I get to make that decision for myself." I would never forgive him for hurting Mom, for lying to me, for the siblings I never knew.

"You won't take money from him."

"I don't need it."

"You will at some point."

"I got a job…at a local bar."

"You know we didn't want you to work in college. We want you to focus on school and lacrosse. How are you supposed to do well in your classes if you're at a bar half the night? It's different if you were doing an internship or honing your skills, but spending your nights at a bar? I don't like it."

I sighed. I knew she wouldn't understand.

I wasn't dumb. I was aware I wouldn't be able to afford my tuition next year. Eventually, I would have to fold. Even if I got money from Mom, it would be the same as getting it from him, but couldn't I try for some independence? At least attempt to break away from my father? My whole life, I'd done everything he'd asked of me. I was like a doll he'd made to be exactly what he wanted, and I was fucking tired of it.

"I love you, Mom, but you don't have to like it."

"You know I'll always support you. Just don't bite off your nose to spite your face, okay? Your decisions will piss your father off, but it's your future they'll affect." Her reply didn't surprise me. Dad would demand I quit when he found out. That was one of the differences between them. Still, I couldn't understand what was so wrong about getting a job. Yeah, they wanted me to focus on school, but shouldn't they be proud I'd taken that step? There were people who didn't have a choice, while my dad would lose his shit and call working at the bar beneath me. That was fucked up when I thought about it.

"Thanks, Ma. I gotta go. I have practice soon."

"I love you, Tyson."

"I love you too." I hung up, then paced around the quad for a while. I was too... I didn't know what I was. Frustrated, for one. And hell, I'd only worked two shifts, but I liked my job at Shenanigans. I'd taken it because it helped accomplish three goals—giving me independence, pissing off my dad, and annoying Brax—but it was sort of fun too.

I chilled for a few minutes, then headed back to the house. I forgot I needed to grab my bag anyway. Collins was still there, so we headed to practice together. Our first game was this weekend, and Coach was riding us hard to get ready.

By the time it was over and I had to get ready for work, I wondered why earlier I'd thought I liked the job. I wanted to just veg out and watch Netflix or something, but then I remembered I'd been a creepy-ass weirdo and checked the schedule last night to see that Brax worked today. Giving him shit would cure whatever ailed me. Plus, maybe he'd want to return the favor and get on his knees for me.

But when I got to Shenanigans, he wasn't there, which was kinda sus. Annoyance prickled down my spine. Was he really going this far to avoid me? All over a little head?

Gwen was working. She'd changed her hair to purple. "Aw, Kings spirit?" I teased.

"Who are the kings?"

I clutched my heart. "You're killin' me."

"My job here is done," Gwen replied.

Before she got busy again, I asked, "Brax isn't here?"

"Nope, he's sick or something." While a part of me worried and hoped everything was okay, I had a feeling this was about us. He hated me so much that I knew he regretted what we'd done. Maybe it had chased him away for good.

The night was busy. People were disgusting. Who knew so many college-aged people played with their food and spilled their alcohol? By the end of the night, I'd gone through a few pairs of gloves and decided I hated the job. At least when Brax was there, I had him to make the time go faster, but nope, he was scared to see me because I'd sucked his cock.

I didn't know who he thought he was dealing with, but I wasn't going to let him slink away.

"Hey, Gwen. I have a question for you," I said, and hoped she had the answer.

CHAPTER SEVEN

Braxton

I WAS GOING to kill my brother.
I didn't know what in the hell he was doing and why he was banging on the door, which, at the moment, felt like he was slamming his fists down on my skull. He was notorious for losing his keys but, like me, knew how to pick a lock, so I didn't know why in the fuck he wasn't doing exactly that.

I had no idea what time it was, and I didn't care. I just knew it was morning and I was sick as fuck, but just like when I was studying or trying to go to bed early, Asher didn't care.

I rolled out of bed, stumbled, and hit my head on the wall. Fuck, I was dizzy, but I managed to make my way down the hallway, unlock the door, and pull it open.

"What the fuck, Sunshine? Are you really going to skip school and work every day just because I blew you?"

Jesus, had I hit my head harder than I thought? Was I hallucinating? But then, if I were having any kind of Tyson Langley fantasy, he'd be on his knees for me again and not being annoying as shit. "Not everything is about you, Lacrosse. How in the fuck do you know where I live?"

"I asked Gwen, and yes, it is."

As always, he was dressed like a jock, douche-bro in a Kings T-shirt with his number on it—11—and a pair of nylon shorts. He looked like the frat boy next door. I wanted nothing more than to tell him that, but I was hit with a wave of dizziness, my legs suddenly feeling weak, and then he was there, inside the doorway with his arms around me.

"Jesus, you almost passed out. You're burning up. Guess this really isn't about me."

"You sound surprised."

"I mean, it's me. Do you blame me?"

I tried to think of something witty to say, but my brain was too foggy, and I was pretty sure that if I didn't get back to my bed soon, I'd pass out for real.

"Bed. Dying. Get out of my house. Close the door behind you."

I staggered away from him like half of the drunk people at the bar every night, hitting shit on my way. I heard the door close and said a silent prayer before falling face-first onto my bed. I was really fucking sick.

"Wow…your room is cleaner than I thought it would be."

What the fuck? I opened one eye, and standing in the middle of my bedroom, was Ty. "What the hell are you doing? I don't have the energy to go back and forth with you today."

He frowned. "Have you taken your temperature?"

"One blowjob, and you really are in love with me."

"Don't fool yourself. I'm just not letting you die while you owe me a cock-sucking."

I tried to roll my eyes but was pretty sure I hadn't succeeded because they were closed. I trembled when a cold hand touched my cheek.

"You really are burning up. Where's your thermometer?"

"No idea. We had one, but I can't find it."

"Okay... When is the last time you took something?"

"Only had ibuprofen. Ran out last night."

"Jesus fucking Christ, Brax. You're going to kill yourself. Who was that guy who left right before I got here? He told me to bang on the door to wake you up. I thought he was being funny and wanted to give you shit."

Asher left? "Brother."

"And he couldn't make sure you had some fucking medicine?"

My head throbbed. "Your voice is even more annoying today. Shut up. Go home." I just wanted to sleep. That was all I needed. I curled up and tugged the blanket over me.

I flinched when the bed shifted and something cold pressed against my face. "What the fuck are you doing?" This...wasn't us. This wasn't me and anyone. Except for Grandma, and I guess my best friend Manuel's family, if they'd known. Other than them, I couldn't remember anyone caring when I was sick.

"Blowjob, remember?"

"Not dying."

"Not taking any chances."

He continued to wipe my forehead, cheeks, shoulders, and the back of my neck with a cold cloth. That meant he'd been in my bathroom, in my things. I wanted to tell him to leave, that we didn't do this, and I didn't want him taking care of me. I didn't want anyone to do that. But I couldn't find the words.

"By the way," Ty said, "your ass looks great in those underwear."

It was all I wore, and I hadn't even thought about that. "I know," I mumbled, and Ty chuckled.

I didn't know how much time passed before the bed shifted and he was gone. *Finally* floated through my head, but then there was a beeping sound. "101.2," he said. "Here, take this."

My head, hell, my whole body throbbed, but I forced myself to open my eyes. Ty stood beside my bed with a frown, Gatorade, medication, and a thermometer. "Carry that around with you?"

"Delivery."

"What are you doing?"

"I don't know. Let's pretend it's not happening."

I was down with that. The last thing I wanted was to get help from Ty. I took the medication, drank some of the Gatorade, and closed my eyes. "Go to class, Lacrosse." Only he didn't.

I fell asleep, and eventually he woke me up to take some more medication, which I did before passing out again.

I dreamed about Ty sucking me off...then me doing the same to him. From there, we were in some kind of TV competition about who could make whose life more miserable, and the motherfucker won, because of course he did.

I woke up to piss twice. Each time I saw him sitting in the corner of my room with his laptop and books. "Why are you still here?"

"Because you'd be sad and maybe cry if I left."

The next time I woke up, my room was empty. The lamp on the bedside table was on. I still felt like shit, but maybe slightly more human than when Ty had first come over. A bottle of water and more medication sat next to my phone on the nightstand. I grabbed my cell and frowned when I saw a text from *The Sexiest Man Alive*.

What. The. Fuck.

My screen opened, and I clicked the message.

The Sexiest Man Alive: I used your face ID to unlock

your cell, but I didn't do any snooping...or did I? Now you have my phone number, and I have yours. Had to leave for practice. I called Oscar and told him you're still sick and won't be in tonight. I helped you, so you should come to my game this weekend.

My fingers hovered over the screen. I wasn't sure if I wanted to respond or not. This felt...like a really bad idea. But him blowing me had been too. Bad ideas were often the most fun.

Me: No.

He sent me back a screenshot, showing he had my name as **Brooding Bad Boy**. I smiled just a little bit. Not a real smile, though.

Me: You're an idiot.

The Sexiest Man Alive: I'll let you blow me afterward...

I hadn't been to one lacrosse game the whole three years I'd been at FU. Hell, I hadn't been to any sports games, and I didn't plan to start now. In high school, I'd go. I'd sit there worshipping the first boy I'd ever kissed—in secret. When people found out about us, he treated me like shit, making up lies about me and what we'd done.

Me: No.

The Sexiest Man Alive: You're in denial...you want to watch me play...you sure as shit want my dick in your

mouth... Stop brooding and say yes.

Me: I'm not brooding.

The Sexiest Man Alive: hahahahahahahahahahahaha.

I shook my head. A second text came through.

The Sexiest Man Alive: hahahahahaahahaha. Sorry. I wasn't done.

Goddamn, I hated him...I thought.

Me: Letting you blow me gave me the flu. I might get hit by a bus if we hook up again. Evidently, we messed with the universe. The last thing we need is to do that again.

But I did owe him and I did want to make him come his brains out, if for no other reason than to show him how good I was at it.

Me: I get off work at six on Sunday.

The Sexiest Man Alive: It's a date.

Me: After that, we're done. Tit for fucking tat or whatever.

The Sexiest Man Alive: Agreed. What's a couple of blowjobs between enemies?

Me: I'm getting off now.

The Sexiest Man Alive: You're coming right now?

He was such an idiot.

Me: Getting off the phone. I'm starting to feel like shit again.

It was clear, though, that the rest and the medicine he'd brought over were helping.

The Sexiest Man Alive: You need anything else?

This was unnerving. I couldn't figure out what was going on or if I liked it.

Me: Stop being nice to me.

The Sexiest Man Alive: After my blowjob!

I exited out of my texts and tossed my phone to the other side of the bed. I wouldn't smile... I *wouldn't*.

The front door opened and closed, my brother's voice and a few others' coming from the living room. He'd known I was sick since yesterday. He hadn't checked on me, hadn't offered to run to the store and pick shit up for me. I wasn't mad. I didn't need anyone's help anyway, yet I couldn't help wondering why Ty had, why he'd cared, and how I felt about that.

CHAPTER EIGHT

Ty

BRAXTON AND I didn't text the next day. A couple of times I thought about checking in on him or just making some smart-ass comment to get on his nerves, but I didn't. I'd already done…whatever the fuck that had been the other day when I sat at his house all day to make sure he didn't die. Clearly, his brother hadn't given a shit.

Between that, swapping numbers, and basically being hard all week just thinking about him getting on his knees for me, it was already bordering on obsessive territory. The last thing I wanted was for him to think I actually *liked* him. I just craved using his mouth, and to do that, he couldn't die of the flu. There was a method to my madness.

And also, it might have been partly because the

medical field had always interested me—something I ignored most of the time.

Today was Saturday, and our first game of the season. The field was packed with nearly every FU student...except for Brax. I'd even seen Peyton, Cobey, and some of the football guys there, repping their FU pride.

I reveled in moments like this, in this game. Ever since I first started playing, I knew I wanted to be a middy so I could get in on both the offensive *and* defensive action. There were three of us, and we were the only ones playing the whole field rather than sticking to one side.

We all took position, the cheering and screaming making my heart beat faster. While I had no real interest in anything computer-related or spending my life working with them, I did share a love of lacrosse with my dad. I felt alive when I played and invincible when I won, my whole body pulsing with uncontrollable energy.

It could also be because of the attention I got. I couldn't lie, I was an attention slut and didn't see anything wrong with it. I was sure Brax had his thoughts on that.

I watched through my helmet as we won the face-off, and everything else slipped into the quiet, dark place in my mind—Dad, whom I hated, but I wouldn't let him take this away from me; Mom; my career choice. Hell, even Brax.

The next four quarters, the only thing that mattered was defending the net and scoring, which we did a lot of, winning the game easily because we were fucking awesome like that.

"We should throw a party at the house tonight!" Ford shouted over the voices of everyone who'd crowded around to congratulate us.

I opened my mouth to say yeah, but what came out was, "Let's hit up Shenanigans! We don't have the stuff for a party at home anyway."

"Bet," Watty jumped into the conversation, those around us already in agreement and spreading the word to each other. I mean, it made sense we'd go there. Oscar often gave half-priced drinks to the team on nights we won. Plus, I hadn't been lying about not having beer at the house. It had absolutely nothing to do with what would be a grumpy-as-hell Brax when we arrived. Nope, nothing at all.

We got home and fought over the two showers,

Collins and I winning. After washing up, I put on my favorite jeans that I knew made my ass look fantastic, along with a button-up, long-sleeved shirt, which I rolled up to my elbows. I kept the top three buttons open, styled my hair... Fuck, I looked really good.

When I hit the living room, it was full of people as if we were, in fact, having the party here. Some were already pregaming it, passing a bottle of vodka around. I could smell the familiar scent of weed in the air. I partook in both sometimes. They were legal, and I was of legal age, so why not? Pot was against NCAA guidelines, but luckily Coach didn't randomly test.

Tonight I was bouncing on the balls of my feet, ready to get out of there, not caring about the buzz. "We leaving or what?"

"Why are you in such a hurry?" Collins asked.

"Because we just won our first game of the season and I don't want to be home?" I lied—well, partly.

"Hell yeah!" Ford yelled. "Go Kings!"

Everyone started fist-bumping and chest-thumping, and while I couldn't pretend I wasn't right in the middle of it, all I could picture was Braxton rolling his eyes if he saw us. He'd think it was ridiculous, but I didn't see the problem in enjoying things. We were only young once. Why not have some fun?

Everyone stumbled out of the house. People were barbecuing, chilling in the hammocks, and enjoying the fact that it was January and we lived in a place where we weren't freezing our balls off at night.

It was a quick walk to Shenanigans. No one driving by would think twice about the crowds of college people filling the streets. It felt like San Luco was our town, like it was made for FU and all of us who went there. It had always been the plan to move back east when I graduated, to work for Dad, but I wasn't sure I could imagine leaving here.

Shenanigans was right by the beach, the sand and ocean not far behind it. As it normally was on the weekends, the place was packed. The second we walked in, people cheered, congratulating us on the win. Peyton approached me right away. "One and zero, baby," I told him, boasting our win and no loss record.

"You play a sport or something?" he asked. "I didn't realize FU had any, other than football."

"Oooh!" Cobey, one of the guys from his team, said. He was a big guy, over six feet—friendly with a killer smile, but I wasn't sure he had a lot going on upstairs.

"Yeah, not all of us play basic games like you," I teased back, making him chuckle. "Don't act like you weren't in the stands, cheering for me."

"Good game, Langley."

"I know," I replied, and Peyton shook his head like he didn't know what to do with me. I got that reaction a lot.

"Yeah, good game, man," Cobey added, and we bumped fists.

The crowd around us was thick, making it nearly impossible to move. It wasn't so much that the bar was *that* full, more that everyone wanted to give their props to the team. I glanced toward the bar, and when I did, I saw Braxton watching. When I smiled, he gave me the finger, making my stomach feel strangely fluttery. Fuck, was everything foreplay with this guy? I was stuck between wanting nothing to do with him and needing more. He was that addicting.

"Hey, Ty. You played well today." A small hand wrapped around my bicep, and I looked over to see a gorgeous girl with long red hair and a really great mouth.

"Hey yourself. And thank you." I grinned. She did the same. She was really hot. I should stick around. Normally, I would, but there was this pull inside me, luring me toward the bar. I hadn't gotten a chance to flaunt my win to Braxton yet.

My gaze made its way toward him again. He wasn't looking at me while he poured a drink, but I had a feeling he had been, that if I'd checked seconds earlier, our eyes would have caught again.

"Wanna get a beer?" she asked.

I fucking loved to flirt, loved when people went after what they wanted—man or woman. Still, I found myself saying, "I'm actually meeting someone tonight."

"Oh. Well, your loss." The redhead winked, and I couldn't even deny that she might be right.

"I'm sure it is."

"Good game, though." She slipped away. I had no doubt she would find exactly what she was looking for. It just wasn't me. Not until I got this shit with Brax out of my system.

It took me at least twenty minutes to work my way to the bar. Every time I tried, I got stopped by someone. Brax was just finishing ringing up a customer when I leaned over the counter, elbows resting on the wood.

"Aren't you gonna congratulate me?" I asked with a grin.

"Nah, I'm good."

"Aw, but I won for you, Sunshine. I feel so unappreciated."

"What happened to your girlfriend?" he asked, making heat zing down my spine. So he *had* been watching us.

"Jealous?"

"You wish."

"Don't worry, there's enough of me to go around." I waggled my eyebrows, and he looked at me like he either wanted to punch my mouth or kiss it. I wasn't sure he even knew which one. It totally got me hard.

Ridiculously, I was on pins and needles, waiting to see how he was going to respond, how he'd flip the script the way we seemed to do with each other, but just as he opened his mouth, hands slapped down on my shoulders.

"Langley!" Ford gave me whiplash, he shook me so hard.

"What the fuck, man?" I pushed him away.

"We need drinks. Excuse me, Mr. Bartender, can we have drinks, please?"

Brax scowled. "Will just anything do, or did you have something specific in mind?"

"Wow, you're grumpy," Ford replied.

"Cut him some slack," I found myself saying, before turning to Brax and ordering a couple of pitchers of beer.

He filled them, Ford thankfully paid, and then I had to help him carry them back to the table. I tried not to show my frustration that I'd been pulled away from Brax before I found out what he was going to say.

Our group had grown since I'd made my escape. Everyone was drinking, joking, flirting, all the shit we did when we went out, but I was distracted. I nursed my cup, my attention continually drawn to the counter where Brax was working.

He was pretty busy for a good hour, and then there was a lull. I was about to head over when a guy standing by our table started rehashing the game, so I refocused on the conversation and said, "It was fucking badass, right?" And by *it*, I meant *me*.

The next time I glanced over, Braxton was talking to Felix, the flirty guy from Freidman House. Felix looked really hot with his reddish-blond curls and banging body that he definitely had on display tonight. He wore a T-shirt that was cut off to show most of his torso. If rumors were correct, Felix was a good time. Even though he hit on me and my lacrosse friends, like I said, I knew we weren't his type, but tonight, he didn't look all that picky.

Brax laughed at something he said, and…what the fuck? It was like pulling teeth to get him to laugh, and Felix did it in two point two seconds?

I watched like a stalker while Braxton made him a drink and handed it over. Felix leaned over the counter, his feet dangling above the ground, his ass out, and his mouth close to Braxton's ear.

Nope. Hell no. All the nopes that had ever noped. I shoved to my feet and went over there. Braxton and I were hooking up this weekend. Felix could find his own man. Not that Brax was mine, and I totally didn't want him to be, but still.

"Hi," I said, standing next to the twink.

"Hi," Felix replied.

Brax's brows pulled together. "Ignore him. That's

what I do."

"You like me too much to ignore me," I countered.

Brax turned to Felix. "Anyway, you were saying?" He *ignored me*, just like he'd said, his voice more smoldering than usual, and holy fuck, he'd never used that voice on me. Did that mean he'd never flirted with me? That couldn't be possible.

And who gave a shit what Felix was saying? Brax was supposed to pay attention to me.

"I'd like a drink," I said, my gut uncomfortably tight.

"Ask Gwen, or Casey, or whoever's available." There were four bartenders there tonight, along with the waitstaff.

"I'm asking you."

He groaned, and *that* sound I was familiar with, though I doubted he was really annoyed. Braxton enjoyed this game we played more than he would a night with the twink. "Why have you made it your mission in life to bother me?"

"Because I'm so good at it, and we both know you like it."

"No, I don't." Braxton grabbed a glass and started

making a rum and Coke, and fuck yeah, Felix, he knew my drink.

"Yes, you do."

"No, I—I'm not doing this with you, Lacrosse. Go play with your friends."

"Aw, but then you'll miss me."

"No, I won't."

"Yes, you will."

"Are you two banging? Because if not, you really need to," Felix said before sashaying away.

"Oh shit. Did I screw with your hookup?"

He growled.

My dick perked up.

It was way too hot.

"I'm taking my break," Braxton told Gwen before turning his dark gaze on me. "Let's go."

Without another word, he walked away, and I followed. Braxton went through the swinging doors and into the kitchen.

"What's up?" SpongeBob said, but neither of us replied as Brax went down the hallway, straight for the storage room. My dick was fully hard now because I was pretty sure I knew where this was headed.

Brax turned into the room, and the second I was

inside, he closed the door and turned the lock. "Want—" His lips crushed mine before I could tease him about wanting me so much.

My back hit the door, the knob jamming into me, but I didn't care. Brax held his hand to my throat, not hard, but enough that I felt it. His tongue pushed past my lips, and I let it.

"God, I hate you," he said, biting me before kissing his way down my throat.

"I hate you too."

"Shut up." He licked the hollow spot at the base of my throat. "You wanted to get under my skin all night, didn't you? Got dressed up so I'd take one look and want you."

"Yes," I whimpered. I couldn't believe he could reduce me to that, but he did. My cock throbbed, my body prickly and tingly as I grabbed his hips and pulled him closer.

"I hate that you turn me on so much."

"The feeling is mutual." Was it, though? I was fairly certain I liked it and wanted to know more about his aversion to jocks…to me. Brax tugged my collar down and bit into my shoulder. "Oh fuck." I rolled my hips so our erections rubbed together.

Braxton hissed.

With his forearms pressed against the door on either side of my head, he sucked my earlobe. "I can't wait to work a load out of your balls...you know, show you how it's really done."

"Oh, fuck you. I know how to give head."

"Do you? I've basically forgotten it already."

We frantically worked open our jeans, shoved them and our underwear down our thighs, thrusting together as Braxton took my mouth in another searing kiss. He knew how to work his tongue. I couldn't wait to feel it on my cock.

Braxton wrapped his fist around us, jacked the two of us off together, my balls dangerously close to release.

"No...fuck no. I want your mouth." I didn't know if we'd get this chance again. I shouldn't hope so, but a part of me definitely did.

"Say please," Brax told me.

"No."

"Then no." He pulled back.

I dropped my head back, banged it against the door. I knew him well enough to know he wouldn't suck me until I said it. "Ugh. You motherfucker!

Please."

He smiled, a big fucking smile, much wider and happier than the one he'd given the twink, then knelt, and in one swift movement, took my dick to the back of his throat. He swallowed around it, making my knees go weak. I fisted my hands and bit my bottom lip, which still stung from his teeth.

His mouth was so hot and good, sliding up and down my cock. He nursed the head for a moment, jerking me while he did. When he pulled off, my legs nearly gave out.

"Jesus, Sunshine. Get your mouth on my cock."

"Look at me while I do it, then. You have to watch, have to see who's giving you the best head of your life."

Not a hardship, but still I said, "Mediocre so far."

It earned me another grin.

Our gazes held while he swallowed me down, buried his nose in my pubes, then pulled back some and got to work again. My balls were ready to unleash, my whole body hot like I was going to pass out.

It was really good head. I didn't know whether to be thankful because it felt awesome or pissed he was so great at it.

I thrust my hips forward, and he took it, my orgasm already bearing down on me. "Fuck, I'm not gonna last long. You want my load?"

The heat of his gaze seared me, made my whole body go up in flames as I thrust forward again, balls drawing up, spurt after spurt filling Braxton's mouth. He swallowed it down, licked it off my crown like it was his favorite treat.

"Jesus," I hissed. "I'm gonna die… I needed that… Fuck, I like your mouth."

"I told you." Brax stood, wrapped a hand around his shaft, but I swatted it away.

"If this is our last time, I want that." Was this going to be our last time, or was Sunday still in the plan?

"Get on your knees, then, and suck my dick, Lacrosse."

He didn't have to ask me twice, and only a minute or two later, I was swallowing down Braxton's load too.

I stood, and he was quiet as we wiped up and got dressed.

"Okay, so I have to admit, you know how to blow

a guy. Are we still meeting up tomorrow? I mean, it's head. Who says no to getting their dick sucked?" He didn't respond. His eyes, his whole damn body, sort of closed down. "Hey, are you all right?"

"I'm fine. And nah. We got it out of our system. We're done now."

"Oh-kay. This is Brooding Brax on steroids."

His lips twitched. He wanted to smile.

I couldn't deny I was disappointed, but he was probably right. This was for the best.

When Braxton opened the door, Marshall was standing there with pink cheeks and his beefy arms crossed. "I'm ninety percent sure I know what was going on in there and a one hundred percent sure I don't want you confirming anything."

"Are you sure? It was hot," I replied.

"I don't wanna know." Marshall bent and picked up a box of liquor. I could have sworn he mumbled something wondering why he'd lingered outside to wait.

"I'm hard to resist," I joked, then turned to hear Brax's response, only to find he was already gone.

CHAPTER NINE

Braxton

O N SUNDAY, AFTER work and finishing the grading for my TA class, I made plans with Manuel so that I wouldn't let my dick talk me into doing something I knew I shouldn't be doing. We grew up one street away from each other. His dad worked construction, and his mom had been making authentic Mexican food at the San Luco's Cantina restaurant for as long as I could remember. She was the best cook I knew. When Asher and I would fight as kids or Dad would do dumb shit, I always went to Manny's.

Even though he was my age and wasn't going to school, he still lived at home. SoCal was expensive as fuck, and a lot of people did that—stayed home longer, or parents moved in with their kids when they got married and started a family.

"Hey, Mama G," I said when Lucia opened the door. I might as well call her just Mama since my own had never been around. She left a long time ago and never came back.

"It's good to see you, mijo. You keep too busy. Between work and school, we never see you."

"I'll be better about stopping by," I promised. I should. The Gonzaleses had always treated me like I was family. "Manny in his room?"

"Yeah, he's back there. That girl just left. You tell him she's bad news."

I laughed. Lucia never liked Manny's girlfriends. I'd been nervous when I'd come out. I didn't give a shit about my own dad, and I'd known Grandma wouldn't care, but I'd been nervous about how Manny and his family might take it. I couldn't imagine losing them. But none of them had given a crap, and Lucia had just said, *"I already knew, and I've always loved you."* I had no idea how in the fuck she *had* known, but I remembered the overwhelming feeling of relief.

"I'll tell him," I promised, then made my way upstairs to Manny's room. I knocked and pushed the door open. He was sitting on the bed, looking through what I thought was the schedule book for the week. He worked with his dad. "'Sup?"

"Not much. What's up with you, College Boy?" We bumped fists, and then I sat down in a beanbag chair.

"Nothin'. School and work are kicking my ass. Asher is partying at the house every night. Dad's still in prison. You know, the usual shit."

"I feel you. Your brother fucking sucks. How's Grandma?"

"She's good. Spunky as ever. You should go see her sometime."

He nodded.

"Who's the new girlfriend? Mama G doesn't like her."

"She doesn't like anyone I'm with. She probably wants me to date you. She's always going on about how proud of you she is. *Brax is going to college*, blah, blah, blah."

"You're not my type," I teased, then, "she's proud of you too."

"Yeah. I know." For some reason, my annoying-ass thoughts went to Ty. I'd always been attracted to men I shouldn't want, men I couldn't have, or not really. There was something about a cocky, pretty boy that did it for me every time. Maybe because that was so different from my reality? I didn't know, but after it had come back to bite me in the ass once, I'd never let myself do more than fuck them. And I sure as shit didn't enjoy myself with them outside of orgasms, the way I did with Ty.

"Yo. You're spacing off. What's up with you?" Manny asked.

A sexy, frustrating jock was up with me, and I didn't like it at all. "Nothin'."

"You staying for dinner? Mom's making tamales."

I smiled. "You know it." There wasn't a chance in hell I was turning down Mama G's food.

But the whole night, I couldn't stop thinking about Ty and wondering what he was doing.

HE SAT BESIDE me in class the next day.

"What are you doing, Tyson?"

"Oh, is this seat taken?" he asked innocently.

"Yes."

"Liar."

"You really want my cock again, don't you, Lacrosse?"

"Nah, I don't even remember what it was like. You're not that memorable."

"Is that why you're stalking me?"

"No, that's just because I like to bother you."

I definitely hadn't seen myself as a masochist until I met Ty.

Students were still filing into the room when our professor entered. He didn't give a shit and immediately jumped into today's lesson.

It was confusing at first, but as I took notes, I was pretty sure I understood it. Ty had his laptop up, but he was in his email, then started searching sex toys, which I knew he only did to see if I was watching him.

And I was.

Damn it.

Of course he would be naturally smart too, so he probably didn't need to take notes like I did. Or maybe it was just that he was so spoiled, he didn't have to care. No matter what, he would have a job with Daddy.

"You just huffed like you do when I annoy you, but I didn't even do anything," Ty whispered.

"You don't have to," I replied, a little surprised that he could read me so well.

We finished taking notes, then worked on a lab that made it obvious Ty had no idea what the fuck he was doing. "Not like that," I whispered, unsure why I was helping him. "You're building the program all wrong."

"I fucking hate this." He ran a hand through his hair, clearly frustrated, and I frowned in his direction.

"Maybe you picked the wrong field to go into, then?"

"No shit." His reply was soft, but with a sharp edge of painful truth to it.

Before I could respond, class was over and we were packing our shit up. I followed behind Ty, wondering what the hell I was doing, but doing it anyway. "Why are you spending all this money on a degree you don't want?"

"I'm not spending money. Spoiled, remember?"

My insides froze up. "Must be nice. I'm working

my fucking ass off and will start my life in debt, while you don't care enough to try and don't have to pay for shit."

"Fuck," I heard Ty grit out as I walked away and around the back of the building, heading I didn't even know where. He caught up to me and grabbed my arm. "I didn't mean to say that."

"But it's true. You're so fucking lucky, and you don't even realize it. I need my job, you don't. I wouldn't have time to play a fucking sport even if I wanted. I don't have a built-in position with Daddy. Hell, my dad is a prick who is in prison. You have everything handed to you on a silver fucking platter, and you don't even see it!"

I didn't know why I was doing this, why I cared how he lived his life or if he knew how good he had it. We weren't friends. We had nothing in common besides the fact that we liked to suck each other's dicks.

"You don't think I know that?" he said too loudly, then looked around. We were in a pretty secluded place, people in the distance but no one close enough to hear us. "You don't think I see it, but I do, Brax. Just because I don't walk around wearing a sign stating my privilege doesn't mean I don't know I have it."

"Then why don't you at least try to do something good with it?"

"Because I can't! I spent my whole life idolizing my father, doing everything I could to follow in his footsteps, even when it couldn't be further from what I wanted, only to find out he's nothing but a fraud."

He ran his hand through his hair again, pacing back and forth in front of me. We were both breathing heavily. I wanted to walk away, not to care about what he had to say, but my feet were rooted in the dirt.

"My dad always told me I had to be a good man, responsible and respectable. I was going to be just like him. I'd work with him, and then one day Langley Enterprises would be mine. My mom and I did everything for him, and now we find out their whole fucking marriage he hasn't been able to keep it in his pants. I have a brother who's one year younger than me that I never knew about, never met. He kept him a fucking secret, paying his mom through a private account we knew nothing about. And he's not the only one either. He left Mom recently so he can be with his new girlfriend, who has a toddler he also fathered. And *that's* why I don't give a shit about this class and why I need that job. I know I'll never make enough money to do it on my own, but I sure as shit don't want to be dependent on a liar forever."

He leaned against the wall, eyes closed, pulling heavy breaths in and out. I couldn't do anything but watch him, trying to find words that were nowhere to be found.

Ty said, "Wanna know something stupid? I've always wanted to be a nurse, and no one knows...well, no one but you now. I didn't even let myself seriously consider it because all I cared about was being exactly who my dad wanted me to be."

I thought about the photo on his Instagram, the one hashtagged *heroes*. How he'd been so insistent on taking care of me when I was sick. That was Ty's dream, hidden away inside the manufactured version of himself he showed the world. "What are you going to do about it?" I asked.

"About what?"

"Your life, your dad...everything. You just gonna keep being who he wants you to be? If I did that, I'd be in prison for armed robbery with my pops." I rested against the wall beside him.

"Shit...you really are a bad boy. So the rumors about illegal stuff are true?"

"Most aren't, but some are." We were quiet for a moment, our arms touching, nothing but our long-sleeved shirts between us. "No one can force you to be anyone you don't want to be, Lacrosse. I refuse to fucking believe that shit. People might look at me and think I'm nothing, but they don't control who I am."

"It's not that easy."

"So? What does easy have to do with anything?"

"I think we're having a moment here."

"Until you opened your mouth and ruined it."

We chuckled, and he said softly, "No one knows any of that...not just the nurse stuff."

"Who am I gonna tell?"

"The twink from the other night?"

"So fucking jealous. Get off my dick," I replied, secretly liking it. I'd always liked Ty wanting me.

"You love it when I'm on your cock. Don't pretend you don't."

Eh, he had a point. "I still don't like you."

"I still don't like you either."

But he wasn't a total asshole. "Let's go."

I pushed off the wall, and Ty did too. "Where are we going?"

"I'm gonna help your dumb ass study. It's not your dad it's gonna hurt if you flunk out of school."

"I wouldn't let that happen. Then I couldn't play lacrosse."

"Shit, I was hoping you didn't really like that game either."

"I do, and you're coming to one of my games, Sunshine. I don't care what I have to do to make it happen."

"Nah, I'm good."

"Just you wait and see."

Jesus, he better not be right.

CHAPTER TEN

Ty

WE'D BEEN STUDYING for an hour, and I still couldn't believe it was happening. That I was at Braxton's house, in his room, with him at his desk while I lay on his bed, with books and computers and... "Want me to suck you off?"

"No," he replied.

Fuck, he had willpower for days. "Do you want to suck me off?"

He groaned. "We're studying."

"*Braxton.*"

"*Lacrosse.*"

"I can't believe you're interested in this stuff. It's so boring." I'd pretended to care most of my life, bonding with Dad over things I had no interest in. I liked that I didn't have to with Brax.

"No, it's not. I like that it makes sense in a way people don't. In case you haven't noticed, I'm not fond of humans. Computers, I like."

"Wait...you don't like people? I never would have guessed."

"Fuck off, pretty boy."

"Aw, you think I'm pretty!"

"I gotta get this shit done before work." Brax didn't look at me when he spoke, instead facing his laptop screen. I could tell he was serious. Before our conversation earlier today, I probably would have continued to tease him, but I could feel how important this was to him. I'd gone to school because that's what Langleys did. It was never a question that I would go to college or that I'd have the money to do it.

Brax *had* to work for it. He wasn't expected to get a degree; he'd chosen to, and that was really fucking cool.

Not that I planned to tell him. Despite what happened earlier, we didn't work that way.

While I wouldn't say we were friends, we had a new understanding of each other.

I really didn't feel like doing schoolwork, but Brax

had been cool enough to help me understand what the fuck I was doing, so I kept my phone silenced, knowing Watty, Ford, and Collins were blowing me up, and said, "Let's do this."

He looked at me, frowned, and then we got to work.

"WHERE THE FUCK were you today?" Collins asked after practice.

"Around." I couldn't say why I didn't want them to know I was with Brax. For some reason, I wanted to keep it to myself. They'd talk shit, which I understood because it was weird that I'd spent time with someone they called Asshole Bartender. But we had, and I'd enjoyed it. Besides, I didn't always know where they were either.

"Around? What do you mean *around*?" Watty asked.

"I mean I was doing shit. What does it matter?"

"Oh damn. Who are you fucking?"

I could see why their thoughts went here. Normally it *would* be about sex. It definitely wouldn't be about homework. "Wouldn't you like to know?" I teased, and they went with it, patting me on the back, Ford pushing me into Watty, who shoved me into Collins. All fist-bumps and bro hugs.

"Stop." I laughed. "I need to get ready for work."

"I can't believe you got a job. It's like you're growing up right before our eyes." Watty wiped fake tears from his face.

"You're an idiot."

"You act like that's something new. I've always been an idiot."

We snickered because none of us could argue that truth.

Once we were back at the house, I got ready, made a sandwich, then headed to Shenanigans.

"The dish bitch is here!" Chuck, one of the bartenders, shouted when I walked inside.

Brax was wiping down the beer taps and not making eye contact with me. This wouldn't do at all.

I walked over and let myself behind the counter. Shenanigans wasn't too busy yet, and I'd come a whole ten minutes early and everything. "Did you miss me?" I crossed my arms.

"Yeah." He shrugged, and I froze, not expecting that answer. "It was tearing me up inside. I just...don't know how I'll ever be happy if you're not with me every minute of every day. It's like a piece of my heart—no, *all* my heart and my lungs and—"

"Shut up." That hadn't been nice. For a moment I'd thought he was being almost sweet. I was definitely an idiot.

Brax laughed, rich and deep, and fuck, it was a really hot laugh.

"But, Ty...I feel so empty without you. Like I'll never be complete again. Every time you walk out of the room, it's like you take all the air with you."

"I feel like you've legit written love poetry about me. You're too good at it."

"I'm just speaking the words that are in my heart. You're my sun...my moon...my very reason for getting out of bed every morning."

Gwen and Chuck snickered. I was pretty sure a customer joined in too.

Brax tossed a towel over his shoulder, letting it rest there, his hip against the counter where he leaned beside me. He twisted one of the rings on his finger.

"I like you better when you're brooding."

"I'll always brood for you..." Then he bent over and fake-vomited.

I couldn't help but join in with the group and laugh. "Ha-ha. We get it. Braxton made a joke. Everyone can stop pretending he's funny now."

Though there did seem to be some lightness to him this afternoon that I didn't often see from Brax. I'd wondered how it would be between us. If our admissions and him taking me home to study would make him close down. It was always a toss-up with Brax. I had to admit, I was pleasantly surprised.

"You gonna stand around and watch me all night?" Brax asked, standing up straight again.

"No, because I don't like you again."

"When did you ever like me?"

That was a trick question. The first response that came to mind was, *When you were on your knees with my dick stuffed in your mouth*, but I didn't figure he would appreciate me putting our hookup on blast. Or our study session. "What do you mean? You're my best friend. My ride or die. The Bert to my Ernie. I'm gonna tell everyone."

"Why you gotta ruin my rep like that?"

"Aw, come on, Sunshine. You know you secretly love it." A group came in, so I backed away from him with a playful wink. "I'm gonna clock in and grab my stuff from the back. See you soon, bestie."

The stare he gave me was basically *fuck my life* in visual form. Strangely, it was one of my favorite looks from him.

I headed to the back. SpongeBob wasn't working today, and someone else was manning the food. I used my app to clock in, then put on an apron. There were dishes stacked up, so I put those in the dishwasher before grabbing my cart and heading to the main part of the bar. There hadn't been any tables to clean up when I first got there, but there were already a couple now.

I tugged the rubber gloves I'd purchased out of my pocket and got to work. They had some here, but I didn't like the quality. It was still gross, and I couldn't pretend I liked messing with people's dirty utensils.

I scraped old food into the trash, stacked dishes into the bin, and wiped the tables down. Was it ridiculous that I knew my father would be horrified if he saw me? Sometimes I couldn't believe I'd spent most of my life idolizing him the way I had. I looked at Brax and couldn't imagine a situation where a person would look down on him for how hard he fought, but my dad would. He sure as shit would freak the fuck out if he knew we were screwing around. Well, that we had screwed around. It didn't look like that was happening again.

As the evening went on, things got busier. More and more people came in, some that I knew from school. It was crazy to me how often people chilled at a bar. There were even people doing homework with earbuds in, which blew my mind. I mean, I wasn't gonna lie. I spent a lot of time at Shenanigans, but not as often as some.

"Are you really wearing rubber gloves?" Brax asked as I made my way past the counter toward the back.

"No." He eyed me, and I added, "I can't help it! This stuff is gross."

"You've been lucky. You haven't even had to clean up vomit in the bathrooms. Maybe I should talk to Oscar about that. You should have a turn on bathroom duty."

I froze. "Wait…we have to clean it up if people puke?" I'd puked in here before, and…hell, I never thought about who'd had to clean it up. I was a dick.

"Did you think it magically disappears on its own?"

He had a point. "No one better upchuck on my shifts, that's all I'm saying." A light bulb went off, and I looked at Chuck. "Hey, Upchuck. That can be your new nickname."

"Only if you want me to kick your ass, Rich Boy."

The title he'd labeled me with felt like sandpaper against my skin. Of course, I'd just called him puke, but that was different. We all knew he wasn't literal throw-up.

"Whatever," I grumbled and made my way to the kitchen.

I kept to myself most of the night. We stayed steady, but not crazy-busy, which was good. A little after eleven, I came out of the bathroom, ready to head out for the night, only to see Brax lingering around in the kitchen.

Ridiculously, my pulse sped up. "Hey, bestie."

"It's Sunshine to you," he teased back, which made me grin. This was a pleasant surprise. "So you got a handle on that shit for class?" he asked, the two of us walking out the back door.

"As good as I'm going to, I imagine."

A rush of cool air hit me the second we walked outside. It was probably only in the fifties, so it wasn't bad for me, but Brax had on his leather jacket—it was his proper bad-boy look—though I didn't think Brax was a bad boy at all. Not really.

"You didn't like it when Chuck called you rich boy," he mused, and damn. How had he been able to tell? Was I that easy to read, or did Brax just pay more attention than most people?

"No, I don't suppose I did. Should I have?"

"It's true, though. You can't help who you are any more than I can."

He started walking toward his bike, and again, I found myself following him. "Wait. Slow your roll there, buddy. You *hate* who I am, and now you're telling me I can't help it."

"I'm telling you there are some things you can change and some you can't. Being a spoiled rich boy is in your DNA. How you approach it, *that* makes all the difference."

"Wow…are you sure you shouldn't be getting a degree in psychology?"

He threw a leg over his motorcycle, and I couldn't

help watching, taking in the way his jeans stretched tight around his thighs. He was so fucking sexy. I hated myself for how much I wanted him.

Brax just shrugged. "Maybe. And stop looking at me like that."

"Like what?"

"Like you're remembering what it's like to be on your knees for me and you're dying for a repeat."

"Um...no lies detected," I replied. "Though I guess it could be the other way around—you sucking me."

"Be good."

"Aren't you supposed to like being naughty?"

Brax gave me a half-grin that said he did. The two times we'd fucked around had both been in public places, and he'd been the one to lead the way to each. "Yeah, I guess I do, but I don't like trouble, and you're trouble with a capital *T*." He tugged his helmet on, started his bike, and drove away.

Damned if I didn't stand there and watch him go.

CHAPTER ELEVEN

Brax

TY TEXTED ME on and off all week. That part didn't shock me as much as the fact that I'd replied to them. Each and every one. A few times I might have even messaged first. It was weird and confusing. I didn't like it...and yet I did. We'd had a strange dynamic from the start. There had been no reason for us to enjoy bantering back and forth with each other, but we always had. While there were a whole lot of people I didn't vibe with, his friends especially, I didn't seek them out the way I often did with Ty. I didn't wonder what the next thing to come out of their mouth would be or work through the best way to get the upper hand with them. I couldn't make sense of it other than...well, he was *fun*.

Which was gross. He was Tyson fucking Langley,

after all.

But now add our study session and texting, and yeah, it boggled my mind. Every time a message came through, I told myself I wasn't going to respond, but I always did.

And I waited for him after work this week.

And, and, and… "Fuuuuuuck!" Now I was lying in bed and thinking about him too.

"You dead in there?" Asher banged on my door.

"Do dead men typically yell fuck?" I got up and unlocked it.

"I thought maybe it was a murder in progress."

No, but this thing with Ty might be slowly killing me. "No such luck."

"What are you doing today?" Asher asked. It was a Friday, and I didn't have class. Ty didn't either. It was frustrating I knew that.

"Going to see Grandma. You should consider it. How long has it been?"

He blew out an annoyed breath. "Yeah, I get it. You're a better grandson than me. She knows I love her. I'll get over there soon. Shit's just been busy." And by shit, he meant partying. "What about you? When's the last time you went to see Dad?"

"Haven't and don't plan to. That's totally fucking different. He's serving time for armed robbery, something he tried to get his sons to go in on with him, if you remember. She's in an assisted-living facility. Fuck off with that comparison."

"You always act like you're better than me, Brax, but you're not. It doesn't matter that you're trying to be someone you're not by going to that stupid fucking school. You came from the same piece-of-shit parents, and no matter what, we'll both likely end up just like them. There's no shame in the game."

"Fuck you." I shoved him. Asher just shook his head, pushed me back, and walked out of the room. "Clean up your mess from last night!" I called after him, trying my best to ignore the voice in my head that told me he was right. Like always, I failed.

"IT'S GORGEOUS OUT today." Grandma reached back and patted my hand as I pushed her wheelchair into the courtyard. She'd had health problems for years, but then had broken a hip, which was what had made her decide to stay in a facility. I would have kept her at home, where she belonged, and taken care of her, but she'd insisted.

"It is." I found a grassy spot for us to relax, locking her chair before sitting on the ground beside her. Palm trees dotted the scenery around the Spanish architecture of her facility.

"How's school going?"

"All right." *There's this guy, Ty, who's driving me crazy.*

She tapped me with her foot. "Geez, don't be too talkative."

I chuckled. "Sorry. It's going okay. I helped this lacrosse player study the other day. Also, Manny has a new girlfriend. Mama G hates her."

"Mama G hates all his girlfriends. Tell me about this lacrosse player."

"It's not like that." Her mind likely went to a potential boyfriend, someone I might *like*.

"It's okay if it was, ya know? Have fun, Braxton. Date boys and have sex. That's what college is supposed to be about."

"Um...aren't you too old to talk about that?

Aren't you supposed to be telling me to be responsible and focus on my future?"

"No. If I were talking to your brother, I would tell him to keep it in his pants and get his shit together. You're my sweet boy wrapped in a brooding package, who likes to pretend his heart isn't the size of San Luco."

Brooding. First Ty and now my own grandma? "I don't brood."

"You're the definition of brood."

If I didn't know better, I'd have thought Ty got to her. Ty, who wanted to be a nurse and—*stop thinking about that motherfucker.* "You're being very mean to your favorite grandson."

She laughed. "You're a joy, Brax. I just wish you knew it."

Pressure built in my chest, suffocating me. "I know how awesome I am."

"No, you don't. So…the lacrosse player?"

"There's nothing to tell." When she cocked a brow, I knew I was fucked. "I don't know… He's blond, rich, spoiled, cocky as fu—heck. He's decided it's his mission in life to annoy me as much as possible. Unfortunately, he's good at it."

"You like this lacrosse player."

"Huh?" My pulse sped up. "No, I don't. He makes me crazy."

"Which is how you know. Your grandfather drove me crazy."

"Grandpa wasn't Ty. I don't date jocks."

"You don't date anyone."

I lay back on the grass, wishing my pulse wasn't suddenly running the fifty-yard dash. "Gee, thanks. Way to boost a guy's ego."

"You know that's not what I meant. It's okay to let people in, Brax. It's okay to care about someone other than me and Manny. I know you haven't had great role models, but you're not your father, and your relationship won't be the same as his was with your mom. You're more worthy of love than anyone I know."

This wasn't the conversation I'd thought I would be having today. Was it possible to melt into the ground? Maybe turn camouflage so she couldn't see me? "Who I am has nothing to do with my parents, and you're getting way ahead of yourself here. There's zero chance of anything even close to love ever happening between me and Lacrosse. He's hot, sure, but even the thought of falling in love with him gives me hives."

"Maybe you should see a doctor."

I looked at her and smiled. "Ha-ha."

"Okay, fine. Ignore what I said about love. Do what all the kids are doing today. Hook up. My friend Mallory said her grandson called it banging. That sounds awfully violent, but if that's what the youngsters are saying nowadays—"

Laughing, I covered my ears. "Oh my God, stop. Please don't talk to me about hooking up or banging someone. I'm traumatized, I'll have you know."

She joined me in my laughter. Not for the first time, I was thankful to have her in my life. I didn't think anyone understood me or cared about me the way she did.

"Fine. Then maybe you can at least be friends with this lacrosse boy. You don't have enough friends."

"You're really determined to bust my balls today, aren't you?" But the truth was, I knew what she was saying, and she was right. I just didn't know if I could do anything about it.

"If I'm not allowed to say banging, you're not

allowed to mention your balls." *My grandma, ladies and gentlemen.* But I loved her. She leaned over and patted my leg. "Be friends with your lacrosse boy."

"Yeah, yeah, I hear what you're saying. But I kinda like *not* getting along with him."

"Pfft. If that's the case, you're already in trouble, Brax. There's no helping you now."

"Can we talk about something else?"

"Yes. Did I tell you I'm helping with sets for a play? It's all for us old people. They provide transportation for multiple facilities in the area to one of the local theaters."

"Have you ever done something like that before?"

"Nope, but there's a first time for everything."

I loved that about her. There was nothing she wouldn't try and nothing she couldn't do. Life hadn't been easy for her, but she'd never let that get her down.

We chatted about her play, and game night at the facility, and two friends she was trying to play cupid with. Apparently, that was a new thing for her.

When my cell buzzed, I tugged it out of my pocket to see a text from Ty.

The Sexiest Man Alive: I'm booooored.

I really needed to change his name in my phone.

Me: So? What does that have to do with me?

The Sexiest Man Alive: I just figured since you don't have a life, you might need me to teach you how to have a little fun.

Me: No, you can't suck my dick.

The Sexiest Man Alive: Gasp! I'm shocked! I can't believe you would suggest something so crude!

Me: You're obsessed with me.

The Sexiest Man Alive: I'm more honest than you.

He might have a point because my cock was definitely interested in playing in his mouth again.

The Sexiest Man Alive: You can also help me with my homework. Take pity on me. Please...

The Sexiest Man Alive: Please.

The Sexiest Man Alive: Please.

The Sexiest Man Alive: Please.

The Sexiest Man Alive: Please.

Me: JFC. Meet me at my house. You're like a fly who won't quit buzzing around my ear.

The Sexiest Man Alive: I love you too.

"Is that your lacrosse player?" Grandma asked, and shit, I'd forgotten I was sitting out here with her.

"He's not mine."

"You were smiling."

"I'm not talking to you anymore."

Grandma yawned dramatically. "I'm *sooooo* tired. I

think I'm ready to go back inside now. I'm going to take a nap, so you should head home."

She wasn't fooling anyone, but I pretended she was. "Rest is good for you, after all."

"So is lacrosse." She laughed, and I ignored her. There was a reason she was my favorite person in the world.

CHAPTER TWELVE

Ty

I WONDERED IF it was possible I'd been abducted by an alien. If they'd taken me onto their ship and hooked electrodes to my head to alter my brain. Maybe they were controlling my actions and feelings. Making me *want* to spend time with Brax and *push* to spend time with Brax.

I'd never chased someone in my life, until now. But let's face it, that was basically what I was doing with Brax. I was motherfucking *chasing* him without an endgame in mind. I didn't want to be his boyfriend. That would be weird. We were too different and didn't like each other too much. I wasn't sure I was trying to be his friend either, for the same reasons. So was all this for sex? Or because I got a kick out of bugging him? None of that felt right either. I just knew he'd always fascinated me, and now, after telling him about my dad, I was even more obsessed with the thought of spending time with him.

Alien abduction was the only thing that made sense.

I turned my gaze to the sky as if I could expect some kind of answer there. Maybe a flash of a spaceship and my real body peeking out the window to say hi.

I turned at the sound of Brax's front door opening and closing. I knew it wasn't him because he'd texted to let me know he was busy and helping someone with something before he could leave. I'd already been close to his house, and now my car sat on the curb while I paced on the sidewalk as if I'd been casing the place.

"'Sup?" his brother said.

"Hey." I crossed my arms. His gaze slid the length of me, not in a you're-hot way, but in an I-don't-trust-you. "I'm Brax's..." What the fuck was I? Brax's alien-abducted associate? "Coworker." There. That worked.

"Oh yeah. You're that guy who was here the other morning."

The morning he didn't give a shit that Brax was sick. Obviously, I was feeling some kinda way about this.

"He's not home. He's visiting our grandma at the assisted-living facility. When he goes, he's usually there almost all day."

His grandma was in a facility? He'd said he was helping someone but didn't mention he was spending time with his grandmother. Guilt pricked at my insides. I hadn't meant to take him away from something important...something that seemed to be important to him. Something that was sort of sweet. *No, no, no, no.* I would *not* allow myself to think of Braxton Walker as sweet. Hell, my other friends had grandmas too, and that didn't automatically make my insides turn mushy.

"I talked to him a little while ago," I told him. "He should be here soon. I just wanted to stretch my legs."

"Are you his man? You don't seem like Brax's type, and he doesn't look like yours. He never has guys here unless it's a fuck and go. But this is twice with you. Is coworker code for fuck buddy now?" He laughed.

Well, at least I knew for sure that Brax was out to his brother. I was always careful about what I said around the family of queer people if I didn't know their situation. It was sad that I had to think that way, but the world was fucked sometimes. "No, I'm not his boyfriend. And how can you look at someone and say if they're someone else's type?" Forget that he was right. The statement still rubbed me wrong. Like, Brax and I couldn't be anything because we were too different?

You thought the same thing five seconds ago, dumbass.

"Oh, gotcha. You like him, but Brax thinks he's too good for you. I get it, man. He's the same with me." He held out his fist, wanting me to bump it in support. I was really starting to wish I'd just stayed in my car. Sure, I might have tormented Brax by telling him the same thing, that he thought he was better than me, but it felt gross to do that with his brother. Like I was betraying him somehow.

A car pulled up then, three guys in it. Brax's brother—I didn't even know the guy's name—gave me an up nod before climbing in and driving off with them. Less than a minute later, I heard the familiar rumble of Brax's motorcycle. He rounded the corner, pulled into the driveway, and killed the engine.

He tugged off his helmet, which had flattened his black hair. "Got here early. Excited to see me?"

"I figured it'd been a while since you've had any fun and took pity on you."

He shook his head, but a small smile teased his lips. He always tried to hide it, like he couldn't let on that he enjoyed something, and I couldn't help wondering why. What all had Brax lost?

"So, homework, huh?" he asked.

"Wait. We're really doing that?" School was boring. It was a Friday, and we'd amazingly somehow both gotten off work.

"What else did you have in mind?"

"Hmm... There are literally hundreds of options that sound a whole lot more fun than school." I couldn't help checking him out because, I mean, Brax was gorgeous. There was no denying that, and I wouldn't even pretend to try. He wore jeans like he always did, just loose enough to be hot but still show the goods. His stomach was flat, his black T-shirt tight against it. He still had the necklace on, but he was missing his rings today.

He gave me a half-grin, then walked closer. He didn't stop until he stood right in front of me. I could feel the heat of his cinnamon-scented breath, and damned if it didn't make me tremble slightly.

"You want me, don't you?"

Yes, yes I did. Who could blame me? "You want me too. You're just determined to deny it more than I am."

Brax leaned in the same way he'd taunted me countless other times, lips close to my ear. "Get your backpack, Lacrosse. We have homework to do."

"Oh, fuck you. I might have to rub one out real quick when we get inside. I'll let you watch."

"You wish," Brax replied.

I jogged over to my car and got my bag, which I'd brought in case he really forced me to do this.

As soon as we went inside, he cursed. There were beer cans everywhere, a couple of bottles of liquor on the living-room table, discarded bags of chips. The kitchen counters were covered in dirty dishes with food on them. "I fucking told him to clean up his shit." Brax went toward the hallway. "Asher!"

"He left a few minutes before you got home." Jesus, I really didn't like Brax's brother. He clearly didn't give a shit about all the pressure already on Brax's shoulders.

"You should just head out." Brax moved toward the kitchen. "I can't do shit until I get rid of this mess. It'll drive me crazy."

This was one hundred percent where I should exit, but instead I set my backpack on the couch and said, "I can help."

"Shut up."

"Geez, I was expecting at least a no-thank-you."

"This isn't your responsibility."

"I don't think it's yours either."

His dark brows pulled together. "It's my house."

"No offense, but your brother sucks." I pushed the sleeves up on my Lacrosse Kings T-shirt. "He didn't give a shit when you were sick, and now he leaves this mess from a party I'm pretty sure you had no part of, while you were going to visit your grandma."

As soon as I said the words, the air in the room thickened around me.

"How do you know about her?"

I looked at him, his eyes stormy with an expression I couldn't read. "Asher mentioned you were seeing her, said you usually stay all day. That's really—"

"Oh my God. Do *not* say something nice to me."

I laughed. "Thank you, for stopping me before I did that. It would have been painful."

"Not as painful as hearing it," he replied, then…smiled, without trying to hide it. Fuck, Brax was sexy when he did that. "We are so weird."

Yeah, we were, but for whatever reason, we worked that way. "Where's a trash bag?"

"Lacrosse…"

"*Oh my God. Do not say something nice to me,*" I repeated his earlier words.

He didn't. He just went into the kitchen, grabbed a bag, and handed it over. I started cleaning up the trash while he did the dishes.

"Who's the dish bitch now?" I teased, and he flicked soapy water at me.

I couldn't help wondering how much this happened. His house had been a mess when he'd been sick too. How often did his brother have parties? Did he ever clean up after himself, or was it always Brax doing it for him?

We chatted some. The whole time I had to force

myself not to ask questions, not to muse about his grandma or all the bits and pieces of Brax's life that I'd never considered before getting to know him better.

When I was done with the trash, I rinsed while he continued to wash. Working together, it didn't take us long to finish up. When we did, he tossed me a towel and grabbed another so we could dry our hands.

"So...homework?" I fake-gagged.

He shook his head before asking the last thing I expected from him, "Do you want to get out of here for a while?"

"Sure. Where to?"

"Hold up a sec." He went to the garage, coming back a second later with a motorcycle helmet.

When he tossed it my way, a fireworks display went off beneath my skin. The thought of riding Brax's bike with him was hot as hell.

"You scared?" he asked.

"Fuck no."

"Let's do this, then." On the way out, he grabbed his leather jacket, then handed another one to me, which I immediately put on.

We made our way outside, Brax locking the door

behind us. He tugged his helmet on, turning to check mine afterward to make sure I latched it correctly. He swatted my hands away, tightening the straps on my chin. It was half sweet and half gross because I could take care of myself.

Without a word, he threw one leg over the bike, started it up, then nodded toward the back, and…Jesus, my dick was plumping up. It would be an interesting afternoon.

I climbed on behind him, legs squeezing, arms wrapped tightly around Braxton. I didn't know where we were going, and I didn't care. I liked this Brax. The one who didn't seem quite as brooding, who wanted to hang out without getting begged to do it.

I'd never ridden on a motorcycle before. There was a kernel of fear inside me, but strangely, I trusted him. Or hell, maybe I just wanted to look badass to him, didn't want him to know that part of me was nervous. Also, I knew my dad would hate the idea.

Brax walked the bike backward out of the driveway, then sped off down the street. My heart jumped into my throat, throbbing there and echoing throughout my whole body. My stomach flip-flopped as Brax headed for the Pacific Coast Highway. I wasn't sure how fast we were going, but it was…fuck, it was freeing, like stress and tension I didn't know I was carrying fell away, evaporating into the asphalt with each mile he drove.

The ocean was to our left, the scenery changing as we went, from sand and beach to bluffs and rocky cliffs. The smell of salt water filled my senses, along with the heat of Brax's body.

My stomach dipped and flew each time he went around a curve, my body leaning with his, while I prayed that this wasn't a dumb decision that would get me killed.

Braxton drove through Encinitas, then slowed down and pulled off into a small parking lot that said Beacon's Beach. This was…surprising.

When he parked, I climbed off the bike and removed my helmet. I wasn't familiar with this beach, but it wasn't that far from campus. Brax must have been able to read the look on my face because he said, "Mostly locals come here. It's a hell of a lot quieter. Especially this time of year or this late in the day."

It was no surprise that Braxton would go in search of the quiet beaches. My friends and I never did. We loved all the commotion. We went to the water to meet people and have fun, not to chill and relax, but…I did go by myself sometimes. Especially at sunrise. It's what I'd done the morning after I found out I had siblings.

A second later, something else clicked—it was late in the day, and I had practice. I didn't want to mention it to Brax. I…fuck, I didn't want to leave. So I pulled out my phone and tried to covertly send out a text while he led me toward the other end of the lot.

Me: If Coach asks, I'm at home puking my guts out. I'm trying to get well before the game tomorrow.

It was a group message between me, Watty, Collins, and Ford. I figured they would start responding in three…two…

Ford: What the fuck!

Watty: You can't miss practice the day before a game.

Collins: Are you legit skipping practice to get laid?

Me: Nah, it's not like that. Don't be dickheads. Cover for me. I've never done this before. It's important.

Was it really, though? Going to the beach with Braxton?

But then, I didn't think he did normal things like the rest of us, so I was basically studying rare phenomena, which made it important.

Watty: Okay…you cool?
Ford: Yeah, you all right?
Collins: You've been weird lately.

I could see why they thought that. I'd been different. And I was good…but I also wasn't. I just didn't think I could tell them that.

Me: Yeah, no worries. Talk to you later.

I was just putting my phone on vibrate when Brax stopped, cocking a brow at me. "Is this getting in the way of your texting?"

"Jealous? I'm not talking to anyone I want to fuck."

"As if I'd care."

"I love you too," I replied, then pressed a playful, loud, dramatic kiss to his cheek.

Braxton shoved me away…but he was smiling.

CHAPTER THIRTEEN

Braxton

WHAT. THE. FUCK. Was I doing?

First, I'd left Grandma to hang out with Ty. Then we'd cleaned my house together before I took him for a ride on my motorcycle and to my favorite beach?

He'd been cool about the house, though. He hadn't had to help me. My own brother wouldn't have. And for whatever reason, spending that kind of time with him had made me think about those photos of Ty on the empty beach on his social media.

He had apparently broken me, and I didn't fucking like it.

Still, I went first toward the steep dirt trail. It wound its way in a zigzag pattern down the cliff to the white sands of the beach below. Grandma used to bring us here.

Ty's foot slipped. He immediately reached out for one of the wooden rails on the barrier that kept people from tumbling down the cliff, and I grabbed for him. My hand landed on his bicep, feeling the tight ball of muscle through the fabric of the jacket I'd lent him. The thought was kind of hot—Ty wearing my things. "I just saved your life."

"I'm surprised you didn't let me fall."

"I thought about it, but I don't really want to go to prison. Family reunions aren't my thing." *Aaaaand*, why had I said that? Ty's blue gaze softened. "Jesus Christ, don't. Don't look at me with pity, Lacrosse. I can't take that shit. I'll push you down the cliff."

"I would expect nothing less. Also, we have the strangest relationship."

"Great. You don't think I'm your boyfriend, right? When two boys meet and share orgasms, that doesn't mean they're in a relationship. It's called hooking up."

We started walking again. "Only we're not. You're just taking me on dates now. Please, for the love of God, when you get married, let your significant other give your kids the sex talk. Oh, and wait…are you bi or gay? I've never seen you with women."

"This isn't a date. And I'm not getting married. Or having kids. Gay."

"I'm an equal opportunity lover, myself."

"Yes, I know. I've seen. And don't say *lover*. You sound like you're eighty."

"What eighty-year-olds do you hang out with, and can I meet them?"

"Like them older, do you?"

He laughed. "No. I just like cool people, and they sound cool. I can't explain why I spend time with you, though."

"Thank God I'm not cool, and the feeling is mutual."

Ty surprised me by wrapping a hand around my wrist and tugging me faster along with him. "This is such a sweet date. I can't wait to get down to the sand."

"Not a date," I reminded him. I really needed to get my shit together so I could get the upper hand again. Ty had it incredibly too much lately.

Still, I didn't pull away and he didn't let go as we navigated our way down the cliff. When we got to the bottom, he immediately took his shoes and socks off, and I did the same. We weren't dressed for the beach. I hadn't planned on us coming here. At first, I was just going to drive by, but then this weird, unexplainable part of me had wondered if Ty liked sunsets over the water as much as those photos led me to believe he liked the sunrise.

There were a few people on the sand, a couple of people surfing, and random stragglers walking down from Beacon's Beach toward Moonlight, which was always busier.

"There's a lot of erosion around here," I told him. "A lot of the sand is covered at high tide."

He froze. "Did you bring me out here to drown me?"

"Fuck, how'd you know?"

We didn't go toward the water, instead walking a little ways down, stopping close to an area in the cliff where the rocks jutted out. It wasn't safe to sit beneath it because rocks sometimes fell, but we could stay close. Unfortunately, the cliff was being eaten away.

We both lowered ourselves, setting our shoes beside us, and then…nothing.

"Wanna make out?" Ty broke the silence.

"Do you ever shut up?"

"It was an awkward silence. I had to break it up somehow."

He was right. This whole talking thing we'd started to do lately was fucked up, but now that we were sitting here, hanging out in this planned way, I didn't know what to say.

I shrugged. "Sure."

Ty whipped his head in my direction, eyes wide before he narrowed them and scowled. "You fucker! I thought you were serious."

A laugh tumbled out of my mouth, deep, making my stomach and chest vibrate. "Aw, did little Ty get his hopes up?"

"You've had my dick in your mouth, Sunshine. You know there's nothing little about me."

"Oh God. You're such a fucking jock." I didn't know how I could forget that, but sometimes I did.

"Because I like to talk about how impressive my junk is?"

"I mean, partly."

"What's your issue with jocks?"

There was zero chance of me sharing something so personal and embarrassing with him.

Before I could figure out how to respond, Ty frowned. He tugged his phone out of his pocket and groaned. "My dad, because of course it is. I wonder if Coach called to tell him I'm missing practice."

He was missing practice. Shit. "Why didn't you say something? I can bring you back." I'd just taken him here with me, assuming he didn't have anything else to do. I didn't even think about lacrosse.

"Nah, it's okay. The guys are covering for me. I'm currently puking my brains out."

So, he'd thought about practice and messaged them to help with an excuse? I remembered him texting before we'd made the hike down. Had that been what he was doing? My stomach twisted, and my heart raced at the thought. I wasn't sure how I felt about it. Ty had chosen hanging out with me over the game he loved so much? It didn't compute.

He rejected the call, but it immediately started to buzz again. "He can't handle not being in control of everything," Ty said. "The more I ignore him, the more insistent he'll be to talk just so he can tell me all the ways I'm fucking up and how much of a disappointment I am. Langleys don't fold. They don't get their emotions involved. They care about the bottom line, and that's all." He scooped up a fistful of sand, then slowly let it sift through his fingers. "Sorry. I don't talk to my friends about stuff like this, so it just sort of comes out when I'm with you."

I almost joked about him basically saying I wasn't his friend, but it didn't feel right. "It's cool. You know my dad is in prison, and you saw my brother's shit. Families are fucked up."

"Yeah, but the difference between mine and yours is mine tries to pretend they're not. Even my mom… I love her to death, but she just acts like nothing happened. I'm supposed to forget the fact that my father is a cheating asshole, that he wasn't a real dad to my brother, and just keep following in his footsteps."

"Maybe she thinks it's what you want too. If she knew you wanted to be a nurse, she might change her mind."

"I'm in my third year of college. I can't switch things up now."

"I'm pretty sure you could," I replied, then, "Do you want to get to know them?"

He knew who I was talking about without me specifying. "Yes and no. The no probably makes me an asshole. It's like...like I know it's not their fault, but I blame them too. Like, they can't control that they exist, but it's hard because...fuck. I don't know. It's not true, I realize that, but part of me feels like they ruined my family. Screwed up, isn't it?"

"Nope. Sounds like normal human emotions to me. Not that I have those," I joked, and Ty laughed. And then because Tyson Langley had somehow short-circuited my brain, I added, "There was this guy in high school...quarterback."

"Aren't they always?"

"No shit." It was my turn to play with the sand and not let myself look at him. But he'd shared with me, so I figured I owed him the same. "Anyway, he was the first guy I ever fucked around with. We used to find spots around school. I legit blew him under the bleachers for the first time. It was...exciting. It went on for almost two years. At first it was just because sex was new and fun, but then...hell, I was a dumbass kid and thought he really liked me. He would tell me he did, would say all this stuff about coming out and being my boyfriend. He had girlfriends on and off while hooking up with me, but I still thought... I don't know why I was stupid...or why in the fuck I wanted to be liked by him. Jocks have always gotten me hard, I guess, but he was the only one I thought it meant something."

When I was quiet for a moment, Ty asked, "What happened?"

"Typical story. We got caught, he pretended I was hitting on him and wouldn't leave him alone, that I'd gotten him drunk and had taken advantage. Of course everyone believed him because he was him and I was me."

"Shit." Ty cursed. "I'm sorry."

I shrugged. "It is what it is."

"No, it's not. That guy was a dick. He live around here? Let's go egg his house."

I rolled my eyes. That had been such a Ty thing to say. I was one hundred percent done talking about this, though. "Be quiet. The sun is setting. Don't you like this shit? You took photos of the sunrise and—" Fuck. Fuckity, fuck, fuck.

"What? Do you follow me on Instagram or Snap?"

I almost rubbed a hand over my face before realizing I would get sand all over myself. Fuck my life. Tyson turned me all upside down. He powered his phone back on and looked.

"I don't see your name… Are you secretly internet-stalking me? Aww. How cute."

"I think you're broken. If someone is internet-stalking you, that shouldn't be cute."

"Not just someone. *You.* Seriously, so sweet. So how long have you had this crush on me?"

"Can we go into the ocean so I can drown you now?"

"What's your secret stalker name?"

"Shut up."

"Are you in love with me?"

"Really, shut up."

Then he surprised me by opening his camera and taking a photo of me. "Spank-bank material," he said, then gazed toward the water. He took a few pictures of the sunset, watching it while I watched him. "It really is beautiful."

My skin got tingly in an unfamiliar way, small bursts of pleasure rocking through me.

I wanted to get the upper hand with him, wanted to make him come again. Wanted… "Lacrosse?"

"What?" He turned to me, and I moved in, went for his mouth, saw the second he realized what I was doing. Just before my lips touched his, I changed directions, went for his ear, licked the lobe, then sucked on it. This was so much fucking easier than talking. This was all about sensation and not real shit like my dad, my brother, or that stuff with Wayne in high school. This wasn't about his family or the siblings Ty had complicated feelings for.

"Should I kiss you? I'm still trying to decide." I nipped at him, then brushed my lips behind his ear and down his neck. "Yes or no? Decisions, decisions."

Ty sucked in a sharp breath. "You're such a tease."

"You like it." I circled my tongue around the hollow spot at the base of his throat. "Hmm...what do I want?" I brushed my nose against his cheek and felt him tremble.

"Kiss me, you asshole." Ty's mouth went for mine, but I backed up.

"Now, now. All good things come to those who wait." My lips were so close to his; each breath I took was the air he'd just breathed.

He tried to kiss me again, but I jerked my head back.

"Jesus, why is this so hot?" Ty asked. "Who knew I liked to be edged this much?"

"Just because I'm so good at it," I replied, before

the pull of tasting him again was too much to deny. I kissed him, slipping my tongue inside. Ty opened up for me, kissed me back, this dance of dominance between us. I cupped his face, brushed my fingers down his neck, fought to hold on to control.

My dick was aching. I wasn't sure anyone had ever gotten me as hard as he did. The whimper he fed me said Ty felt the same.

He pressed his palm against my erection, rubbing me.

"So hot!" someone yelled, and we jerked away from each other. A group of women who looked around our age laughed and cheered before jogging off.

"Shit," I cursed.

"You can say that again. I forgot where we were."

"Me too. Though that part of it is kinda hot." We'd fucked around in an empty classroom, a storage room, and now on the beach.

"For real, Mr. Public Sex." Ty chuckled. "You made me miss the rest of my sunset."

"Are you complaining?"

"No, I'm just saying it was a nice place for you to take me on a date, and it's a shame I missed it."

"Not a date." I stood and held my hand out for him. Ty took it and let me pull him to his feet.

Strangely, he didn't let go of my hand until we got back to the trail leading up the cliff.

Even more strange? That I let him hold on as long as I did.

CHAPTER FOURTEEN

Ty

I HOPED THAT once we got back to Brax's place, we'd finish what we started at the beach. When we pulled up, there were a couple of cars in his driveway, one of them the vehicle I'd seen his brother leave in earlier. As soon as we were off the bike, he said, "Fuck. I'll go grab your bag real quick."

I nodded, concerned at the worry creasing his brow, but he came out a minute later and handed it over, looking more like normal Brax, so I figured I must have imagined it. As I slipped one strap over my shoulder, I said, "So I'll see you at my game tomorrow?"

Brax gave me an exaggerated laugh, complete with knee slaps.

"You're lucky I know how awesome I am, otherwise you might give me a complex."

"*I'm* lucky, huh?"

"Well, yeah, since you like me so much the way I am."

"Why would I give you a complex talking shit if I liked you so much?"

"Because it's basically our form of foreplay?"

Brax's dark, sexy grin made my balls tingle, and then he backed me against his bike, brushed our noses together, his lips a breath away from mine. "You're gonna be thinking about that kiss all night, aren't you?"

"Yes." I didn't even pretend to deny it. What was the point? We both knew it would be a lie.

"You gonna jack off thinking about me?"

"Obviously."

He licked his lips, the tip of his tongue touching my mouth as well. "Me too," Brax admitted before pulling away. "Night, Lacrosse."

"You know we can do that together, right?"

He was walking backward toward the house and gave me another of his smiles, the real one that said he was enjoying himself. He didn't have to speak for me to know the answer.

"You're killin' me here, Brax. Why you gotta be so mean?"

It wasn't until he got to his door that he said, "Maybe I like knowing you'll be thinking about me." When he slipped inside the house, I realized I was smiling too. I liked playing these games with Brax, even if they gave me blue balls.

I climbed into my car and took a photo of the prominent bulge beneath my track pants.

Me: I hate you. I attached the photo.

Brooding Bad Boy: And that's new how?

I didn't bother replying right away. Let him sit and wonder what was going through my head like I so often did with him.

I didn't go back to campus yet. It was too early, and I didn't want to risk seeing anyone since I'd skipped practice for the first time ever. I drove around for a while, then let myself splurge on some In-N-Out. I parked and pulled out my phone, looking at my photos of sunrises to see if I could figure out who Brax was.

It didn't take long. There was a random account with a photo of the San Luco pier as the profile picture and two photos uploaded, one of the beach we'd just been at and the other of an older lady with a wide smile and hazel eyes similar to Brax's.

She must be the grandma he'd been visiting today. If Brax was the one taking the shot, she was smiling at him like he was her whole damn world, and I found myself wondering about their relationship. There were too many things I was curious about when it came to Braxton Walker.

By the time I made it back to the house, it was empty again. The guys had to have made it home and gone out. Practice would have been lighter since we had a game the next morning. Maybe Coach would go easy on me missing.

I locked myself in my room, hoping they would leave me alone when they got back. I ignored the voice mails from my dad because I wasn't in the mood for that shit. He could bitch at me later for whatever he was upset about this time.

I definitely rubbed one out thinking about Brax.

Once I wiped the cum off, I posted a photo of the ocean from earlier, and my fist. He could take that to mean whatever he wanted.

"DID COACH SAY anything when you said I was sick?" I asked the guys the next morning.

"Nah," Collins replied. "He was just worried about his star player possibly missing a game."

"I mean, makes sense," I teased, and Ford flicked me in the ear. "Ouch. Damn it."

"What the fuck is going on with you lately?" Watty asked. "You love lacrosse. This is our third year playing together, and you've never skipped practice. You sure as shit haven't skipped the day before a game."

No, no I hadn't. And I wasn't even sure what to say. I didn't figure watching the sunset with Braxton was a good answer. "I just have stuff to deal with."

"I thought you were getting laid?" Collins asked.

"Holy shit, are you hooked on someone?" Ford added.

"Jesus Christ, can we not do this so early? I'm not hooked on someone, and if I was getting laid or not isn't anyone's business but mine." I absolutely one hundred percent wasn't hooked on someone. Like...at all. Right? "Shit's not always perfect, ya know? I have my own stuff going on."

They were all quiet as if they didn't know how to take that. I could understand because I wasn't sure how to handle it either, or why I'd said it. Maybe because I could talk to Brax so easily about stuff, it just slipped out? As much as these guys were my boys, it just felt different sharing with them. It was like I had to keep a mask in place, always being the Ty they were used to, not wanting them to see my secrets.

Ford patted me awkwardly on the shoulder. "Bro...you know you can like, talk to us and shit...about whatever's going on with you. Is it the job? Because it's seriously cutting into your college experience already."

"Yeah, man. It's the job," I lied. "We should get going."

We headed to the locker rooms, where we met up with the team. Coach made a beeline for me. "How you feeling, Langley?"

"I'm all right, Coach. I slept it off, and I'm ready to get us the *W* today."

He slapped me on my back. "That's what I want

to hear. We need to talk after the game."

Fuck. I had a feeling something like this was going to happen and that I'd be pissed about it, so it was a good thing we weren't doing it before the match.

Coach went over a few things with us, and then we climbed in the bus and headed for Los Angeles. I kept my earbuds in the whole drive, and luckily, no one bothered me.

There was a wreck on the I-5, because when wasn't there a wreck on every Southern California freeway? It slowed us down a bit, but we always left early enough to make sure we had time regardless.

We were in the locker room at USC, just having gotten dressed and listening to Coach give us a speech about winning, playing as a team, winning, having a good time, winning, and how important it was to win.

"Let's do this. On the count of three—one, two, three, Kings!" We all shouted the last word in unison. Something made me glance at my phone one more time before closing my locker, and when I did, the biggest smile stretched across my face.

Brooding Bad Boy: Good luck. Break a leg or what the fuck ever I'm supposed to say.

I was going to win this game if it was the last thing I did.

LA was killer on defense, and we really struggled to get the ball downfield. I was knocked on my ass too many times to count, but had managed to score and also make some good defensive moves. The game was tied in the fourth, though, and nerves were buzzing down my spine. If we lost, would Coach blame me because of practice? Logically, that didn't make sense, but he rarely did. It was almost the end of the game when Watty managed to break through the pack and throw the ball my way. It fell perfectly into the scoop, and I took off, dodging defenders before jumping in the air and shooting. Their goalie tried but missed the block, my shot landing right in the net.

"Fuck yes!"

It hadn't been a pretty win, but it was a *W*, and that's what mattered.

And when our team high-fived and hugged after our win, I thought of Brax. It was so stupid because he didn't really care about me or my sport despite the text he'd sent, but I still wanted him to know how badass I was. I wanted to impress him.

We showered and loaded the bus again, everyone

lively and celebrating much more than we had been this morning. I'd almost forgotten that Coach wanted to talk to me until we got back to campus and he said, "Langley, can I have a quick word?"

Concern activated. That easily I went from *Fuck yeah, this is gonna be a great day* to *Fuck no, this is gonna be the worst day ever.* There was a small possibility I could be seen as dramatic, but in my opinion, most people were.

I went into his office and closed the door. "Yeah, Coach?"

"I spoke to your father yesterday." I was fairly certain that in the history of the world, there had never been a good conversation that started with *I spoke to your father.* It was basically the number-one rule in the book of life. "I didn't tell him you were sick, but the fact that you were, it nailed home some of our concerns."

Their concerns…because apparently they were a unit now? Yeah, my dad had gone to FU and he'd had ties to the college ever since, but was it really fair that he got to call my coach to have *concerns* about me? "I'm fine. It was just a stomach bug."

"Yes, but our worry is that you're working yourself

too hard. The late nights at the bar can't help. You shouldn't have to worry about anything other than your grades and lacrosse. I know I said I'd give it a chance, but we're only a couple of weeks in and you've already missed a practice. And if I'm being honest, I've noticed a change in your performance."

"I just won the game for us today…sir." I forced out the last word, fighting to bite back my frustration. "I haven't missed a single practice in three years until yesterday. I've been the highest-scoring middy on the team every season so far. I work my ass off when it comes to lacrosse, and I don't really think it's fair to hold one stomach bug against me." The stomach thing was obviously a lie, but the rest of it was true. "I like this job. I think it's good for me."

Maybe he would think I was bullshitting him. Maybe it didn't make sense how cleaning tables at a bar made me feel…hell, like I was accomplishing something, but it did.

"I'm not telling you to quit…of course, I can't do that," he said while hinting heavily that he thought I should. "I just know your father feels strongly about it, and he wants what's best for you."

So that was what this was really about. Dad had

Coach doing his dirty work. If I wouldn't talk to him, he'd find another way to get to me. "I'll talk to him," I said through gritted teeth.

"Thank you. And good game today, Langley." The irony of him saying that after making it sound like I'd been slacking wasn't lost on me, but I let it go. "Have a good rest of your day."

Everyone was already gone when I got back to the locker room. The second I stepped outside, I called my dad.

"Tyson, I—"

"I'm not quitting my job. If you pull something like this again, I'll walk away from lacrosse before I leave the bar."

"You're being dramatic. It's a *bar*, and you're only doing it to get back at me. You've loved lacrosse your whole life, and you've worked at that place for only a couple of weeks."

"I don't care. It's my life. Stop trying to dictate how I live it. You have another son you can do that with now."

But he'd always had another son. One he'd thankfully provided for monetarily, at least, if not in any other way. I couldn't imagine how Perry must have felt his whole life, how much he must hate me, and I couldn't blame him.

I ended the call, immediately opening my texts messages, going to *Brooding Bad Boy*, fingers lingering over the screen. What was I doing? I couldn't run to Brax every time my dad pissed me off. I shouldn't want to, and I wasn't sure how I felt about that so quickly becoming my default reaction.

Instead of messaging, I headed home. The guys were all sitting around playing video games and looked up when I entered.

"What was that about? Calling in sick yesterday?" Collins asked.

"Yeah, but it's fine." I waved my hand like it was just a minor inconvenience that didn't make my insides feel like they were burning up. "I need a drink. Who wants a drink?"

A bottle of whiskey sat on the counter. It was a shit brand but would do the trick.

"Is that really a question?" Watty replied.

"And we should have a party tonight," I told them. "Who's down?"

They were all in agreement. I'd have a good time tonight. I'd forget about the shit with my dad and maybe even find someone to hook up with so I could stop obsessing over Braxton Walker.

CHAPTER FIFTEEN

Brax

HIS FIST AND the ocean.

There was no doubt it was for me, and every time I looked at it...I *smiled*. Like, really smiled, and the fact that I could say *every time* when it came to thinking about his post spoke for itself.

I would *not* look at it again because what was the point? The thing wouldn't change. This whole situation was becoming more and more unnerving.

The bar was busy tonight. Gwen was working too. I liked being on shift with her. She'd changed her hair again, this time to green.

Every time the door opened, I found myself glancing that direction. It wasn't because I hoped Ty would show up. Clearly, I didn't, but I liked to know if my night was going to take a trip down the toilet, was all.

That often happened when he was around with his friends.

Or maybe my dumb ass wished he would come in so I could mention the posts.

But none of the lacrosse team showed up, and I'd only checked my phone to see if they'd won so I knew what to expect. They almost always made an appearance if they had something to brag about.

They'd won, though, and of course, all the talk was about Ty. Ty scoring the winning point. Ty's defense. Tyson Langley, Tyson Langley, Tyson Langley. The universe hated me.

"I need three Midori sours, please," a girl said, bringing me out of my thoughts. "Also, you're hot."

I chuckled. "Thanks, but I'm gay."

She groaned. "All the hot ones are."

She was cool and chatted with me while I made her drinks. Two friends joined her just as I gave her the change.

"Thank you, hot guy!"

When I heard a chuckle, I looked over and saw Chris, this stoner guy I'd done edibles with once. He pushed his dirty-blond hair behind his ear, but it fell forward again. "That happen to you a lot?"

"You know how it is." I shrugged, then reached up and massaged the tight muscles in my right shoulder.

"If you want, you should head over to the massage school. I can help you work that out." He nodded toward me with a laid-back smile. I used to think he was flirting when he said stuff like that, but I didn't think he was. It was just Chris. He was chill like that.

"Nah, not really my thing. Thanks, though."

"No worries. I just thought I'd offer." He took a drink of his beer, and when someone on stage started singing, turned to listen.

"Since we have a little lull," Gwen said, "do you want to take your break now?" There were three bartenders there, so if Gwen got busy, she'd have backup.

I headed toward the back so I could chill outside.

"'Sup?" SpongeBob said, and I gave him a quick up nod on my way out.

This time, when I accidentally on purpose found myself on Ty's Instagram page, there was a video. One *click* showed him in the middle of a packed house, drink in hand, dancing, his eyes slightly glazed over and a dopey smile on his face. Seemed they'd decided to keep the party at their house instead of coming to Shenanigans.

A guy I recognized approached him. Steve. We had Data Structures and Algorithms together last year. He was also the head of FU's LGBTQ Club, so my hackles rose automatically. "Wanna dance?" he asked Ty, just as Ty mumbled, "Oh shit," and his phone tumbled out of his hand. He picked it up and ended the video.

My gut tightened, this strange feeling twisting around in there, almost like *I* was the one who'd had too much to drink and my stomach disagreed with it. Jesus Christ, was I jealous that Ty might hook up with some random guy from class? If I had to even ask myself that question, the answer was clear.

I closed the app.

I could do this. I wasn't jealous. I didn't like Ty. He could fuck whomever he wanted. Stupid, annoying jock.

I forced myself not to look at my phone and eventually went back inside for my shift. My phone was calling to me from my pocket, a quiet whisper of, *Check me. Open Instagram.*

It was almost midnight when I looked at my

phone again, pulled up the stupid fucking app, and saw multiple photos...of the star-dotted sky, the dark ocean, his feet in the sand. The last one was a shot down the beach. In the distance, I could see the corner of a sign. He didn't get the words or the building or anything, but I recognized it right away. The caption on the post read: *Peekaboo*, and I knew it was for me. Shit.

I turned to Chuck. He was supposed to get off at midnight, Gwen and I staying until two. "I'll give you an extra twenty to swap shifts with me tonight."

"Why would I want to do that?"

"I'll owe you one too. Whenever you need a shift covered, I'll do it."

He shrugged. "Sure. I don't have anything going on tonight anyway. I would have done it just for the extra two hours and tip."

"Fucker." I pulled a twenty out of my wallet and gave it to him. Now I was out money, tips, and hours, all to go see Ty? I was definitely losing my mind.

I told Gwen we were swapping, grabbed my shit, and walked to the beach behind Shenanigans. It didn't take me long to find him. Ty was close to the water, sitting in the middle of the sand, in a T-shirt…at midnight in winter.

Fucking jocks.

I stopped beside him. Ty had his arms around his knees, feet in the sand. "Peekaboo. I see you," he said without looking up.

"Are we leaving secret social media posts for each other now?"

"Makes things easy since you internet-stalk me."

I didn't try to deny it. There was no other excuse for why I was there.

Ty looked up at me, his eyes bloodshot. "Let's go skinny-dipping."

"Let's not and say we did."

"You're so boring, Sunshine."

"Maybe you should have brought Steve out here instead, then."

Fuck. I realized my mistake the second his eyes widened, and then he said, "I mean, you took me on a date, but I didn't know you wanted to be exclusive."

"Ha-ha." I sat beside him.

"Wanna dance?"

"No."

"Make out?"

"Fuck no."

"You don't want to do anything with me. Live a little." He stood up and started doing cartwheels. On his third, he fell.

"I think you're living enough for the both of us."

"I'm drunk." Ty literally crawled over to me and sat down again.

"You don't say." When he sighed, I nudged him. "What's wrong, Lacrosse?" Clearly, something was.

"You'll just think it's stupid and say I'm spoiled, and you wouldn't be wrong."

"Yes and no."

"Gee, thanks. You were supposed to say, *No, Ty. I would never tell you that. You're awesome and smart and really fucking hot.*"

I chuckled. "Keep dreaming and stop stalling." Because I knew that was what he was doing. Over the past two weeks, I'd gotten to know him, to understand him.

"I just… I *am* spoiled, and I get that. I skipped practice yesterday, and though it was the first time, I did it because I knew I'd still be able to play. And I shouldn't have been able to, not without talking to Coach myself about being sick. But he wouldn't want to risk upsetting my father. So I get it, why you think that stuff about me, but it's not my fault. I don't control it."

"But you use it to your benefit sometimes."

"Who wouldn't?"

He had a point there. I would. I couldn't fault him for that.

"What's wrong, though, Ty? It's more than that."

He looked up, the moon glistening in his eyes. "My dad called Coach so he would try and talk me into quitting my job. Who does that? He hates not being in control. He hates that I'm not doing what he wants, and all I can think is, how was I so blind all those years? How did I not see who he is? I wanted to be just like him. What does that say about me?"

I...hadn't expected this. Ty had surprised me in so many ways, I'd lost count. He wasn't who I'd thought he was. Which meant he was even more dangerous because he could make me like him. "It doesn't say anything about you. He's your dad, and you love him. I... When I was a kid, I used to pickpocket for my dad."

I didn't look at him, didn't want to see the disappointment in his gaze.

"I was really fucking good at it, so he always had

me do it. Asher used to get so pissed because he's older, but Dad always took me with him since I was so much better. It was our secret from Grandma. I knew it was wrong. I hated myself for doing it, but he was my dad. I wanted his love and wanted him to be proud of me. It makes me sick now." I couldn't believe I'd told him. But maybe it was better that way. Now that Ty knew I'd been a thief, he'd want nothing to do with me.

"He really asked you to do that?"

I nodded.

"Shit, man. I'm sorry." And then…then he wrapped an arm around me and rested his head on my shoulder. "It wasn't your fault."

"Then it's not yours."

"Yeah, well, I think you have a harder time believing it." He was right. We were both quiet for a few minutes, just listening to the ocean, watching the dark waves wash ashore. "I want to meet him…my brother, Perry. Both my siblings, but it's different with Ainsley. She's only one year old. She'll have my dad. All I can think is that my father knew about him, provided him money, but wasn't a part of his life. My dad is a dick, but at least I had him. Perry didn't. If I were him, I'd hate me for it."

"You didn't have a choice to be in his life when you were younger. You didn't know. It wasn't your fault."

"Not sure that changes much of anything when it comes to feelings."

No, I wasn't sure it did either.

"I didn't hook up with him—Steve, I mean. I turned him down."

My body relaxed. "You didn't have to."

"But you're glad I did."

And damned if he wasn't correct. I also really fucking wanted him.

I turned to Ty, leaned in. He didn't pull back when I licked at the seam of his mouth. He opened for me, let me in before hungrily kissing me back.

Eat shit, Steve!

Because Ty had turned him down and come to find me. He wanted me, and I was so fucking tired of pretending I didn't want him too.

We deepened the kiss, and when Ty dropped onto his back, I rolled on top of him, grinded our erections together. He tasted like weed and alcohol but like himself too. Minty and familiar.

Still, I pulled back because when we fucked around again, he wasn't going to be drunk or high.

He smiled. "So glad you're admitting you have a crush on me."

"I'm not admitting a damn thing."

He seemed about to reply but then frowned. "I'm not feeling so hot."

I jumped off him, and he lay there, breathing heavily, but didn't throw up. I got into an app on my phone and ordered us a ride, knowing he wasn't in any shape to hold on to me on my bike. Plus, I didn't have my extra helmet with me. I trusted that my bike would be safe at Shenanigans.

"Our ride is three minutes out," I told him. "Can you get up?"

"Can you help me?"

I took his hand and pulled him to his feet. He didn't let go of me, and I didn't either. We took a few steps, and then he started to… "What the fuck? Why are you singing 'Mary Had a Little Lamb'?"

"Distraction so I don't puke."

"Fuck my life."

He didn't ask where we were going, and I didn't tell him, not when we got in the car or on the drive.

He closed his eyes as we went, and when the car stopped, he sucked in a sharp breath. "Shut up."

Asher was there, but thankfully there wasn't a party. He and three guys were playing video games, and when he saw us, he raised a brow at me.

"No comment."

"Hi! I'm Ty. Oh cool, that rhymed." Ty laughed. I shook my head. "Ooh, I love this game!"

"Nope. We're going to bed."

"Why are you so boring?"

Asher snorted, but I just kept walking with Ty to my room. When we got there, I unlocked the door and let us in.

He cocked his head slightly, clearly not drunk enough not to understand I kept my door locked in my own house because there were so many people coming and going.

"I have to pee. I might sit down to do it." He swayed.

"Jesus, Lacrosse. Maybe don't drink so much next time."

"Jesus, Sunshine. You're not the boss of me."

He went into the bathroom, giving me a leery look when I followed him in. I watched him piss, then wash his hands. He pulled off his shirt and tossed it to the floor, then stepped out of his shoes, tugged his pants and underwear down, went straight to my bed, and collapsed on it.

Well, okay, then.

I took a leak too, washed up, and stripped, leaving my boxer briefs on. I plucked a bottle of water out of my mini-fridge for him and set it on the nightstand beside the bottle of ibuprofen he'd bought when I was sick.

Then…then I turned off the light and climbed into my bed with Ty.

CHAPTER SIXTEEN

Ty

MUSIC WOKE ME up. I rolled over and looked at Brax, who I was pretty sure had been watching me sleep. The second our eyes met, I gave him a half-grin, the look in his eyes no doubt reflected in mine, and Brax's mouth slammed down on mine. He kissed me like he was starving and I was his last meal, like he'd been chained just out of reach of water for days, weeks, and he was finally free to drink—and drink he did.

We didn't part as Brax jerked off his underwear. He rolled on top of me, his hard weight holding me down in a sexy-as-fuck way. He thrust against me, kissed down my throat, making me feel like he was savoring the taste of my skin. "I want you so bad, Ty."

"I want you too." I grabbed his ass and pulled him tighter against me.

The music got louder. It didn't seem to bother Brax, so I tried to ignore it. He reached for the condom and lube on the nightstand…just as his door busted open. His brother stumbled in, along with the other guys who'd been there last night.

"Um…Brax?" I asked.

"What's wrong? Do you want me to stop?" he asked. "It's fun with an audience."

The blankets flew off us, which was my first clue that something was going on. We were lying there naked and hard, and suddenly Watty, Collins, and Ford were there too. Nothing like a little exhibitionism first thing in the morning.

But then we were on a stage, and they were the audience, eating popcorn and watching. I tried to ignore them, tried to kiss Brax, but he wasn't Brax anymore. He'd turned into a giant bottle of whiskey, and I was…drinking him?

My eyes jerked open, heart punching my chest. It was morning, but clearly still early. Brax's room was fairly dark, but light filtered around the curtains. I was on my back, Brax on his side, curled up in a tight ball. It was cute as shit, and I'd have to tease him about it. He looked like he should have a stuffed animal in his arms to hug tightly. He'd hugged me at some point during the night. I was sure he'd been deeply asleep and hadn't realized he was doing it, but I remembered waking up once to feel him, arm thrown around my waist, his face in my neck as he'd spooned me from behind.

Braxton Walker was a cuddler, and I liked it. I sort of wanted to see if I could snuggle into his arms right then, but I had to piss and my mouth tasted like trash.

As gently as I could, I sneaked out of his bed. He'd set a bottle of water and painkillers on the bedside table, which was sweet. I thought about how Brax had seen my photos and had automatically come to me last night. The way he'd listened to me and hadn't made me feel like a spoiled shithead for my thoughts. How he'd taken a car home with me. He'd left his bike at the bar. He'd brought me to his house... Jesus, Brax really was sweet. Infuriating and annoying, but sexy and caring.

I grabbed both bottles and headed to the bathroom. I took two pills, which I hoped would help the throbbing in my head, drank all the water, then took what might possibly be known as the world's longest pee. I seriously got tired of holding my dick for so long. Luckily, my morning wood had already started to go down. After washing my hands, I found Brax's toothpaste and finger-brushed, swished some mouthwash around, then sneaked back into bed with him. I'd just nuzzled in when his eyes opened. "Shit. You're gonna kick me out, aren't you?"

"Have you done something to annoy me?"

"Breathe. That's usually all it takes."

He smiled, then yawned. His hair was a mess, sticking up in every direction and clearly not in the styled way this time. It was adorable. I liked Sleepy Brax. He seemed much more chill.

"Is it me, or was there music last night?"

"There's music every night. That was nothing."

His brother…fuck, I really didn't like that guy. Did he throw parties on the daily? I liked a good time and had one often. We had people over to our house a lot. But I had a feeling Asher didn't worry about Brax needing rest or when he had to study or anything like that.

"I had a dream that we were having sex in front of

a room full of people, and then you turned into a bottle of whiskey and I drank you."

Brax cocked a dark brow. "You are the weirdest person I've ever met."

I liked being the most of something to him, even if it was weird. I just liked knowing Brax thought something about me. It was annoying, and I didn't understand it, but I wasn't one to stress about things as much as he did.

"Thank you for last night. I was all up in my head. I can't talk to anyone else about all this stuff. They wouldn't get it." But he did. In a way I was still piecing together, Brax understood me, and maybe I understood him too.

"No biggie."

"You got me water and pills."

"I owed you from when I was sick. Now shut up and go back to sleep. It's early."

I was tired too, but I didn't think I'd be able to go to sleep right away.

Brax closed his eyes, and I tried, I really did, but all I could think about was being in a hot guy's bed, one I really, really wanted to bang. I tossed and turned, going from my left side to my right, then to my back.

"Why am I not surprised?" Braxton groaned.

"What did I do?"

He didn't respond to my question, instead saying, "Now I have to pee."

"I'm not sure how that's my fault. I drank you. You didn't drink me."

He chuckled as he climbed over me. The second he did, my dick took notice, blood rushing to my groin.

I watched him go. He left the door open, but because of where the toilet was, he was hidden.

When he came back in, I could see his bulge beneath his black boxer briefs. I didn't take my eyes off him, saying a silent prayer that he watched me too. Brax had such a sexy body—a tight six-pack, solid arms—and that damn chain hanging against his chest. He stopped when he reached the side of the bed. I didn't touch him, but I couldn't help licking my lips. I wanted him so fucking bad. He was this constant ache beneath my skin that only grew each time I saw him.

"Fuck. Why do I want you so much?" he gritted out, his voice low and gravelly.

"It's like you took the thoughts right out of my head."

Brax cursed again, then shoved his underwear down mid-thigh, his erection springing free. Veins throbbed beneath the skin. I wanted to trace my tongue along each and every one.

He held the base of his cock, angling it toward me. I loved how confident he was, that he didn't second-guess offering his dick to me with the expectation that I'd suck it. I was a safe bet. "Hell yes." I circled his crown with my tongue, took him deep for one long, languid suck, smiling when Brax hissed.

"Proud of yourself, are you?"

"So proud."

"I kinda hate that you're so good at this."

"I can be bad if you'd rather?" I replied. "Maybe use too much teeth?"

"I take it back."

"That's what I thought." I licked him again, nuzzled his balls, sucked one, then the other. Brax's fingers threaded through my hair, guiding me back to his leaking erection. Mine throbbed and begged for attention too. I rested on my elbows, bobbing my head, blowing him, taking in the salty taste of his skin and the slight musky scent of him that went straight to my head and turned me on even more.

"Jesus, I'm already going to blow my load." Brax pulled back, jerking his underwear the rest of the way down and stepping out of them. He took a condom and lube from the drawer and set them on his nightstand.

"Fucking finally. You're gonna be pissed at yourself that you waited so long to have someone so good."

Brax tugged the blanket off me and straddled my thighs. "When will he get here? Should we wait?"

I laughed. "Fuck you." I held on to his waist, ran my hand up and down his back.

"Yes, or I can fuck you." Brax leaned down, kissed my throat, then moved over to suck my earlobe. He seemed to like that. "What do you want, Lacrosse? I'm vers." He nipped my ear.

"Me too," I replied breathlessly as he kissed my throat. I wasn't sure how else to answer because I wanted it all. This couldn't be a one-time thing. We had to do this at least twice just so I knew what it was like to have him both ways. "Fuck me."

"You're welcome." I felt him smile, a zing of electricity shooting down my spine as he kissed and licked his way down my torso.

"What am I supposed to be thanking you for?"

"I'm about to give you the best dick you've ever had."

"Promises, promises." I'd just gotten the words out when Brax took his turn sucking me. He took my dick to the back of his throat, surrounding it in wet heat. I arched off the bed, choked him with my cock, but he didn't seem to care. He took it, kept giving me so much pleasure, I thought I'd die from it. My nuts got his attention next, wet laps with his tongue before he went back to my erection again.

My whole body thrummed with need. My bones felt like they would melt, and I knew I'd come any second, but before I could, Brax pulled back. I pouted, complete with my lip out and everything.

"So fucking spoiled," Brax said playfully before settling between my thighs and kissing me again. We rutted together, our shafts dragging against each other. He fed me his tongue and then took mine, squeezed my hip with his hand, then moved it up to tease one of my nipples, his mouth never leaving mine.

It felt like I'd been waiting a whole-ass eternity for us to get here, like I'd wanted him for longer than I had, which was unnerving as shit, so I pretended those crazy thoughts hadn't infiltrated my brain.

Not breaking our kiss, I reached up, trying to find the lube. I knocked it over, but the bottle didn't fall to the floor.

"Impatient?" Brax asked.

"You should be thanking me for the quality hole you're about to receive."

When he laughed, I couldn't help doing the same, our bodies dancing together with the movement. "We'll let my dick be the judge of that," Brax said.

I wrapped my hand around his shaft, rubbed my thumb over the tip. "He's drooling. He says you should hurry."

Brax cocked a brow. "You're talking for my cock now?"

"We're tight, he and I." I looked down between our bodies at his erection. "I got your back, buddy. We'll get you all tucked into your favorite ass in no time."

"Jesus, you're ridiculous." He was smiling when

he said it, and Smiling Brax made me feel like the luckiest man in the world. I took it as my personal responsibility to make him do it as often as I could.

Brax grabbed the lube and slicked up his fingers. He rolled to his back, pulling me with him. I took the hint and straddled him, which left me wide open. I took over where he'd left off, kissing his neck, ears, the hollow spot at the base of his throat, then sneaking my way up to his lips.

His slick finger circled my rim, sending shocks of pleasure up my spine. "Fuck yessss," I hissed when he breached me. Sinking my cock into a tight ass, or hell, a pussy too, was fucking fantastic. But having something inside me? It was next-level shit, intense in a way nothing else was.

"Been dying for this for a while, haven't you? For my fingers…then my cock?"

I thrust back, working with Brax to finger my ass. Each time I moved, it made our dicks rub together, adding to the sensation that already had me wanting to empty my balls.

"Well, the sooner I have you, the faster I can stop talking to you, so yes."

Brax pushed a second digit in, twisting them,

sliding them in and out. I had to fight the urge to call out his name and show him just how much I was enjoying this.

"I don't think so," Brax said. "You wanted me to take you on a date, remember? You're always teasing me about liking you. You want to be my secret boyfriend, don't you? So you can ride my cock whenever you want."

"I mean, the riding-your-dick part sounds good. It's dealing with the rest of you that's difficult."

Brax silenced me with his mouth, pushing his tongue between my lips as he continued to work me open. When I was a needy mess on top of him, he finally took mercy on me.

"I want inside you," Brax said, raspy and lust-filled.

"Hell yes."

He nudged me, and I climbed off him, getting on my hands and knees. I looked over my shoulder, watched as he opened the condom and rolled it down his shaft. He lubed that up too, then grabbed my ass cheeks and spread them. "Fuck, Lacrosse. That's a pretty little hole. So nice and pink and begging for my cock."

Yes, yes it was. "Then why don't you give it to me?"

When his gaze caught mine, fire and want ignited in his stare. The tip of his cock nudged at my rim. I pushed out slightly as Brax worked his way inside. The head was thicker than his fingers had been, and my hole stung slightly with the stretch. But he was careful with me, taking his time. "You good, Ty? Need me to back off a second?"

"Fucking perfect." This time, I didn't stop myself. I let my satisfaction show, my eyes rolling back, a whimper slipping from my lips. Brax cursed, took it slow, until his groin met my ass, all of him stuffed inside me.

Then he pulled back, leaving only his tip inside before slowly pressing forward again. "This is so fucking hot, watching you take me, seeing my dick disappear inside you while your whole body is damn near vibrating with need."

"Fuck me."

"I am."

"Fuck me faster."

"You're not the boss of me," Brax teased, but the edge to his voice had changed. The time to tease and take it gently was over. His hands squeezed my hips, and he let loose, railing into me, his cock dragging over my prostate with each measured, on-fucking-target thrust of his hips.

I fisted my hand in the pillows. His bed banged against the wall. I didn't give a shit who heard us, if we woke up the whole house, because it felt too good to care. I grabbed my dick, stroked, but Brax knocked my hand away.

"This is my cock when I'm inside you. I get to play with it. We're tight, he and I."

I couldn't even laugh because I was too distracted by the feel of him pounding away at me while jerking my cock with his slick hand.

I knew I wouldn't last long. Next time I'd draw it out, but right now, I just wanted to shoot my load all over Brax's bed so it smelled like me. "Fuck, I'm gonna come. You're already gonna make me shoot."

"Give it to me. Empty your balls for me."

He thrust harder, faster, jerked with even more perfect skill. I couldn't hold myself back. Pleasure exploded behind my eyes, tingles shooting down my spine as I orgasmed, spurt after spurt in his hand and on his bed.

"Me too…" Brax called out, his dick jerking inside me as he filled the condom with his release.

I fell into my cum and didn't even care. "That was… I can't speak. Later."

He chuckled. "Go to sleep."

I closed my eyes. The bed dipped, and even though I was already slipping, I knew Brax had left. I wanted to tell him to come back, but I didn't need to. He did. He climbed back in, likely after getting rid of the condom. He pulled the blankets over us, tugged me into his arms, and right before I lost myself to sleep, I was pretty sure I felt his lips press a kiss to my shoulder.

CHAPTER SEVENTEEN

Braxton

TY WAS A restless sleeper, which didn't surprise me at all. His body was a little like his mouth and never stopped going. Luckily, I was used to not getting peaceful rest, so I still managed to pass the fuck out.

After screwing Ty.

Which I *so* knew would happen one day but was still kinda angry with myself for doing. We were getting way too cozy, like right now, after I'd woken up again and he was all tucked in my arms, the two of us snug like two bugs in a rug or whatever that really weird saying was. People said the craziest shit.

It was about eleven when I said, "Hey, wiggle worm. Wake your ass up," because I knew he had to work this afternoon.

"No," he mumbled in a half-asleep, slurred voice I would *not* let myself call cute even though it was.

"You have to work today."

"Adulting sucks."

"I've been doing it since I was five. I think you can handle it at twenty-one." His eyes fluttered open, his blue gaze snagging on me all soft and caring. "Oh my God. Stop looking at me like that."

"Like what?"

"Like you want to say something nice to me."

"Why? I'm pretty sure we do nice now—at least sometimes. Me hanging out with you is nice. Me giving you my ass is nice. Me posting a photo last night so you knew where to find me was nice. Me sleeping over was nice."

My chest was light and airy in this way he brought out in me. "You did all that stuff for me, huh? None of it was for yourself? You were just blessing me with your presence?"

"*You* don't do nice to me, remember? But I never said that. I'm like…I don't know, someone who's really fucking considerate. Captain of the nice police…King Niceington of Nicetown. Nice—"

I shut him up with my mouth. It wasn't that I

wanted to kiss him. He just wouldn't stop blabbing, and it was the only course of action I could take.

Ty twisted to his back, taking me with him. I settled on top, slowly thrusting my groin against his while tasting every millimeter of his mouth. When I pulled back, he smiled at me, and my pulse started doing this foreign dance beneath my skin. "What?"

"You like kissing me."

"I like shutting you up."

"By kissing me, but geez, stop distracting me. I'm trying to be an adult here. I need to get up because I have to work today."

This fucking guy. I rolled off him and watched as Ty got out of my bed. He rummaged around for his clothes, and I couldn't pretend I wasn't enjoying the view. He was all hard, his ass tight, and my dick perked up at the memory of what it was like to be inside him. When he grinned, I knew he'd realized I was watching him, but he didn't call me on it. Instead, he faced me and stretched.

"Oh my God."

"What? Just being *nice*."

Not this again. I sat up on the side of the mattress when Ty went into my bathroom, sand falling out of his clothes. He cleaned up and got dressed. Once he had his shoes on, he said, "Thanks again for last night."

"No problem." Hello, awkwardness. We just chilled there like neither of us knew what to do. "You don't have a ride."

"There's an app for that." I crossed my arms, and he added, "Shit. I should pay you back for taking a car here last night...or at least so you can go get your bike today." He pulled out his wallet.

"What? No. Fuck that." It felt like charity. I didn't think he would do the same if I were one of his friends.

"Stubborn," Ty said before leaning in and pressing a quick kiss to my lips. "I'll see myself out and will call you later."

He slipped out of my room without another word. I sat there long after he'd left and wondered if he realized how boyfriend-y that kiss goodbye was or if it was just me.

"WHO'S THE GUY?" Asher asked later when I'd just finished cleaning up the house and he woke up.

"What guy? I don't see a guy."

"You're an idiot."

"I'm rubber and you're glue."

"Wow…you really don't want to answer that, do you? Is my little brother in love?"

"He's nobody." I watched as Asher pulled the milk out of the fridge and began drinking it from the container. "You're so gross."

"What? We're family."

We were, and as crazy as Asher made me, I loved him. But he did make me really fucking nuts. "Speaking of family, you should go see Grandma today. I'll go with you."

"I'll text her."

"Jesus Christ, Asher. Go fucking see her. Even if it's just an hour. Hanging out and getting high can wait." I shoved him.

"You act like you don't get high too. Your boyfriend was drunk off his ass last night."

I shook my head. I didn't know why I tried. It wasn't about the weed or anything else. Hell, nearly everyone I knew did it, but they visited their grandmas too. "That has absolutely nothing to do with what I'm saying. I get my shit done, and that's what matters. We wouldn't even have this house if it wasn't for her."

"She only lets us stay here because you're her pride and joy. The only Walker man who isn't a fuckup."

"Grandpa wasn't, and I'm just as much of a fuckup as you." How could I not be with our dad as a role model?

"I'm not doing this with you today." Asher pushed past me and went to his room.

My heart thudded. I ran a hand through my hair, tugged on it slightly. "Fuck." I didn't know why I let him get to me so much.

I messaged Manny, but he was with his girl at her place.

I still had to get my bike, so I showered, got dressed, and headed to Shenanigans. I told myself I wasn't going inside, but I knew that was a lie, so I didn't know why I tried to pretend otherwise.

How could I go to the bar and not take the opportunity to give Ty shit? I wouldn't be me if I didn't.

Ty had his back to me when I walked in. He was cleaning a table, his stupid rubber gloves on his hands, his tight little ass on display.

I sneaked up behind him, mouth close to his ear. "You missed a spot."

"What did you say? You want me to sit on your face?"

"Yeah, because that's what came out of my mouth." Though I couldn't say the thought wasn't tempting. I was excellent at eating ass. "I just came to get my bike."

"I missed you too." Ty winked.

I was tired of letting him get the upper hand. He'd been on his game lately, and I was failing miserably. I wished I could have stuck a finger in his belt loop and pulled him forward, but he lived in athletic gear, so I grabbed his hip instead and sneaked my finger under his apron and shirt so I could dance it over the pointy bone there. "I've been thinking about you since you left. I've never had a boyfriend before." Surprise flashed in his eyes, so I added, "Meet me in the stockroom. I'll get on my knees for you again. It'll hold me over until you show up at my place tonight."

He was slightly breathless when he said, "I, um...didn't know we had plans. The guys were pissed I bailed last night, so—"

I jerked back. "You're ditching me for them?"

Concern creased his brow. "Huh?"

"I thought you liked me, baby. I thought we had something." I could see when the light bulb went off in his head, the playfulness that curled his lips. "But I love you, pooky butt. I can't be without you. If I can't have you, no one can."

"Ha-fucking-ha." Ty flipped me off, and I bit the tip of his finger. "Ouch. And go away. I'm working. Also, what the hell is a pooky butt?"

"You...and I can't be without you. Ty...you're my world."

"Security!" he called out.

Marshall was carrying a box from the back, and he shook his head, laughing at us. "When's the wedding?"

"I told him no," I replied.

I slipped out of Shenanigans, my mood lighter than it had been when I went inside. Ty was good at that. I should hate it more than I did.

CHAPTER EIGHTEEN

Ty

I DIDN'T TELL the guys I'd gone to meet Brax last night, and I couldn't really say why. I'd never purposefully hidden who I'd had a hookup with just because I wanted to...protect it? *Ding! Ding! Ding!* Holy fuck. I wanted to *protect* whatever this thing with Brax was, even though I couldn't even say it was a thing we'd do again. But I wanted to.

That was...confusing, to say the least.

When I'd gone home yesterday before work, they'd talked shit at me for leaving the party and asked me where I'd gone. I'd played it off as if it was some big secret when it shouldn't have been. *Oh, hey. I went to the hot bartender's house, and he fucked my brains out.* That wasn't so hard, but then it would become a thing. They'd mention it at Shenanigans, and I wasn't sure how Brax would react.

He had my head all twisted up.

Class was boring as shit on Monday morning. I couldn't wrap my head around why Braxton liked this shit, why any of these people did. Maybe it was just too tied into my dad, but I knew that wasn't the case. I'd never enjoyed it. I'd just been able to fake it a whole lot more before I lost all respect for him.

"What are you up to?" I asked Brax when we'd been let out.

"Library. You?"

"You're a really shitty bad boy."

"You're the one who made that ridiculous assumption. I am who I am, and that's all."

He had me there, but he'd also used to be a pickpocket and who knew what else, so who could blame me for my assumptions. "We should head to the empty room again. I want to work a load out of your balls."

Brax paused, and I could see the war raging in his eyes. He wanted me on my knees. He wanted to come down my throat.

He groaned. "Why did you have to say that? I have shit I have to do for class. You have shit you need to do too."

"Yeah, well, doing *you* is more fun."

He frowned, and I knew it was because of my dad and the fact that I fucking hated computers. "Come to the library with me. We'll get some work done together. I can help."

"Wanna help me get off instead?"

"You get your work done, and I promise there's an orgasm in it for you."

"Bet." I didn't mention I was the one who was supposed to blow him and now *he* was making *me* come. I'd enjoy myself either way, but I wasn't going to turn down him emptying my balls.

More than that, the offer to help was nice. I thought he was more King Niceington of Nicetown than he let himself see. He could've gotten an orgasm out of me and been on his way, but instead he wanted to work with me on my homework? It was pretty cool.

We headed across campus together. I loved that you could see the ocean across the street, that the air always smelled like salt and summer. It was hard to imagine that in a year and a half I'd be expected to move back east again. The coastline was just as beautiful there, but there was something special about Southern California. "Do you ever feel like you're waking up in paradise every day?" I asked Brax.

"Nope," he replied simply. "Have you seen the traffic on the I-5?"

"I'm not talking about traffic, just…I don't know. You suck."

He nudged me with his arm, chuckling. "I guess I don't see things the same way. I've only lived here, so I don't have much to compare it to. Is it beautiful? Fuck yes. Would I call it a paradise? Probably not."

"I'm not saying it's perfect, but life could be a whole lot worse."

"You're leaving when you graduate?" Brax asked, but didn't wait for me to answer. "Is it different because of your dad? Makes sense, ya know? That you'll question every little thing now."

"Yeah, I do question everything. I'm expected back home so I can work for Langley Enterprises."

"If you don't want to, don't go."

I turned to look at Brax, forehead wrinkled and a look in my eyes that I hoped told him he was crazy. "It's not that easy."

"So? Does everything have to be easy? Seems like

most things have been that way your whole life, and you're not happy."

"I'm happy," I argued. Who did he think he was?

"Are you? I mean, surface level, yeah, but you're over halfway through school for a career you don't want and planning on moving to a place where you don't want to live, with a person you're angry with and don't want to work for. Maybe you need a little difficulty to shake up your life."

"I'm pretty sure that's where you come in." I tried to keep my voice light, but the truth was, Brax was right. Not that I'd never had to work hard for anything. I wasn't a natural at lacrosse, but I'd trained and practiced until I was the best. I was shit with computers, but before I found out about my dad, I'd studied my ass off to get good grades. I took the job at Shenanigans, determined to start making my own way—and, okay, mostly to piss my father off—though I guess I wouldn't call the latter that hard. Still, when it counted, I took the easy way. But what did it matter if I ignored my dad's calls and worked at a bar if I was still going to follow the path he'd carved out for me?

"You like that I don't make anything easy on you.

If I had, you would have lost interest already. Everyone gives you what you want without you even having to ask for it, but not me."

"That's not why I want you. I want you because you're hot."

We stopped walking. Brax didn't seem to have the same issue I did about wanting to protect what we were doing. He stood close, cupped my cheek, traced my bottom lip with his thumb, which made me chub up because, again, he was hot. "Truth, but it's also because I don't kiss your ass, and I don't sugarcoat shit for you. Eventually, that'll get old and you won't want someone who makes you work for it." For a second, I thought he was going to kiss me, right there under a palm tree, in the middle of campus, but instead he dug his teeth into my bottom lip and bit gently. "I'll never stop making you work for it, Lacrosse."

Please fucking don't. I touched my bottom lip, lost for words. It wasn't the first time he'd done something brazen like he just had, but it made warmth spread through my chest in an unfamiliar way. It made my blood rush faster through my veins and my pulse beat harder against my skin. I seriously doubted this would ever get old, and that…that was scary as fuck and something better thought about another day, so I said, "You like biting."

"I like biting *you*."

"Because you think I'm hot too."

"Clearly." He started walking again, but I was rooted to the ground for a moment before catching up with him. I still wondered why we were going to the library instead of somewhere we could fuck around and he could bite me all he wanted.

I followed him, though, and went up the stairs leading to the white-stucco library building. Brax skipped a bunch of empty tables, working his way toward the back, then to the second floor, and finally into a quiet, nearly empty corner there.

He took one of the chairs and sat with his back to the library and facing a window. I went to sit across from him, but Brax shook his head. "No. Sit beside me."

Why was it so hot when he got a little bossy? "What if I say no?"

"Believe me, you don't want to."

Well, when he put it that way, I figured I should listen. But all he did was pull out his laptop, a notebook and pen, which surprised me since hello, computer. He eyed me, waiting for me to do the same. Grumbling, I tugged mine out of the bag too, and then...then we fucking did homework. Not what I had in mind.

But Brax did help me. It was him, so of course he didn't make it easy on me, like, doing the work for me, but we spent over an hour there together, working through codes and processes until my head hurt and I wanted to cry thinking about this being my whole life. Every time I lost focus, he pulled me back into it, surprisingly without being a dick or seeming like he was losing patience. He didn't have to do this; he could have walked. My friends wouldn't have pushed, wouldn't have kept me there and kept my head in the game, but Brax did.

"You really hate this, don't you?" Brax asked. Behind us some people came in, others were browsing the shelves, but no one was close enough to listen to our conversation.

"Yes." I looked away because it was embarrassing as shit. Why did I let my dad control me so much? Why did I do nothing more than pretend to rebel with a stupid-ass job? Why didn't I call it a day?

"Why nursing?"

No one had ever asked me that before, but then, no one had known before either. My gaze found his again. "I don't know. No real reason. I'm not one of those people who had a sick family member or whatever. I just…I don't know. I like the idea of helping people that way. Of doing something that feels like it matters."

His features softened, and he gave me an almost insecure smile, like it was him who had just shared something personal. "You did your work, and now you get your reward." I went to close my laptop, thinking we were gonna get out of here so he could blow me, but Brax grabbed my wrist and stopped me. "You don't want to come, Lacrosse?"

My eyes widened. "Here?" I'd never done something like this before. It was way fucking different than getting on my knees in an empty classroom with a locked door.

He shrugged. "Unless you don't want it."

"I want it," I rushed out, making him chuckle.

"You're responsible for making sure we don't get caught." I nodded dumbly, my body coming alive like a lit sparkler. Brax pulled my chair close. "Put your arm around me."

I did as he said. He was about to jerk me off in the library. It wasn't as if I'd argue with anything he told me.

Brax reached over, shoving his hand under my waistband and deftly pulling me out of my underwear and track pants.

I was already hard as a steel post, my dick leaking. I turned my head slightly so I was looking at him but could also see if anyone came up behind us. He licked his hand before wrapping it around my shaft for a long, lazy stroke. I groaned and almost shot my load right then and there.

Sex in public was fucking hot.

But then, anything with Brax was.

"Shh. You can't be loud, Lacrosse," he whispered, rubbing his palm over the head of my erection, then back down again.

"Easy for you to say."

"If you're loud, I stop."

"Fuck you."

"I told you I won't make anything easy on you."

He sped up his hand movements. Handjobs were a whole lot better with lube, but I was so horned up, my precum and Brax's spit were doing the job.

"Fuck...Jesus God, that's good," I said breathlessly.

My eyes drifted closed, but then I heard, "Where do you want to sit?" and they jerked open. I would fucking die if the group of girls came close to us and we had to stop...or I'd throw Brax on the table and give them a show. I was so damn turned on, I didn't think I could stop.

"Look how full your balls are already."

"Can't...look." I eyed them, one of the girls gazing at me, but something in my expression must have said, *Don't even think about it*, because she frowned and pointed in the other direction.

"Let's go over there." They left, but there were still people around the space behind us. The possibility that we'd get caught remained a constant worry, yet all it did was turn me on more.

"Such a pretty cock. I bet you want to fuck me with it, don't you, Lacrosse? Wanna know what it's like to have my ass hugging you tight? Should I give it to you before we end this?"

"Yesssss. Hell yes."

My eyes rolled back, and I nearly melted into the

seat, but I forced myself to chill the fuck out before I ruined this.

He took his hand away and spit in it again, then jerked me faster. My breathing picked up. I didn't know how no one realized what we were doing, but I didn't care.

I watched him while he pleasured me, took in the way he licked his lips, the cut of his jaw, the way he styled his hair so it was messy and sticking up, the flare of lust in his eyes when he turned to me, and said, "Tick-tock. You better come for me before it's too late."

I didn't know what it was about those words, but the way he'd spoken them, coupled with his hand twisting around my crown and then down my shaft, had my whole body tensing, my balls letting loose, spewing my load all over Brax's hand, my groin, and my pants. "Fuck...*fuck*." I was a mess in the goddamned library, but I didn't care. "That was the hottest thing I've ever done."

He smiled, used his clean hand to tug a hoodie out of his bag. He wiped his hand before giving it to me, when I heard, "What the fuck, Langley?" Watty basically shouted across the library.

"Shhh!" someone hissed.

I dropped the sweatshirt to my thighs, covering my softening cock, emptied balls, and the cum all over me.

Watty walked up with Ford. "We've been texting you." Ford looked back and forth between me and Brax.

"I was…um…"

"Studying?" Watty finished for me.

Yeah, that. I was a fucking idiot. "Yep. Homework." I nodded toward Braxton, unfairly angry with my friends for ruining this moment.

"I gotta bail." Brax shoved his laptop into his bag, glanced at me, and winked. I was going to fucking kill him. I had my dick out and my friends there, and he was leaving? He stood and said, "See you at work tonight, Lacrosse, and just so you know, it's your turn next time." He walked away without a word to my friends.

"Your turn for what?" Ford asked.

"Nothing."

"What's going on with you and Asshole Bartender?" Watty questioned.

"Nothing. It's school stuff," I said, trying to figure

out if I could discreetly clean the jizz from myself before it dried.

"Is he who you were with the other night?"

"Jesus, man. What is this, fifty questions?" I bit out, being more of a dick than the situation warranted.

"What the hell is your problem?" Watty crossed his arms while Ford gave me a penetrating stare.

"Nothing, sorry. Just shit for school that I hate. What are you guys doing here?"

Watty said, "I need this book for class, and then we're out. Want us to wait for you?"

"Nah, I gotta finish something real quick. I'll meet you guys back at the house, and we can go to practice together."

They looked at each other. This whole thing was totally sus, and I got that, but they nodded and went on their way.

I cleaned up my jizz, tucked myself away, and couldn't wait until work that night when it would be my turn to work a load out of Brax's balls.

CHAPTER NINETEEN

Brax

TY AND I kept hanging out—after class, and my TA stuff, before work, after work. The day I'd jerked him off at the library, he'd given me head in the stockroom again. Poor Marshall had interrupted us again, and I was fairly certain he was now scarred for life because this time, the door somehow hadn't locked and he'd actually walked in to see my dick hanging out of Ty's mouth. I'd never seen a face turn so red or a door close so quickly.

We'd messed around in the empty classroom again too, and he'd come to my house a couple of times to study, which we did, but I rewarded him with orgasms afterward. Ty hadn't fucked me yet, but I'd had him again, and he was right—it was, in fact, quality hole.

Two weeks had gone by since the first night he'd slept over, and we just…kept playing this game with each other. We didn't put a label on it. Hell, we didn't even talk about it. We just participated in the two *H*'s: hooking up and hanging out. We acted normal around everyone else, didn't do couple stuff because we weren't a couple. We were two horny guys who liked getting off with each other and giving each other shit, but I was pretty sure some people had realized something was up.

Tonight Shenanigans was pretty busy, even for a Friday night. Ty was supposed to get off early, but Gwen had asked him if he could stay a little longer and help us. Around midnight the doors opened, and a group of lacrosse players came in. Just what we needed. "Langley!" they yelled, one of them adding, "I can't believe you're a dish bitch!"

I didn't know how in the fuck he hung out with them. I could hardly handle being in the same room as his teammates, but then, there was a time I'd felt that way about Ty too.

There were six of them, Ty's usual three friends among them. Ty glanced at me from where he was wiping down the bar, before giving them his attention again. "I'll make *you* my bitch," he replied, grabbing his junk.

Jesus fucking Christ. Sometimes I couldn't believe I liked him.

"Anytime, sexy," one of the guys replied. I didn't know who in the fuck he was, but I already didn't like him. Heat burned across my skin, settling in my gut with lingering embers. "You know I love you." He grabbed Ty and playfully tried to kiss his cheek.

Ty shoved him away. "Get the fuck off me. I don't know where your lips have been."

I was pretty sure the guy had been teasing, but still, there was a sharp edge to my voice when I interrupted, "Can I get you guys something to drink?"

Ty must have sensed my annoyance because he cocked a brow my direction, but I ignored him. They all ordered beer, and while I poured a pitcher, I heard, "What are you doing when you get off? After this we're heading to a party. Jessica Rodriguez said you should go. She legit told me to tell you she wants you."

The pitcher of beer decided to jump out of my hand and clatter to the floor. "Fuck," I gritted out. There was beer everywhere, all over the wooden floor and my shoes. *It's not because of what fuckface said. I don't care if someone wants to ride Ty's dick. Nope, I'm not jealous. Not at all. Not of the woman or the dickface who tried to kiss him.* "Watch out," I told Gwen when she headed my way. "Don't slip."

I didn't let myself look at Ty, partly because I didn't want to see the cocky grin on his face that said *busted* and also because I didn't want him to make a decision based on what he thought I might want. We were just fucking around. We weren't exclusive.

"I'll help with this." Marshall brought over a mop and began cleaning up while I started to fill another pitcher.

"You gonna go, or what?" the jockhole asked.

"Ah, no, I don't think so. I'll probably turn in early tonight," Ty replied.

I smiled. Fucking *smiled*.

"Come on, man. You've been ditching us all the time lately. What the hell is up with you?" Watty asked—and seriously, that was the stupidest fucking nickname in the world.

"Nothin's up with me. I just have plans. That okay with you?"

"He's hiding out with some piece of ass," Ford

replied.

I clunked the pitcher onto the counter and handed them mugs.

"Maybe he's in love," came another response, and they all started laughing.

Yep, it was time for me to get the hell out of there.

I took the payment and moved down the bar to get this guy Charlie a drink. He came in from time to time, but I didn't know him well. Just that he was probably one of the most friendly guys I'd ever met.

The whole time, my gaze kept making an unexpected journey back to Ty and his friends. They were drinking and talking shit to Ty. Fortunately, they didn't stay long. Ty and I hadn't officially decided to hook up tonight, so he could have gone with them if he'd wanted.

We finished our shift, dancing around each other when we walked outside.

"So...whatcha doing tonight?" Ty asked as we stepped into the cool February night.

"Eh, I'll probably head home and crash. You're not going to meet up with Jessica?" Shit. Why the fuck had I asked that? The stupid question just slipped out.

I leaned against the building, under an overhead light. Ty's grin grew into an uncontrollable smile as he stepped closer to me. "Hey, remember that time you threw a pitcher of beer because you were jealous someone else wanted a piece of me?"

Here we went. I'd been expecting it. "I wasn't jealous, and it slipped."

"Slipped out of your jealous fingers because you want me all to yourself."

"You wish, Lacrosse." But I did in a way, at least while we were fucking around. When we ended this, he could do whatever he wanted.

"Should I call you Jelly now? Jelly McJellerson from the house of I Want Tyson Langley?"

"If you don't want me to answer." I grabbed onto his hips, pulled him close so his groin met mine. "You could have gone. I don't own you."

The curl of his lips turned downward. "I know, but I didn't want to go."

"You heading straight home too, then?"

He cocked his head slightly before shaking it. "Shut up."

"You shut up."

"Did you bring my helmet?" He pulled back and

headed for my bike.

"That's not shutting up."

"If it wasn't for my mouth, your life would be boring, Sunshine."

"Nah, I could find someone else to suck me off." I laughed when Ty pushed me.

"I meant because I make you laugh. You think I'm funny. You have a good time with me. It's why you hate Jessica. Oh, and Tim for trying to kiss me."

So that was the jock's name. Fuck Tim.

I scoffed. "I don't hate Jessica. I don't even know who she is." But I didn't want her hands on Ty any more than I did Tim's, so there was that.

"But you like me. I knew it. You didn't deny how much you enjoy my company. I feel like we're turning over a new leaf in our relationship."

I tossed him the helmet. "You're still not shutting up."

"Don't plan on it either."

No, he wouldn't, and I was secretly glad of that.

It was a short ride back to my house. Luckily, it was blissfully quiet. I didn't know where Asher was, but there was no party, so that was all I cared about. We'd basically ignored our fight from a couple of weeks back. That was the way we worked: one day pissed at each other, the next pretending it never happened. Basically, we were great communicators.

I let Ty inside, and he headed straight for my bedroom, only moving for me to unlock the door. Once inside, he opened the cabinet by my minifridge. "Thank fuck." He tugged out the sea-salt-and-cracked-black-pepper chips he'd brought over the other day, took his shoes off, then sat beside my laptop on my bed, like he was at home, like he'd done this a million times in the past. "Want some?"

"Nah, I'm good." I took my shoes off too, trying to ignore the comfort of this, how natural it now felt to spend time with him.

I headed into the bathroom for a quick piss and to wash my hands, and when I came back into my room, he was looking at my laptop. The screen had been black before, but he must have touched it and woken it up, my search from earlier right there for him to see. My stomach flip-flopped like a dying fish.

"Brax?"

"I was bored and just looking out of curiosity. It's not a thing."

"You planning on going to nursing school?"

I pulled my tee off, trying to act normal. "No, dumbass. Clearly, I was looking at it for you. I was curious what you'd need to do." I shrugged. "You should know what your options are if you decide to follow your dream instead of your dad's."

I grabbed my laptop, closed the search, and plopped onto the bed beside him. He was sitting up, but I lay down, head on the pillows, legs crossed at the ankles. We were both quiet, Ty's gaze on me, then on his chips, before coming back to me again.

"Jesus Christ, Ty. Why are you looking at me like that?" His stare was softer than it had ever been and annoying.

"I know this might come as a surprise to you... I know it does to me, but...you're kinda sweet."

I hit him in the face with a pillow. "Take it back."

He set his chips aside and straddled me. "Your name just changed. Sweetie McSweetson but still from the house of I Want Tyson Langley. You have a big heart."

"I think I just threw up in my mouth."

"And such a way with words," he teased, brushing his fingers over my chest, right where the muscle in question sat. "Show me what you found out."

"Yeah?" I hadn't been sure he'd be interested. Well, I knew he would be on some level, but not that he'd allow himself to be. I got up, turned on the lamp beside my bed and the main light off. After making sure my door was locked in case Asher showed up with a houseful, I took my pants off while Ty did the same, followed by his shirt.

A minute later, we were lying on our stomachs, computer in front of me, while we researched the nursing program, both at FU and at other local schools. Currents of hope and excitement radiated off him. He wanted this so bad. I couldn't believe this wasn't what he was going to school for. "You should do it. It's your life, Ty."

"You think so?"

His question surprised me, as did his intense stare. He watched me like he cared what I thought, like he respected my opinion. "It doesn't matter what I think. It matters what you want."

"I'd basically have to start over."

"Not totally. Some prereqs and stuff would transfer over."

"I'd have to talk to my dad...like really talk to him. It's something I need to deal with anyway. I can't pay for school next year. I'm fooling myself, acting like this job matters in the grand scheme of things. I mean, Mom has money too. She'd pay, but it's just like getting it from him. She put her career aside for him to be the perfect wife and mother. Right now, all her money is from him."

"You should take the money. I respect what you're trying to do, but fuck, Ty. You're so goddamned lucky. That doesn't mean you have to agree with him or be close to him. There are people who would die to be in your position. But if you don't take the money, you'll still be okay. That's what loans are for. Tell your dad how you feel and what you want, and then make that shit come true, with or without him."

Ty bit his bottom lip, grinned, and my pulse beat a little too fast. "See? Sweet. I can't believe I ever thought you were a bad boy."

"I'm a badass motherfucker is what I am." We laughed, and Ty closed the laptop.

"I can't look at that anymore tonight. Fuck, Sunshine. I might do this. I might really fucking do it." I hoped he did. "I'm all stressed out now. Do you have any weed?"

"Yep. I just went to the dispensary yesterday."

I grabbed the stuff from my drawer and packed a bowl. We sat up. I put the pipe to my lips and lit the green bud. Once it was burning, I inhaled.

"You didn't even offer me green," Ty said, so I leaned in, smoke still in my lungs. He nodded and moved closer, sat between my thighs with his legs over mine, wrapped around my waist so we were close. He brushed his lips against mine, then opened his mouth. When I exhaled, he breathed in, shotgunning the smoke into his own lungs, straight from mine. He coughed some.

"Good?" I asked.

"Yeah."

I took a second hit, and Ty rested his hand against my nape, pulling me in so our mouths touched again. Smoke billowed out from between my lips, Ty sucking it up, taking it into his body. This was really fucking sexy.

We smoked the whole bowl that way—some hits I kept for myself, some I shared with him, but each one Ty took into his body came from my mouth. When it hashed, I set the pipe on my nightstand, my body sufficiently buzzing.

"I'm high." Ty snickered, making the same action

bubble out of me.

"I think that's the point."

He wrapped both arms around me and took my mouth, dipped his tongue inside, tightened his legs around me, and we kissed for a while. I ran my hands up and down his back, teased the crease of his ass, but we didn't go further.

"I kinda want to laugh, but I don't have a reason to," he said, which of course resulted in both of us cracking up. "Guess what?"

"What?"

"Chicken butt. I'm kidding. That was dumb. I'm not responsible for what I say when I'm feeling this good."

"Clearly."

"Come to my game tomorrow."

"I'm working."

"I'll win for you."

"You'll win for you."

"I'll win for us?"

"I'm working," I reiterated, because I did have an earlier shift. Ty poked out his bottom lip, and I bit it, then sucked it into my mouth. God, I wished I wasn't scheduled. If I hadn't been, I'd go to Ty's game, and that was…unnerving. I laughed.

"Um…did I miss something?"

"*Unnerving* is a funny word."

Ty's brows pulled together. "Is it?"

"It is tonight."

We dissolved into laughter, untangling ourselves from each other, only to lie down together and twine our bodies again. I turned off the lamp.

"I used to go to his games—my high school jock. I'd watch him and be stupidly fucking proud like…like he was mine, this boy everyone wanted, and we had this secret that was just between us. I ignored the girls who were there for him too, the shit-talking from his friends. He liked having me there, said it would make him do better, but I think it was just because he liked having that control over me."

"That's not me." Ty's breath ghosted against my cheek. "I mean, I like attention, but I'm not him. I want you there because I…fuck, I want to *impress* you."

He did, more than he knew. "I know you're not him." I danced my fingertips down his face. "I have to work." It was the only excuse I had, so I'd keep using it.

"Okay." He pressed a kiss to my lips. "I might become a nurse."

"You should. Don't let anyone take that away from you."

"Next time we fuck, we should play doctor." More laughter, followed by quiet. "Tell me something nice…about you…your life."

"Like what?"

"I don't know. You gotta tell me. I can't tell you."

He had a point. My heart beat a little too hard. I took a couple of deep breaths to slow it. "I don't know… My grandma used to play hide-and-seek with me when I was a kid. It was my favorite game. She was always the best hider, and it would take me forever to find her."

I felt Ty smile. "She sounds awesome."

"She's the best. She used to let me have cereal for dinner too. I fucking love Golden Grahams."

"Shit, now I want Golden Grahams."

"Me too." I was quiet for a moment before admitting, "If it wasn't for her, I wouldn't be doing crap with my life. She's the only person who ever told me I could do something, that I could be different. She wouldn't lie to me, so I had to believe her, ya know?"

Fuck, the weed was giving me loose lips.

"Brax…"

"Don't get mushy."

"Don't tell you that you're fucking smart and hot and that I believe you can accomplish *anything* you put your mind to?"

"I guess you can tell me that."

We laughed, wrestled around together, before I settled on top of him, grinding my groin against his. "Go to nursing school."

There was a pause, and then a soft, "Okay."

We kissed lazily for a while, just savoring each other's mouths, like we didn't have the munchies for both food and each other.

I didn't know what time it was when we finally fell asleep, but we did so in each other's arms.

I was too high and comfortable to let myself worry about it too much.

CHAPTER TWENTY

Ty

I FIGURED I had two choices. Well, make that three. One, I could text Brax and see what he was up to today. Two, I could stop obsessing over the guy and do my own thing or chill with my friends. I hadn't been spending as much time with them lately. They were always asking what I was up to or who I was fucking, and I still hadn't told them.

The third possibility was to show up at his house unannounced. Considering this was me, I went with option three. It was the only one that went along with Ty logic when it came to Braxton Walker.

Unfortunately, as soon as I got out of the car, Brax was leaving the house, heading toward his motorcycle, and frowned when he saw me.

"Wow, I'm not used to that look," I told him.

"I look at you like I don't know what the fuck you're doing ninety-five percent of the time."

"It's usually mixed with a little more *God, I want you, Ty. What did I ever do without you?*"

"Lived peacefully."

"Huh?"

"That's what I did without you."

"Ha-ha."

Brax shuffled his feet, looking slightly unsure, which wasn't an expression I was familiar with when it came to him. Maybe I shouldn't have come. Things had been a little different between us Friday night, something I swore not to think about, so I wasn't going to.

"What are you up to?" he asked. "I'm heading out."

I shrugged. "Was bored, so I thought I'd see what you were doing. I figured you must be missing me by now."

I got the reaction I'd been hoping for when Brax chuckled. "It would appear it's the other way around. You jonesing for my cock, Lacrosse?"

"I mean, I wouldn't turn it down."

He groaned low from his gut like he wanted exactly what I'd said. "I have to go. Someone's expecting me."

It didn't matter that I had no business doing it; I tensed up. Was he heading out to hook up with someone else? *I don't care. Nope, not at all. This is me not caring.*

I didn't move when Brax reached out and rubbed my bottom lip with his thumb. "You're frowning." And then surprise bloomed in my chest when he leaned in and brushed a kiss over my lips. "Don't be jealous. I'm going to see my grandma."

"Dude, I totally want to meet your grandma. Take me with you." I liked the way Brax talked about her, like she was his bright spot in all the shit he'd been through. She sounded great, and I couldn't pretend I wasn't curious about Brax's family. I'd only met his brother, and I couldn't say I was impressed, given how he treated Brax. But his grandma was special. Even through his stories I could feel their love for each other.

"No," Brax replied.

"Yes."

"Why would you want to go to an assisted-living facility with me and see my grandma?"

"Because I'm hoping to get more dirt on you. I need material for fresh jokes."

"Maybe that's just because you're not funny."

"Then why can't you stop smiling when you're with me?" Brax's lips immediately straightened into a hard line. "Too late. Let's go. Wanna take the bike or my car?"

"No," Brax said again.

"Please. I'll do anything." I fluttered my eyelashes dramatically.

When Brax dropped his head back, I knew I had him. "You're so fucking spoiled. Fine."

There was a rough edge to his voice that told me he was nervous about this. I had a feeling I was likely the only guy Brax had taken to meet her, and that felt better than winning any lacrosse match. It felt right in a way I didn't want to contemplate. I was thinking that about a lot of things lately, but there was just too much going on in my head to sort through it all. I'd rather focus on having fun with Brax. "You know I was giving you shit, right? You don't have to take me. If you'd rather I didn't go, I won't." I *wanted* to go. Probably too much, but I didn't want him to feel forced.

He sighed. "Let's go before I change my mind."

"Sure, I'd love to go meet your grandma with you," I teased. He went for his bike, and I followed.

Brax glanced my way, his face spelling out a look I was familiar with by now. It said: *God, I hate you* and *You're so fucking ridiculous*, but mixed a little with *You make me smile* and *I have fun with you*. I wasn't sure he'd acknowledged the last two parts yet.

Like he often did, Brax batted my hands away and strapped my helmet. "You know I'm capable of doing that, right?"

"No," he replied, and I fake-gasped. "No shit, but when you're on my bike, you're my responsibility."

Okay, so was that supposed to make me go all soft inside? Because it totally did. "Look at you being all sweet and protective."

"Look at you not knowing when to stop."

He had a point. We climbed on. It was a twenty-five-minute drive to the facility, more because of the Southern California traffic than because of the distance.

I liked riding with him, liked the feel of the wind around us, Brax between my thighs, my dick close to his ass, and how I had to lean with the bike when he did.

He didn't say anything when we parked at the facility and I got off the motorcycle. He was still quiet when we removed our helmets and put them in the packs. He made it all the way to the door, spine stiff, before I wrapped my fingers around his wrist to stop him. "I don't have to go in there, Sunshine." I wanted to make sure he knew I was serious. I hadn't suggested it to make him uncomfortable.

"Fuck. I know." He rubbed a hand over his face. "She's asked about you."

My pulse kicked up like it did when we were riding. "You told her about me?"

"Just that you're annoying and drive me crazy. I had to tell her something that day I left to see you."

Nope. I refused to believe that was the only reason. "I want to kiss you right now."

"I'll bite your lip."

"Is that supposed to deter me? It's kinda hot when you bite me."

"Only kinda?" Brax cocked a dark brow, looked toward the door—there was no one there at the moment—and leaned in and nibbled my earlobe. "If you're good, we'll go home and get naked together.

It'll be better than *kinda* hot."

"Yes, please. I'd like that. Now don't give me a boner in front of your grandma. I'm a respectable young man."

He laughed way too hard as we made our way inside. We checked in, gave our IDs, and then Brax led me down the hallway toward his grandma's place. We passed a large room where people were sitting on the couches, watching TV, or at tables playing board games. It smelled like antiseptic and old people but also like warm cookies and good times.

"How long has your grandma been here?"

"A few months."

"You miss her a lot."

"She's close. I see her every week, sometimes more than once."

"Doesn't mean you can't miss her."

Brax sighed. "No, I guess it doesn't." He nodded toward a door, and I turned for it.

I stood behind him as he knocked. When a soft, "Come in," drifted through the door, he opened it.

"You're scowling, Braxton. You're too pretty to look so annoyed half the time," was the first thing she said, and I immediately fell in love.

I peeked out from behind him and smiled. "Right? I tell him that all the time. He's such a brooder."

Her eyes widened, and her smile grew. Her hair was black like Brax's but being taken over by a lot of gray. She was little, both short and skinny, but somehow I knew you didn't fuck with her. That there wasn't anything this woman couldn't do.

"This was a mistake," Brax said, but I just slipped around him and went for his grandma, who sat at a table by the window.

I held out my hand for her. "I'm Ty. It's so nice to meet you."

"Matilda, and it's nice to meet you too. The lacrosse player, I take it?"

"Fuck my life," Brax mumbled behind me.

"The one and only. He still hasn't come to one of my games, though."

"Well, that's not very nice of him," Matilda replied.

"I agree."

"We'll work on him today." She winked.

"I like you, Matilda."

"I like you too, Ty."

CHAPTER TWENTY-ONE

Braxton

"DOES YOUR PERSON appear to be a man?" Ty asked Grandma. The facility was busy today. We'd gone into one of the main hangout rooms, where they had lots of games, but many were already taken, so the three of us sat at a table in the corner, Ty and Grandma playing Guess Who. Ty choosing a game for eight-year-olds should surprise absolutely no one.

"Yes," Grandma replied. "Does your person have glasses?"

Ty looked down at his board, rubbing his chin as if he had to put such deep thought into the question. "Hmmm."

"You're a dork," I told him.

"I'm thinking."

"Thinking about what? It's not your opinion she's asking for."

Grandma swatted my hand. "Let the boy think, Braxton."

"Yes, let the boy think," Ty added.

"You're a traitor, Grandma."

"He's quite charming."

Ty's smile grew. "I am, aren't I? I've been trying to get Brax to see that for years now." He turned to me. I was sitting next to him, Grandma across from us. "See? I'm charming. Matilda said so."

"You're annoying is what you are."

Ty faced Grandma again. "He likes me more than he's willing to admit. I think I'm one of his favorite people."

"It would appear that way to me," Grandma replied.

"Can you two stop ganging up on me?"

"For now." Ty winked, and I found myself reaching out and resting my hand along his nape. When his muscles tightened, I almost pulled back, but him resting his palm on my thigh told me I shouldn't. I really needed to stop this shit. We were acting like a couple. I'd brought him to meet my *grandma*. I liked to keep things about myself and the people important to me close to my chest. I hated exposing my vulnerable spots, but time and time again, I'd shown them to Ty.

"No glasses," he said to Grandma, and I watched them play, realizing how much I enjoyed this, how much I liked seeing them together, and that he got to see how fucking cool my grandma was and wanted to spend time with her. Hell, my own brother didn't even do that. "Does your person have red hair?"

"Yes," she replied. "The two of you have the same major?"

Ty nodded, his eyes darting my direction, almost insecurely, before he said, "I'm thinking about changing mine. I've always wanted to be a nurse, but…my dad wanted me to follow in his footsteps."

"But it's not his life," I added, "and Ty should do what *he* wants." When Grandma cocked a brow at me, I shrugged. "It's true. He hates computers. He'd be miserable."

"I thought you wanted me to be miserable?" Ty asked playfully.

"Most of the time, yes, but not in this."

"He's kind of a big teddy bear, isn't he? A brooding one, but still," he told Grandma.

"He is. He's always been like that. Tough on the outside, but with a tender heart. Brax will always do the right thing."

I shifted uncomfortably. "Yes, I know. I'm awesome. Can we not, though? Don't the two of you have a game of Guess Who to play?"

"I think we've embarrassed him enough for the day," Grandma said.

"I guess. Maybe we can do it again sometime," Ty replied.

"I'd like that."

We hung out for about three more hours with her, just visiting, playing games, and going for a walk outside. It was obvious that Grandma loved Ty. I liked that more than I thought I would.

When it was time to go, she pulled Ty into a hug. He gripped her back just as tightly. "Are you going to come and see me again?"

"I would love to."

"And you should think about what Brax said. It's your life. You should be happy." Ty nodded, then kissed her cheek and stepped back. He lingered in the background, giving me space to say my own goodbye without being all up in our business. "I like him, Brax."

"I know." I wasn't sure what else to say. Ty and I weren't a real couple.

"You like him." It was spoken only for me, not loud enough for Ty to hear, but still, discomfort slid down my spine.

"I love you, Grandma. I'll see you in a few days."

"I love you too."

Ty and I didn't say much to each other as we headed out. I fastened his helmet, and he grinned but didn't argue.

I thought about our day the whole way back to my house—how much he seemed to enjoy spending time with my grandma, and the way he made her laugh; how his hand felt on my thigh, and the fullness in my chest when he smiled at me.

I parked in front of the garage and turned off the bike. I didn't offer for him to come inside, and he didn't ask. We simply headed for the door together.

Once I had it closed behind us, something snapped inside me. The magnetic pull between us strengthened, urgent and undeniable, until our mouths collided in pent-up want. I pushed my tongue into his mouth, Ty's hands ripping my jacket off my shoulders and throwing it to the floor before shoving under my T-shirt. He tasted like the lemonade we'd drunk, both bitter and sweet. I'd never enjoyed a flavor more than I did in that moment. I was like an addict for it, *for him.*

We crashed into the wall, my back slamming against it and Ty on me. We laughed into the kiss while he thrust his rigid cock against mine.

"Fuck, you really want me, don't you?" I said, reaching around and grabbing his ass.

"I was just thinking the same thing about you."

I shut him up with my mouth again, teeth clanking, hands searching and tugging on clothes. I really hoped my brother wasn't home because if so, he was about to get an eyeful.

Our mouths didn't part as we stumbled our way down the hall, ripping each other's pants open and kicking out of our shoes. I pulled his dick out, wrapped my hand around it, and gave it a long, tight stroke.

"*Fuuuuuck,*" Ty groaned.

"We're getting there. You gonna give me this?" I rubbed my thumb over his tip, spreading the precum there. "You gonna let me see if you can dick me down the way I need?" It was overwhelming, the sudden need I felt to have Ty inside me.

His cock jerked in my hand, blood pulsing beneath his skin. "Hell yes. I'm going to own your ass."

"I don't know about owning," I replied, a slight tremor to my voice.

"I do." Ty pushed me down to the bed, and I let him. We were both in our pants, mine jeans, and his the stupid athletic gear he always wore. Our dicks were hanging out, the band of his bottoms resting beneath his tight ball sac. "You licked your lips. You want this?" Ty stroked himself.

"I mean, I'm not doing anything else right now, so might as well."

He chuckled and shucked off the rest of his clothes while I watched, jerking myself with slow, leisurely pulls. "Take my jeans off."

"I'm only listening because I want to fuck you."

"Whatever you have to tell yourself," I teased as Ty got me naked. He grabbed the lube and condoms from my nightstand, setting them close before climbing over me, one knee between my legs.

"You're so fucking hot." He licked one of my

nipples, then nipped it before moving to the other one. I threaded my hands through his hair as Ty began to kiss his way down my sternum. "I wanted you from the first time I saw you. You've had my dick hard for three years, Sunshine, and that goddamned mouth of yours just gets me hotter for you."

"Me too. I hate it, but I can't make it stop." It wasn't easy to admit. I blamed it on the way he turned my body inside out and had me ready to blow my load without even touching my dick or ass yet.

"Stop trying." He kissed one hip bone. "It's useless anyway." Then the other. "I think we might like each other."

"Liar." But we both knew Ty was right. There was zero chance I would have taken him with me today if that hadn't been the case.

Ty took my dick to the back of his throat, swallowing around me before slowly pulling off. My body was on fire for him. My brains scrambled. I wanted to tell him I really did like him, that I enjoyed seeing him hang out with my grandma today, that he made my insides feel chaotic but in a way I welcomed because it felt better than anything in my life ever had. Maybe because I'd never let myself feel much, so anything felt like delicious chaos. But instead I answered the way I could, the way he would expect, the one that totally fit us. "Get your fingers in my ass, Lacrosse, before I just jerk off and take a nap instead."

He laughed. "God, you're great."

The affection in his voice made my breath hitch. It wasn't often someone said something like that to me. "I know," I replied, with a silent thank-you in my head.

Ty knelt beside me. "Turn over."

I did, and he grabbed the lube and pumped some onto his fingers. He used the other hand to rub over my ass, then stretch one ass cheek to the side. "Jesus, look at that hole. He's begging for my cock."

"You fluent in asshole?"

"I'm fluent in you."

Oh…well, shit. I didn't know how to respond to that. Ty leaned over me, kissing my shoulders, then each knot of my spine as he sneaked his fingers in my crease, starting by rubbing my rim, then pushing inside. "Christ." My eyes rolled back. It had been a while since I'd had someone inside me.

"You took the word right out of my mouth. You're so tight."

"Quality hole," I teased.

"Whoa there, buddy. Stop trying to steal my shit. That's me."

"It can be both of us."

"We'll see about that."

I ended up on my hands and knees. Ty went from one finger to two and finally three, stretching me out, fucking me with them, making my hands fist in the pillows at that familiar sting and the feeling of fullness from having someone inside you.

"My dick is leaking like a faucet. I've never wanted to be inside someone so much."

I buried my face in the pillows, let his words sink in. Lots of people had wanted me—wanted to fuck me, wanted me to fuck them—so why did it feel so different when it came from Ty? "Fuck me." I pushed back against him, worked my ass on his fingers.

"I'm gonna need you to say that to me a whole lot more often. It's hot."

"Not if you don't get on with it."

But he did. I groaned when he pulled his fingers out. I watched over my shoulder as Ty suited up, lubed himself, then knelt behind me, his hands on my hips, his cheeks flushed pink, but then his grin grew cockier by the second.

"I'm going to get to the owning now."

"About time."

He held the base of his cock and pushed in. His dick was wider than his three fingers had been, filling me, working me open in new ways. I breathed through the initial discomfort, focused on his words. "Fuck...you're so good. I can't believe you're letting me in that ass. Holy shit, Brax. I never thought I'd get to actually have you."

I never thought he would either, but I sure as hell was glad to be wrong.

He was going slow, too slow, so when he was almost in, I pushed back, and we both hissed out a breath together.

It was all Ty needed to let loose on me. He pulled back some, then slammed forward, snapping his hips, fucking into me over and over and over again. My head spun, my balls ached, my cock leaked and throbbed as we took pleasure in each other.

"Stroke your dick for me, Sunshine. He needs a little attention before he gets too jelly of how much love I'm showing your ass."

I didn't know how to respond to that, but then,

half the time I was lost in how to respond to him. No one had ever kept me on my toes the way he did. No one made me laugh the way he did either.

I squirted lube into my hand and got to work, fisting my erection and working it with each pump of his hips. Every time Ty's cock brushed over my prostate, my vision doubled and pleasure shot down my spine.

"Quality. Fucking. Hole." Ty's voice was rasping, his breathing choppy as he lost himself in my ass. "You have no idea how much I want to empty my balls inside you. How much I wish I could watch my load leak out of you."

Hearing him say that, imagining his load inside me, ratcheted up the pleasure. I started to unravel, the small string pulling loose until I fell apart. My back arched, and I squeezed my eyes closed, an electrical storm shooting off beneath my skin, balls tight and my cum spurting out all over my hand and the mattress beneath me.

"Jesus, the way your hole just tightened around me. You want it, don't you? You want my load?" I really fucking did, and even though we weren't going there, even though there was a condom between us, it didn't feel like it. I didn't think it did to Ty either. "Tell me you want it."

"I want your cum," I said, and he cried out, thrust deep, his cock jerking and twitching, filling the rubber, both of us pretending it was my ass instead.

Ty fell down beside me. "Holy shitballs, that was hot."

"Shitballs?"

"Don't know. Just came out. I'm dead." He threw an arm over his eyes. "I've never done that before."

"Fucked?" I asked, though I knew what he meant.

"Wanted my load in someone's ass so much that I pretended it was real."

I didn't know if he was planning on saying more, but I didn't let him, instead keeping his mouth busy with mine, our tongues dancing together.

We napped after that, then fucked again, this time with me on top. And when we parted ways later, I almost asked him to stay.

Once he'd left, I wished I had.

CHAPTER TWENTY-TWO

Ty

BRAX MUMBLED UNDER his breath and let out a soft curse, which led to a groan and then more mumbling.

He lay on his back on the bed, his laptop balanced on his chest. I'd made myself comfortable between his legs, my head resting on his thigh while I looked at my phone. "Oh no."

"Oh no, what?" he asked.

"Brooding Bear is back. How can you be so grumpy? Remember this weekend when I fucked your brains out? Aren't you still riding the high from that?" I knew I was. It had been the best sex I'd ever had, both when I topped him and when he topped me. Two days later I still got hard thinking about it.

"First, Brooding Bear is not going to become a

thing."

"Um…I think it is."

"No it's not," he countered.

"Yes it is."

"You do realize we have a major test coming up, right? Shouldn't you be studying with me?"

Yes, yes I should, but I was so over it. That wasn't the most responsible way to look at things, but I couldn't help it. "I'm going to be changing my major anyway." He sighed and set his laptop on the nightstand. I twisted onto my stomach, arms resting on his abs, and looked at him. "Am I about to get a lecture? This feels like a lecture. How about we skip that and get to the spanking?" I waggled my brows for emphasis.

"You're not going to do anything this semester, and if you fail your classes, you can't continue to play that stupid game you love."

He had a point. "Ugh. I hate it when you're right."

"You must be miserable all the time, then."

I laughed. "And you say I'm cocky." Things had been slowly changing between us for weeks now, but it felt really different since visiting his grandma and the incredible way I'd dicked him down afterward. Again, it had only been a couple of days, but we were cuddling on his bed between class, practice, and work, when it had nothing to do with sex. I leaned forward, lifted his shirt and blew a raspberry on his belly. Like…what the fuck even was that? I'd never done that with someone I was fucking in my whole life.

"What are you doing?"

"I don't know. It's weird as fuck. I was just thinking that."

"Well, stop it."

"Why? Because it's kinda cute and endearing and makes your crush on me grow?"

"No, because your slobber is gross." He grinned.

"You like my spit…in your mouth…on your cock…dripping in your hole. Or like…when I do this." I pushed up onto my knees, bent forward, and licked from his chin to his forehead.

"You're so fucking gross." But he grabbed me and tried to do the same. We wrestled around until I was on my back with Brax on top of me, licking my face like a dog and making me laugh.

"Stop. You're right. It's disgusting." But it was fun too. "Come on. Let's study. I don't want to fail, and even more importantly, I don't want to be a distraction to my Brooding Bear."

"Gag," Brax replied, but he grabbed his laptop. We rolled to our bellies with the computer in front of us and made it thirty minutes of being responsible young men, when my cell rang.

I picked it up from where it sat on his pillow. "It's my mom." If it had been anyone else, I would have ignored it, but I worried about her being alone, what with my dad having moved out to be with his new family and me on the opposite coast. Brax nodded and gave the computer his attention again as I answered. "Hey, you."

"I missed your voice. You've been quiet lately."

Guilt gnawed at my heart. I should have been better at keeping in touch. "Sorry. Things have been crazy with school, my job, and lacrosse."

"Are you overworking yourself, Tyson? Don't do that. Don't put pressure on yourself to get back at your father, not when it can hurt you."

"I'm fine, Ma. I'm a badass. I can handle it."

Brax huffed out a laugh.

"Well, you've definitely got your father worked up. He says you won't answer his calls."

"I don't know why you do that. Why you talk to him after what he did to us. I hate him." But a part of me still wanted to make him proud. How fucked up was that?

Brax looked at me, and then…then he reached over, pushed his hand beneath my shirt, and massaged my lower back, like he just wanted to touch me and for me to know I wasn't alone.

"No," Mom replied. "You don't. That's what makes it even harder. You love him."

I swiped at a stray tear that leaked from my eye. I was not going to do this. I wouldn't cry over him, and I sure as shit wasn't going to do it in front of Brax. "It doesn't matter if I love him. I still don't want to talk about him."

Mom sighed, and I could hear the wobble in it. She didn't like my answer, but she would respect it. "What's new with you? Tell me everything." When Brax cocked a brow, it was obvious he heard her, and weirdly, I knew exactly what he was thinking. I shook my head. He rolled his eyes. "Hello? Ty?"

"Sorry, Ma. My friend Brax was talking to me."

His mouth dropped open like he hadn't been expecting me to tell her about him. I hadn't expected to do it, but he was bugging me, so it served him right.

"Oh, is he one of your lacrosse friends? I don't remember you mentioning him before."

"No, we have a bunch of classes together, and we both work at the bar. He hates sports. He's never even watched me play. Can you imagine?" Brax scowled, and I stuck my tongue out at him in retaliation.

"Why wouldn't he want to watch you play?"

"I know, right? We went and saw his grandma this weekend, and she and I were teasing him about it. He doesn't like jocks; well, except for me. He likes me."

"Well, then, if he likes you, you tell him your mama said he needs to go watch you play."

My smile grew at her response. "Did you hear that? My mom said you have to come and watch me so I can impress you with my mad skills."

Mom laughed. "You might have embellished some."

"I was planning on it," Brax said, making my gaze snap to his.

"Wait. You were?" It was possible he was just saying that since I'd put him on the spot, but Brax wasn't the type to do things he didn't want to do.

Brax groaned and dropped his head. "Don't make me say it again."

I joked with him often about my games, but as far as I'd known, I'd been joking. Maybe that sounded weird, not knowing, but why should I care if he watched me play? And yet, hearing Brax say he planned on showing up made an unexpected burst of joy explode in my chest. I wanted him there. I wanted to impress him. I wanted Brax to see something I was good at.

Oh God. Kill me now.

"You know that's really sweet of you, right? You're sweet Braxton Walker. Admit it. He broods, Mom. Like seriously broods. I didn't know that was really a thing."

"You like this boy," Mom said, which basically stopped my heart. I willed it to beat again because I hadn't been serious about that whole kill-me-now thing. I had a lot of life left to live. "Why didn't you tell me you're seeing someone?"

The way Brax's eyeballs fell out of his head, it was clear he'd heard her. *Mayday! Mayday! Mayday!* This was not going the direction I'd thought it would. "He's not… We're not…"

"I want to meet this boy. Put him on."

"Wait, Mom. We're not... He's not... It was..."

"Brax?" Mom called through the phone. I was back to the whole kill-me-now thing.

"Yes, ma'am?" Brax replied.

"Oh, he's polite. Hear how polite he is, Tyson. Let's switch to video call. I want to see and talk to Brax."

Brax looked a little dumbfounded, like he would bolt at any second and never be heard from again, but he cleared his throat and managed to push out another, "Yes, ma'am."

Mom somehow accidentally ended the call, and I hardly got out an, "Oh shit. I'm sorry," before the video call came in. "We can ignore."

"Fuck that. She already thinks I'm a douchebag for not going to your games. This has backfired bigtime. Answer the call."

Okay, so it was totally sweet that Brax wanted my mom to like him. I wasn't sure if he knew that was the case or not. I answered, and her face popped up on the screen. It took a moment for me to remember we were lying on Brax's bed. We looked awfully comfy, which wouldn't help convince her on the we're-not-boyfriends front.

"I don't want to see you. I want to see Brax," Mom said, and I angled the phone his way. "Hi, Brax."

"Hello, Ms. Langley."

She waved her hand at him. "You can call me Cecelia." I turned the phone to the side and squeezed my head in so we could both be in the frame. "He's very handsome," Mom told me.

"Don't say that. It'll go to his head."

"Well, it's true."

I shrugged. "Eh, he's all right."

"So, you're going into computer science like Ty?"

I shifted uncomfortably as Brax replied, "Yes, ma'am. I mean, Ms. Langley. I mean, Cecelia."

Okay, why was that so adorable? I rested my head on his shoulder. "He's good at it, Ma. Better than I ever could be. He's smart. Don't tell him I said that."

She smiled, and damn it, this was a mistake. I was getting her hopes up, making her think I was dating Braxton when we were just... I didn't know what we were. But I also wanted her to know how proud of him I was. I wanted him to know it as well.

"He looks smart," Mom replied, and damned if

Brax didn't blush. "How long have the two of you been dating?"

Guilt weighed my gut down and started to pull the truth out of me. But before I could speak, Brax said, "Um…just a couple of weeks now."

"You should come out with Ty for spring break. I'd love to meet you in person. Ty's never introduced us to a boyfriend before—or a girlfriend, for that matter. Not since high school."

I lifted my head off his shoulder, and Brax gave me a panicked look I felt down to my bones. "Let's not get ahead of ourselves," I told her.

Mom ignored me. Once she got an idea in her head, she was off to the races. Plus, I figured it felt good to focus on this, to pretend life was normal, and not to think about my dad. I was her only son, while my dad had three kids now. I couldn't imagine what she was going through.

"Do you live close to your grandma?" she asked.

"She lives in an assisted-living facility not far from here. I see her every week, though, sometimes more than once. My brother and I live here together," Brax replied.

"What do your parents do?"

Fuck. It was such an obvious question for her to

ask, but I hadn't even considered it. "Ma." I shook my head.

"No. It's fine," Brax answered. "My mom left when I was young. My dad's locked up." There was distance in his voice, in his eyes too. Brax was waiting for my mom to judge him, for her to decide she didn't like him or that he wasn't good enough for me—not that we really were boyfriends. But that wasn't her. I knew that, but he wouldn't expect it.

"I'm so sorry to hear that. I can't imagine that's been easy on you. But it sounds like you have a lovely grandma and a good head on your shoulders. Family can be tough sometimes. Tyson and I understand that." She gave him an encouraging smile, and I wasn't sure I'd ever loved her more. My mom was badass.

"I, um…thank you."

"It's important to remember that we control our own lives. No one can take that away from us. It's what I've tried to tell Ty since this whole…situation with his father came to light. People hurt us and do the wrong thing. None of us are perfect. Sometimes we forgive, others we don't, but that doesn't mean we let them take our happiness away. No one should have that much power over us." She looked at me.

"Don't let your pain or anger dictate how you live your life. You only hurt yourself that way."

I agreed, wondering how this day turned into Mom giving me and Brax advice while thinking we were boyfriends. "I hear you, Ma."

"Good."

"I should… I have to head to practice." Brax and I said our goodbyes, and when I ended the call, I told him, "I'm sorry about all that. She means well. She's just—"

"Great," Brax said. "She's great. And she loves you. That woman will one hundred percent support you changing your career goals."

He was right. There was no doubt in my mind about that. Maybe it was just me. Maybe I was scared to go for something I really wanted, in case I wasn't good enough to get it. "I know." I climbed over him. "I should get to practice. You don't really have to come to my game on Saturday. I was just giving you shit." Brax nodded but didn't reply, and I tried to hide my disappointment. "I'll see you at work tonight." I put my shoes on, pressed a quick kiss to his lips, and stood. "Boyfriend."

He threw a pillow at my head.

I was still smiling when I got into my car.

CHAPTER TWENTY-THREE

Brax

I WONDERED IF it was possible to get hives from being at a lacrosse game. It had just started, and I already felt itchy while lingering by the stands, with cheering fans all around me, worshipping the men on the field.

I was pretty sure I secretly liked one of those men. A lot.

Ty wasn't what I'd expected, and I was still trying to work out what to do about that, or how I felt about it. My brain was saying *ignore, ignore, ignore*, but Tyson Langley wasn't the type of guy to be ignored. I smiled at the thought.

I didn't know much about lacrosse, but I'd read up on it before coming. The truth was, I'd planned to make his game even before his mom had teased me about it. I was curious about Ty on the field and, shit, he deserved someone there to support him. He'd been pretty fucking supportive of me lately.

As my gaze scanned the stands, though, I realized how ridiculous that line of thinking was. He didn't need *me* there to support him. He had hundreds of people there for that, people wearing his jersey and cheering his name.

I wasn't an idiot. Logically, I'd known that would be the case, but it was a whole new experience seeing it, knowing how much he thrived on that kind of thing and how different we were.

When the crowd cheered, my stare snapped to the field. Ty had caught the ball in his scoop and was running it down the field. Their uniforms were gold and purple, and looked like basketball shorts and a jersey with short sleeves.

Ty threw the ball to Jeff Watson, then ran ahead, and Watson thrust it back toward him. Ty dodged defenders before doing some crazy-ass jump-and-throw thing where he looked like he was a fucking ninja. I swear everything happened in slow motion right up until the ball landed in the net, and then everyone erupted in applause.

Ty jumped in the air again, this time celebrating, a few of his teammates slapping him on the back. He smiled so big, it took over his whole face. And then he looked at the crowd, and…shit…*shit*. I'd been hoping I could watch without Ty realizing. When somehow he brightened even more, I knew he'd spotted me.

Ty nodded in that cocky way he did before pointing at me with his lacrosse stick, then jogging back down the field again. When I glanced around, I noticed a group of girls looking at me. A few guys too. Ty was fucking hot, and everyone knew he was bi, so there was equal opportunity to wonder what the fuck was going on with us.

And they were. Apparently, Ty must not have pointed to people from the lacrosse field often. Noted.

This whole thing didn't feel like it had when I'd watched Wayne play. Ty didn't hide the attention he gave me, didn't keep himself from looking for me, and that somehow managed to wipe out all those old memories that haunted me. Fuck Wayne.

By the second quarter, I was *in* the stands rather than lingering in the shadows like a creepy stalker.

By the third, I was cheering. Fucking Ty. What

had he done to me? There was a small possibility I liked watching lacrosse now. Actually, that was a lie. I liked watching Ty play lacrosse. Hooking up with him had somehow given me a lobotomy.

And Christ, he was good. I couldn't count the number of times he'd glanced my direction during the game, this eager look on his face like he cared what I thought, like he wanted to win more because I was there.

When I heard a loud rumble of laughter, I turned and saw Peyton Miller with a group of football guys. How had this become my life? I was at a sports game, watching the guy I was sleeping with play, while surrounded by even more jocks from other sports?

The biggest kicker was, I didn't feel the urge to rush to change it.

I stopped myself mid-leap when the Kings scored again. I wasn't going *that* far in my annoying enjoyment of Ty's game. But right at the end of the fourth, when Ty scored again, pushing the Kings to a three-point lead and cementing the win, I couldn't stop myself from shoving to my feet and clapping.

As the stands began emptying around me, my goal had been to peace the fuck outta there before Ty could get to me, but I didn't. I lingered, hands shoved into my pockets as people went onto the field to congratulate the team.

There was a big group around him because this was Ty and that was how he rolled. I didn't head over to him, just waited my turn for a chance to talk to the king of lacrosse, but somehow, he managed to move closer and closer to me.

Our eyes caught as Ty and a group of players and admirers walked by me. Our fingers brushed, and damned if the hairs on my arms didn't stand on end, if goose bumps didn't play chase across my skin, simply from the feel of his sweaty digits against mine.

"Wait for me, Sunshine," he said softly, then kept going. He tossed me a glance over his shoulder, a wink and a smile.

I told myself I wasn't going to wait, but I wasn't believing my own lies anymore when it came to Ty.

I hung around until everyone was gone and I was starting to wonder if he was playing some kind of trick on me and had left me there. I was pacing, and I'd just turned in the direction of the locker room, when I saw him. He was still wearing his lacrosse uniform. He had two of the sticks with him, which gave me a bad feeling about where this was heading.

"Remember that time you came to watch me play, boyfriend?"

He'd been calling me that all week, ever since his mom had said it, and Jesus, I still couldn't believe I'd video called with her. "Seems to me you want that to be true. You want me to be your boyfriend, Lacrosse?"

"Do you want me to want you to want to be my boyfriend?"

"Huh?" I laughed, Ty walking toward the field with me following. He set down one of the sticks and stopped.

"I have no idea if I said that right." He was sweaty and had a smudge of dirt on his face. Somehow it just made him hotter. "I won the game for you. Did you like that?"

"You won the game for you."

He crossed his legs and leaned against the stick still in his hand. "I won the game a little bit for you and a lot for me because I like attention and for people to praise me. You gonna tell me how fucking awesome I was?"

I shrugged. "You were all right."

"You're breaking my heart here," he teased, smiling at me, and I was smiling at him, and why was my heart beating so fast? Why did my stomach feel like butterflies were throwing a party in my gut? "Play with me."

Every fiber in my being told me to tell him no, to walk away. What the fuck did I want to run around playing lacrosse for? But instead, I said, "Bet I can score on you first."

"You already did." Ty winked, handed me the stick, then picked up the one on the ground.

He tossed the ball into the air, caught it, then started doing some...dribbling? I didn't even know if that's what it was called, but he threw the ball with the stick and caught it over and over. "Show-off."

"Are you surprised?"

"Fuck no. How we doing this?" Because if I was playing with him, I was doing it right.

"This is called a short stick—"

"Your position plays with the short stick? How fitting." Total lie because Ty was packing, but it earned me a swat on the ass with his short stick.

"You know that's not true." He grabbed his dick. "Back to what I was saying. Run your ass down field and try to put the ball in the net. *Try* being the keyword. I'll stop you…maybe give you one more chance, and then it'll be my turn. I'll win. You'll give me a celebratory blowjob, and that's that."

That was such a Ty thing to say.

"Catch." Ty threw the ball to himself a couple more times before flinging it my direction. It was a whole lot harder than it looked to catch a ball in a small net on a stick. I raised it in the air but missed it.

"Again." I picked it up and threw it to him. "Why is it so hard to get it in the net?"

"Scoop. Why am I not surprised you can't handle it if you're not good at something?"

"I don't know, why are you? It's not like you wouldn't be the same."

He did as I asked, and by the fourth time, I finally got the stupid thing in the scoop. Then? Then I started running.

"Cheater!" Ty called, taking off after me. The fast little fucker not only managed to catch up, but got ahead, blocking me from trying to score. I shuffled my feet, making a weak attempt to fake him out or get around him. A minute or so later I did, maybe because he let me, but I was gonna pretend I didn't know that.

I pulled the stick back, thrust my arm forward, and…the ball flew way to the right. "What the shit? How do you throw with this thing?" Ty bent over, clutching his stomach and busting up. "I'm serious. How the fuck do you do it?" Ignoring him, I jogged to the ball, put it in the scoop, and tried again. I got distance on it but had no real aim. Over and over I kept practicing, Ty laughing the whole time. When I got annoyed and attempted to throw the ball at him, the asshole lifted his stick and caught it like it was nothing. "I hate you."

"No you don't." He walked over to me. "First, you should know by now that I'm extremely good at everything I do, and it's basically impossible to be as good as me." I gave him the finger. "Second, it takes practice, Mr. Grumpy Pants. I wasn't this good when I started playing."

I pouted. "I'm not grumpy." We both knew that was a lie, but seriously, how the fuck was he so good at this game? "Show me how."

"What will you give me if I do?" Ty waggled his brows.

"What do you want?"

He pretended to think, tapping his temple, then

rubbing his chin while he looked up at the sky. "To go with you next time you visit Matilda."

Oh shit. I hadn't expected that. My mind had gone straight to the gutter, wondering about all the sexual things he could ask from me, but he wanted to visit my grandma? I waited for that to feel uncomfortable, for it to make me want to run and maybe swim out to sea and never come back, but it didn't. I shrugged. "Done."

"Also a blowjob, maybe somewhere public again. That's always hot."

"Don't go getting greedy on me."

"Getting? I always have been." He wrapped his arms around me from behind. "Here, pull your arm back like this." Ty danced his fingertips up and down my forearm. "Your grip is all wrong too. Try this." Next, he helped me position my hands, still holding me from behind, his groin against my ass.

"You're getting hard."

"Can you blame me?"

"Not really. I have a great ass."

When he laughed, his warm breath ghosted over my neck, making me tremble.

"It's a lot of hand-eye coordination. The more you

practice, the easier it will get. You'll learn how hard to swing your arm." He thrust his dick against me.

"I think I felt something, but I'm not sure."

"Oh, fuck you." Ty lowered his hands to my hips, pressing his erection tighter and rolling his hips. This wasn't like me. I flirted and talked shit to him, yeah, but real-life PDA wasn't my game. Yet when it came to him, I didn't seem to care. "Throw it."

I did...and it was a shitty one at that. Ty cracked up in my ear. "Fuck you."

He let go, and I missed the contact, which was slightly unnerving.

We spent the next little while with Ty trying to teach me how to have any kind of aim, along with distance. It was annoying, and I sucked. I couldn't imagine why anyone would want to play this game, but I did get better as we went.

The next time he gave me the ball, I said, "Game back on." Then ran for the goal.

"Fucker!" Ty called, chasing me. We were close enough to the net that he didn't have time to catch up this time.

I pulled my arm back, hoping like hell I didn't make a fool of myself. When I snapped it forward, the ball flew…and landed right in the net! "Fuck yes! I won. Looks like you have a little competition. Think they have room for me on the team?" I teased, just before Ty tackled me. He was careful with it, but we both went down, me on my back and him on top of me.

We were laughing. Our bodies shaking together like they were on the same wavelength, our vibrations just as addicted to each other as we seemed to be. I didn't know what I was doing, why nothing felt the same with him, or why it didn't matter that we were lying in the middle of the Kings' lacrosse field, Ty between my legs, his laughter slowing while he just looked at me.

"That didn't count," he said softly.

"Yes, it did. Don't be a sore loser. Though, look where it got you? I guess you didn't lose." I undulated my hips, rubbing our cocks together. How did he turn me into a totally different person? I didn't get how he could make me want him so much. How he made everything more fun, made it better.

"And you say I'm the cocky one?" Ty lowered his head and brushed his lips against mine. I opened up for him, taking his tongue into my mouth, let him taste me and explore me like it was the first time and I was uncharted territory.

He groaned into me, thrust and deepened the kiss. I spread my legs more, wrapped my arms around him, tangled my hand in his hair. "I wish I could fuck you out here, right in the middle of this field. I'd take you hard and fast and make you come all over the grass."

"Fuck," Ty gritted out before kissing me again.

There was a good chance we could both come right then and there, but then we heard, "Um…what the fuck?"

We both stopped moving at the sound of the new voice. Ty looked up just as one of his friends added, "Him? Asshole Bartender is who you've been obsessed with and spending nearly every day with lately?"

"Fuck off, Collins. He's not an asshole," Ty defended, but we both knew I kind of was. "Well, not all the time."

I should maybe be offended, but I wasn't.

"Dude…is he your boyfriend?" Watty asked.

Before Ty could answer, I said, "Jealous?" and cocked a brow.

"Fuck no. He's my friend, and I'm straight."

"Eh, your loss," I replied.

"Be nice," Ty warned.

"You don't like it when I'm nice."

"My mind is blown here," the big one said. "I feel like we're interrupting something."

"You think?" I asked.

"Shut up," Ty told me. Then to them, "I'd get up, but I have a boner right now. I'll talk to you guys later."

I had to admit, I liked that they didn't give a shit that Ty swung both ways.

"What are you doing tonight?" Collins asked.

"We work," Ty replied.

"And after?"

"I don't know. I'll hit you guys back."

"Dude, we never hang out anymore," Watty said.

Was this normal friends stuff? Manny and I were never like this with each other.

"We'll chill. I promise," Ty answered.

"Bro, we better. Friends before dick," the largest one said.

"Aren't you supposed to try and rhyme those?" I asked.

"Huh?"

"Never mind."

They literally fist-bumped Ty while he was between my legs. They said their goodbyes, his friends bailed, and Ty rolled off me. Both our cocks were pointing up. We looked down and laughed until my stomach hurt. It wasn't something I'd ever done before him. I'd never enjoyed myself so much. I didn't know if that was a good or a bad thing.

CHAPTER TWENTY-FOUR

Ty

"SERIOUSLY, MAN? ASSHOLE Bartender? He's who you've been dicking down for weeks and stopped spending time with us for?" Collins asked the next morning.

Brax and I had hung out at the field for a little while longer before going our separate ways. When I'd gotten back to Adler House, my friends hadn't been there. I ended up taking a nap before getting showered and dressed to go to work. I'd expected them to show up at the bar, but they hadn't. Maybe it made me a dickhead, but I'd been glad because I knew this was exactly how they would respond. Any time one of us hung out with a person they were boning too much, it became a reason to talk shit—this was college, we were supposed to be having fun, not tying ourselves down, and so on. Not that I was tied to Brax, and none of us had dated anyone seriously, but I guessed it went back to my wanting to protect this thing Brax and I had. I liked it too much to give it up, and I worried that the more people got involved, the sooner that would happen.

But I also missed chillin' with my boys, and a part of me wanted Brax to get to know them so he wouldn't think they were bigger douchebags than they actually were; and also, so they wouldn't think he was a bigger asshole than he actually was either.

How in the hell had I ended up in this situation?

"Clearly," I replied, "considering you stopped us from going at it on the lacrosse field. Thanks for that, by the way. I'm too pretty to go to prison for public fucking."

"I'm pretty sure it would just be jail," Watty said.

"I'm too pretty for that too," I teased. They'd all ended up in my room somehow, watching as I tossed clothes into a duffel.

Ford said, "Seriously, though. I'm not surprised the two of you fucked because there was some major sexual tension between you, but you're with him a lot, and you sleep over there. That's some boyfriend shit."

Ford scratched his head as if confused.

I couldn't blame him because it was definitely *boyfriend shit*, and I didn't think I would be opposed to that. "You know how that sounds, right? When you say *boyfriend shit*?"

They ignored me, Collins asking, "Are you serious about him?"

Unfortunately, I didn't know how to answer that.

"What do you guys even have in common other than both of you liking dick?" Watty asked.

"You know there's more to being queer than liking a certain body part, right? Plus, not all dudes have a dick. You're coming off as a bit of an asshole."

"You know that's not what I meant. My sister is a polyamorous lesbian."

"This girl I used to bone got off on MMF porn, and I'd watch it with her," Watty added.

"Wow, way to take one for the team." My friends were idiots.

Ford sighed. "Dude…all we're trying to say is, if he's your boy, we're cool with it. If you wanna lock yourself down to one person, we might think you're crazy, but we'll have your back. Even if it is Asshole Bartender. You can bring him around. You don't have to ditch us."

Ugh. My friends were idiots with big hearts. I appreciated what they were doing. "Thanks. I'll be better about hanging out, and I'll see if I can drag Brax over."

I sat on the bed, and Collins joined me. "You guys really are different."

We were. There was no doubt about that, but we also weren't. Somehow, Brax got me. And he was easy to talk to. I couldn't imagine sharing the shit about my dad with anyone but him. "He's cool. You know me, I wouldn't be spending so much time with him if he wasn't."

"Oh shit. Langley's in love." All three of them started singing *Ty loves Brax*. I shook my head but couldn't help smiling.

"Thanks, guys. I appreciate the support. I gotta go, though. We're going to see his grandma."

"Wow. You really are on lockdown. Family visits?" Watty asked.

"She's badass." She was.

I finished packing my bag. I was staying at Brax's tonight. The test we'd been studying for all week was tomorrow, and I knew how important it was for him to do well on it—and not only because he had to keep his grades up for his scholarships so he could afford school.

When I arrived at his place, Brax was already waiting outside for me. "Sorry. The guys bombarded me before I left."

"It's all good. You know you don't have to come…or stay at my place tonight. I'm not that guy who's going to keep you from your friends."

"But then you'll miss me while I'm gone," I teased, and he surprised me by pressing a quick kiss to my lips.

"Grandma will want to see you, I guess."

"Of course. And you too, admit it. You like having me around." He answered by putting the helmet on my head and strapping it. "Also, you like to spoil people."

He didn't even try to deny it.

Brax drove us to his grandma's. Her eyes lit up when he walked in, and then she smiled when she saw me. "You're back."

"I am. I taught Brax to play lacrosse so he would bring me. He's terrible."

"Braxton Alexander Walker, you be nice to him.

Ty can come and see me anytime he wants." She playfully swatted him.

"Okay, but don't you see why I didn't want to get the two of you together again? It becomes the gang-up-on-Braxton hour."

"Be nice, and we won't have to," I replied. Matilda gave me a high five.

"Let's go outside. I want to show off my boys. Plus, it's a beautiful day."

Brax went to her closet and pulled out a sweater. "It's a little windy, so let's get this on you first."

I watched as he helped her in it, my heart doing this foreign *thud-thud* that sounded suspiciously like *Brax-ton*. When he went for her wheelchair next, I took Matilda's arm and guided her to it.

"I can do it myself, but I'll never turn down a handsome man's help," she playfully flirted.

"And I'll never deny a hand to a beautiful lady." I gave her my best smile.

"Flirt," Brax teased.

We headed for the hallway. The first person we saw was a tall Black man in scrubs, and Matilda said, "Hello, Jamal. You've met my grandson Braxton. This is his boyfriend, Ty."

I stiffened, my gaze darting to Brax, who seemed about three seconds away from throwing up. It was one thing for my mom who lived across the country to think we were boyfriends, but something entirely different for his grandma to believe it. I tried to tell him with my gaze that it was okay, and then shook Jamal's hand. Brax recovered quickly and offered a hello of his own.

Every person we met, Matilda introduced me as Brax's boyfriend, and every time we went along with it. The three of us settled under a tree outside, and she told me more stories about Brax growing up. When it started to cool off more, we made our way back inside. I ended up organizing a game of Pictionary with the residents, then judged an impromptu dance competition, and damn, did some of them have moves. When one of the women scratched herself, I helped her clean and bandage it before saying, "All better." I was pretty sure she blushed.

We played board games and cards, and before I knew it, evening arrived and we'd spent damn near the whole day there.

"We should head out," Brax finally said. "We have a test tomorrow to study for."

"Do we have to?" I asked in unison with Matilda's, "Do you have to?" and we both dissolved in a fit of laughter.

"What am I gonna do with the two of you?" Brax asked.

"I'm sure you'll figure it out."

Like the last time we were there, Brax didn't say much as we drove back to his place. When we arrived got my bag out of my car, and we went inside. "You like pizza? I can order us a pizza. Shit, I didn't ask if you wanted to go out and grab something." He appeared uncharacteristically shy, which was cute as fuck.

"I don't wanna go out. Do you have the stuff for spaghetti? Matilda said it's your specialty."

"Probably not. If we did, I'm sure Asher and his friends would have eaten it by now. Plus, it has to cook all day."

"Oh."

"I'll make it for you another day. It's fucking awesome. And no, you don't get my secret recipe."

"You suck."

"Quite well."

"I can't argue with you there."

I watched as Brax came closer, placed his hands on my waist, and pulled me against him. "Thank you. I know I said that last time too, but she enjoys your company, and she hasn't had enough people who care about her in her life. My grandpa and me. My dad, Asher, my mom when she was around, but they've never appreciated her. You do, and that means a lot to me."

Jesus, he was sweet. There wasn't a part of me that thought he knew it, though. "You don't have to thank me for that. I like being around her, and I kinda like being around you too. Wanna know a secret?"

He nodded, still holding me. His fingers slipped under my shirt, brushing against my skin. "Being with Matilda reminds me of spending time with my own grandparents when I was young. They've both passed away, but I used to entertain them, play games with them… It's not like I think that's all there is to being a geriatric nurse. That's probably the smallest part of it, but I think that's what I want to do—be a nurse for the elderly. I don't think enough people go into that, and it's important work."

"I like that. I think you might be the best one I've ever met." He didn't let me respond before he kissed me, making my toes curl.

We ordered pizza, then shotgunned another bowl while we waited for it to arrive. I straddled Brax's lap on his bed. He inhaled the smoke into his lungs, then leaned close to me, exhaling while I breathed it in. Fuck, there was something so hot about that. There was something hot about everything we did, but smoking this way was the most delicious kind of foreplay.

Just before the bowl was dusted, I let my lips ghost over his, brushing in the gentlest of touches, while pulling his air into my lungs. As soon as I exhaled, I pressed my mouth to his, sweeping my tongue inside. My chest was full, so full I thought the seams might rip open, my heart tumbling right out into his lap.

"What are you doing to me?" Brax asked, lowering himself to his back and taking me with him. His hands went to my ass, our tongues taking turns dipping into each other's mouths. My cock swelled, fucking ached; it was so hard. I rutted against him, kissing a trail down his throat.

"Whatever it is, you're doing it to me too." I shoved my hand down his pants, wrapped it around his thick cock, and—*Ding-dong!*

"Fuuuuuuck," Brax gritted out.

"I hate pizza."

Brax laughed, then dumped me on the bed and stood. His hand did as mine had just done, lowering into his pants, but he was just adjusting his erection, trying to make it less obvious before going to the door. He came back a few minutes later with our food, set it on his desk, then plucked paper plates off his mini-fridge. It was shitty that he had to keep things like that locked in his bedroom so his older brother and his friends didn't take them.

He sweetly made me a plate first and handed it over. I took it, heat flooding my chest.

"What?" Brax asked.

"Nothing."

He grabbed a couple of slices for himself. "That look wasn't nothing."

"You're all heart."

"Fuck you."

"Okay, maybe not *all* heart. You might be the only person in the world who would curse someone for a compliment like that."

"I have a rep to keep."

We ate and chatted, Brax talking to me more about nursing and about his grandma. We spent the next couple of hours studying, then watched a movie before he said, "I need to go to bed. If you think I'm a dick normally, you should see me when I haven't gotten enough sleep. I don't want to fuck up my test in the morning."

He took school more seriously than anyone I knew. It made me feel like a bit of an asshole sometimes because I didn't think my friends or I appreciated it the way Brax did.

We stripped down to our underwear, brushed our teeth, and got back into bed. It didn't escape my attention how domestic this was. How Brax and I had slipped into a routine together that was pretty boyfriend-y. But despite neither of us correcting Matilda or Mom, we'd never used the word ourselves yet.

Brax passed right the fuck out, but for whatever reason, I couldn't sleep. I started thinking about my mom, and the siblings I didn't know, and my dad, whom I hated but kind of missed too.

What would he think when he found out I wanted to change my major? *He won't ever know if you don't get the balls to actually do it.* So far I was all talk, and I fucking hated that about myself. I didn't understand it, why it was so hard for me to stand up to him. Why the thought of disappointing him still made nausea boil in my gut and my heart thud against my chest.

Brax turned toward me, wrapped an arm around my waist and buried his face in my neck. I was falling for him. Hell, there was a good chance I'd already fallen. I'd liked hearing Matilda call us boyfriends. I wanted to be with him for real, to take some of the pressure off him because Brax felt like he had to take care of everyone. He did it with his grandma and even with Asher. He let his brother get away with anything and covered for him with Matilda. Even today, he'd made some bullshit excuse for why Asher still hadn't been by.

I heard something hit the wall in the living room, then the *clomp-clomp* of numerous sets of feet, followed by loud voices, laughter, and music. Asher partied a lot. He never gave a shit if Brax was sleeping or studying or anything else.

The noise didn't quiet over the next few minutes. If anything, it got louder. Brax groaned in his sleep and rolled away from me. I was familiar enough with his sleeping patterns that I knew he'd wake up soon.

As gently as I could, I climbed out of bed, tugged on my pants, and slipped out the door. There were at least ten people in the living room, two women dancing with each other while Asher and another guy sat at the table with a bottle of whiskey between them.

Maybe this was stupid because I didn't know how much of a prick Asher was or wasn't, and I was clearly outnumbered, but I walked over to him. "Dude…do you think you guys can keep it down? Brax is sleeping, and he has a test tomorrow."

Asher glanced up at me. "No." The guy with him cackled.

It was official—I really hated his brother. "Why are you such a dick? Brax and your grandma carry all the bills on this place. Brax has to keep food in his room, or he'll buy something only to have it eaten before he gets the chance. You don't go and see Matilda or realize how hard your brother works between school and his job. He's actually trying to make something of his life. Is it too much to ask to let him have a good night's sleep?"

"Who the fuck is this clown?" his buddy asked.

"Brax's girlfriend," Asher replied, and they guffawed obnoxiously, before his gaze zeroed in on me. "Me and my brother don't have shit to do with you. Mind your business. Next time, I won't be so nice about it." There was a hard edge to his gaze.

This was a totally different Asher than the dopey, playful one I'd met before. Still, I wasn't afraid of him. "Fuck you. Brax *is* my business."

When his buddy chuckled, something even darker passed through Asher's eyes. It was clear he didn't appreciate feeling like he was being laughed at. He shoved to his feet. Before he could do or say anything else, Brax was there, pushing between us, going head-to-head with Asher.

"Bro, control your boy. He's out here bitching about shit that has nothing to do with him." Asher snickered like none of this was a big deal.

Well, at least he called me Brax's boyfriend this time.

"Don't fucking talk to him the way you were, and don't threaten him. Ever. You won't like how I respond if you do."

At that, Asher seemed to hesitate. Apparently, he didn't want to mess with Brax, which surprised me.

"He's the one coming out here and talking shit to me in my own house. All we're trying to do is have a good time."

Brax shook his head and moved beside me. "You're so fucking clueless."

"You're such a poser, playing house with your rich boyfriend, pretending you're better than us, that you'll ever be anything more than you are. You know he doesn't really give a shit about you, right? You're a phase for him, and once he's done with you, you'll be stuck here, not doing shit with your life, and he'll move on to someone Mommy and Daddy approve of."

My heart clenched. I hoped Brax didn't believe that. "You don't know shit about us," I said.

Brax shoved his brother. "Fuck. You." Then he grabbed my hand and pulled me with him back to his room. "Jesus… I *hate* him. He reminds me of my dad so fucking much sometimes." He paced the room, hands opening and closing into fists.

"Hey, you know that's not true, don't you? None of what he said. Not the shit about us or the things about you and your future either." When Brax didn't respond, I added, "I'm sorry. I shouldn't have gone out there. I just… You take care of other people so often. I wanted to take care of you too."

Brax froze, gaze snapping to mine, sparks igniting off it and landing in my chest. I could see it in his eyes, how much those words meant to him, how much he'd needed to hear them, no matter how simple they were.

The music raged on in the other room. If anything, it was even louder.

"Let's go stay at my place."

I expected him to say no, but he didn't, nodding instead. We finished getting dressed, got clothes and our school stuff together, and then he surprised me by going to my car with me and getting in.

Watty, Ford, and Collins were awake when we got there. Playing video games half the night wasn't anything unique for them.

"What's up?" Ford asked, all their gazes on Brax.

"Nothing. We're staying here tonight. Make sure you guys keep it down. We have a test in the morning."

"Bet," Collins replied, and Watty turned the television down.

I took Brax's hand and led him to my room, where we stripped, got into bed together, and went to sleep.

CHAPTER TWENTY-FIVE

Brax

"I KILLED IT on that test," I told Ty after class, and he groaned. "You don't think you did well?"

He shrugged. "Whatever. I don't know. Probably not. I mean, I didn't fail it, I don't think, but for once, I'm not nearly as confident as you."

It was shitty that he was doing something he hated so much. I wanted more for him, wanted him to follow his dreams. I wished I could call his dad myself and tell him to fuck off and let Ty do what he wanted to do, kinda the way he'd stuck up for me with my brother.

While it had only been a day, I was still obsessing over what had gone down between Ty and Asher. I'd been pissed at Asher too many times to count, but I'd never wanted to slam my fist into his face as much as I had last night. I was used to his shit. I could deal with it, but Ty hadn't deserved that.

Ty, who'd gone out there for me.

Ty, who'd thought about me, cared, and had my back.

I wasn't used to that from anyone besides Grandma. I'd always been the odd one out with my brother and my dad. I didn't let myself get close enough to guys or friends, except for Manny, and as much as I loved him, he was the kind of person who felt like he just needed to mind his own business. He hadn't ever gotten involved in our family shit, but Ty had, and fuck, there were no words for how much I appreciated that.

The little bastard had been taking up way too much space in my mind lately. Between what went down with Asher, and Ty spending time with Grandma, he had me feeling some kind of something that I should want to evict from my chest but didn't. I really fucking didn't.

"Come on." I took his hand, and he let me. We went back into the building, then up the same stairs we'd used the first time we'd hooked up. I picked the lock on the empty classroom.

"You gonna get on your knees for me?" Ty asked.

"Yep," I replied simply, and I did just that, showing him with my mouth how much I wanted him, how much I appreciated him, until he spilled his load down my throat. I swallowed it down, sucked him for a minute afterward, just liking the feel of his softening cock on my tongue. "I was hungry."

I winked, tucked him away, pulled his pants up, and stood. Ty's mouth came down hard on mine. He opened my jeans and took my dick in hand, stroking me until I was right on the edge before kneeling and taking me into his mouth so my cum spurted down his throat.

We kissed lazily for a few minutes, arms wrapped around each other, tasting ourselves as our tongues tangled together.

We didn't talk about what was going on between us, about the change that crept up on me like the sun slowly peeking over the horizon until it was high and bright, undeniable.

If we didn't talk about it, we could pretend it wasn't happening…because a part of me knew Asher had been right. Even if I wanted us to, Ty and I wouldn't last. We didn't fit, and there was no changing that.

So I slid my sunglasses on and tried to deny the sun had risen.

We walked to Adler House. I sat on his bed, my back against the wall. Ty lay down and put his head in my lap. "Pet me. I want attention."

I rolled my eyes but did as he asked. "You always want attention."

"Are you pissed at me? For last night?"

I frowned, shook my head, wasn't sure I trusted myself enough to speak.

"I know it's not my business, but…"

"I appreciated it. People don't do that—have my back that way. Don't apologize for it."

He looked up at me, my fingers carding through his hair. "Okay."

"I can take care of myself. I'm used to it. My dad and Asher would always gang up on me. I'd tell Grandma not to get involved, but she did. I can handle it. I'm used to handling it, but…" Fuck, I didn't know what to say.

Ty smiled at me, upside down because of how he lay. "But it was nice to have your super-sexy, amazing-in-the-sack boyfriend be there for you?"

I cocked a brow, and his pupils blew wide as if he'd just caught on to what he'd called himself. This wasn't the same as going along with it when Grandma or his mom said it.

"You tryin' to ask me something, Lacrosse?" I'd never had a boyfriend in my life, and I couldn't figure out why I wasn't just telling him to fuck off with that label.

"Do I really have to ask when it's clearly already true?"

"You wish."

"Maybe I do."

"Aww, you're going sappy on me."

"Dude, you should see the way you look at me now. You've been sappy for a while."

"Please, I think you're mistaking me with you. *Pet me, love me, you're the best thing that ever happened to me.*" We laughed together, and then I bent over and kissed him. "Get your ass ready for practice."

Ty sighed, sat up, and with his back to me said, "You know we basically are, though, right?"

I knew he meant together. Ty didn't elaborate, and I didn't either. He grumbled, and I watched as he dressed for practice and complained we couldn't stay in bed all day.

After we said our goodbyes, I realized I didn't want to go home. Fuck Asher for making me not want to be in my own house.

So I went to chill with Manny before work.

"Hey, bro." We bumped fists, and Manny pulled me into a half-hug. "What's up with you? You've been more absent than usual."

I followed him inside. It didn't seem like anyone else was there. He led me straight into the kitchen because he knew how much I loved his mom's food. I started loading a plate with green-chili enchiladas. "Been busy."

"What's that? You smiled when you said it."

Fuuuuck. Goddamned Ty, turning me inside out. For a moment, I thought about denying it, but Christ, I didn't think I wanted to. He had me so messed up, I was stuck between sorta feeling like I wanted to throw up all the time and telling him that yes, I wanted him to be my boyfriend; and then making the announcement to everyone else I knew too. In a way, we'd basically said it earlier. He had, at least, and I didn't tell him he was wrong.

"Just been with this guy a lot lately, is all."

Manny crossed his arms, one brow arching. "No shit?"

"No shit."

"He your boy?"

I shrugged. "I guess so."

"Then I guess I better meet him."

I nodded, waiting for the world to implode or the sun to fall out of the sky or some shit like that. I'd admitted to someone that I was with Ty, and nothing bad happened. It maybe even felt a little good.

What in the hell had he done to me?

I hung out with Manny until it was time to head to work.

I WAS ALREADY on the clock when Ty rushed in, five minutes late. "Shit. Sorry. Coach kept us late."

"It's okay," Gwen told him. "We're not busy yet."

He clocked in, then came to stand beside me where I leaned against the bar.

"Our dish bitch is here," I teased, then pressed a

kiss to his lips. My whole body tensed because I hadn't planned on doing that. At all. It had just come naturally.

"Oh shit," Marshall said, walking in just as we pulled apart.

"About time," Gwen added.

"You guys know we've all been aware you're fucking for a long time now, right?" Casey chimed in.

"Yeah, but we're boyfriends now," Ty replied.

"Gross." I mean, I had to say it, even though everyone there knew it was a lie.

CHAPTER TWENTY-SIX

Ty

"DUDE, DID YOUR boyfriend move in?" Collins asked early on Saturday morning when we were getting ready to head out for our game.

"Shh." My gaze darted down the hallway. I wanted to make sure Brax wasn't coming out and heard him. He hadn't spent one night at his house all week, and when he did go home to get stuff, he said he and Asher just pretended nothing happened. Apparently, they did that often. I mean, I got it. I wasn't one to want to talk about how I felt either. Emotions were often pretty fucking annoying. But it pissed me off because Asher took advantage of Brax. He had no respect for him. Brax deserved better, and I wanted him to tell his asshole brother that. Again. "Does it matter if he stays over?"

"No, I was just curious. You've never been one to get serious enough to have someone in your bed every night."

Brax wasn't like anyone else, but I didn't want to sit around and explain that to Collins. They'd told me more than once that they didn't think Brax and I made sense. And Brax was kind of a dick to them sometimes, but that was just him. I loved it when he was an asshole. It got me hard. What could I say? So I just shrugged. "Well, I do with him." Which I guessed was basically the same as saying he was special.

"Damn, you're really feelin' this guy, huh?"

"Yep." I tossed my lacrosse shoes in my bag. Brax was... I didn't even know how to explain it. He made everything feel different. He made *me* feel different. He made me better.

"Well, I'm happy for you, bro. Your dad's gonna shit a brick, though. You know that, right?"

I groaned because I did. He would hate everything about Brax. "I don't give a shit what he says."

Collins frowned, but it wasn't him who spoke. Ford walked into the room and said, "That from the guy who spent the past three years—and probably his whole life—doing everything to make his father happy."

I…wasn't sure what to say to that. My pulse thudded against my skin, my stomach feeling a little wobbly. How the hell did Ford know? Was it obvious to everyone? "What do you mean?"

"I don't know. You've just always been up his ass. You're not the same Ty when your dad comes out to visit. You don't act like Ty. You act like a mini him." Ford grabbed a doughnut from the box on the counter and shoved half of it into his mouth. "One of the reasons we were shocked you took the job at the bar. Pretty sure he would think that's beneath you," he said around chewed-up food, which was gross as shit, but I didn't call him on it.

I hated that they'd seen this in me and that no one had said anything. I hated that I let myself become exactly who my dad molded me into. *Then why aren't you doing anything to change it?*

My bedroom door opened, and Brax came out. He rubbed a hand over his face as he walked toward me. "You should have woken me up."

"You can stay while we're gone."

He frowned, looked from me, to Collins, to Ford,

who went back to shoving the rest of the doughnut into his mouth. "Whass up, rude?" his question came out instead of *What's up, dude.*

Brax shook his head and mumbled, "Fucking jocks."

"Yes, you're fucking a jock," I replied, trying to joke so my friends didn't make a comment about what he said.

"Yep," Watty said as he joined us. "My room is near yours, so I can vouch for that fact. *Fuck me, Sunshine. Oh yeah, right there. You gonna give me your load?*"

My face got hot at Watty's talking shit. Yeah, I'd gotten into the habit of pretending we went at it raw because it was hot.

"What the—did he say that?" Collins asked.

"More than once. Apparently, Brax dicks him down good. I need to invest in earplugs."

"You're just jealous." I tugged Brax to me, but really, I *was* a little embarrassed. I wrapped my arms around his waist. "Wanna make out before I go?"

"So your friends will get even more jealous that we're having better sex than them?"

"Hey, I get mine," Collins huffed.

Brax grinned. "Go win your stupid game. I'm outta here." I wasn't surprised he wouldn't stay without me there. That wasn't really Brax's style. Hell, I was still surprised he slept over at all.

"Um…did he just call lacrosse stupid?" Ford asked.

"Dude, I think your boyfriend's broken," Watty added.

"Catch you jockholes later." Brax kissed me, then headed for the door.

"You coming to the party tonight? It's kinda fun to see Ty in *L-O-V-E*," Collins sang.

"You can spell?" Brax teased, my friends laughing, which made me a little mushy inside. I liked to see him joke around with my boys. "Unlike you guys, I have to work to pay my bills."

Brax's gaze caught mine, and I answered, "He'll be here afterward, though." For once in his life, he didn't argue with me.

THE BEER WAS flowing freely. Music pumped through the speakers, and the living room and kitchen were packed with people. I had an empty red Solo cup in one hand and my phone in the other, waiting for Brax to get off at Shenanigans so he could come here and hang out with us.

I went to the kitchen for a refill, hoping time would speed up. Why weren't parties fun without Brax anymore?

When I heard a familiar laugh, I glanced over to see some guy trying to talk to Marshall. He got to be off tonight. Why couldn't Brax? Whoever the guy with him was, he was definitely interested, but it didn't look like Marshall realized that.

Just as I was about to turn away, I saw Felix walk over, head high and definitely a man on a mission. He said something to flirty dude, then literally waved his hand like he was dismissing him. Well…wasn't this interesting? Where the hell had I been? Last I'd seen, Felix had been trying to hit on Brax and now he'd just chased some guy away from Marshall?

It looked like hearts flew out of Marshall's eyes, mixed with a little mischief. I chuckled, filled up and made my way over to the couch so I could continue to pout until Brax arrived.

"'Sup?" Todd, this guy I'd hooked up with a couple of times, sat beside me. His dad and mine knew each other. They'd both gone to FU and did business together from time to time.

"What's up?" I swallowed some of the beer in my cup.

"You guys won today?"

"Yep."

"You haven't been around much lately."

I shrugged. "I've been busy with school and lacrosse, and I got a job. I'm working at Shenanigans."

"No shit?"

"Yep." Todd and I weren't close, but he'd been a good lay. It'd been easy with us when we'd decided we wanted to have sex, and the way his gaze worked its way up and down my body told me that was exactly his hope for the night. But as good as he was in the sack, there wasn't even a small part of me that wanted him, so I found the easiest way to clue him in. "My boyfriend works there, and he's really fucking hot, so any extra time I get to spend with him is a win in my book."

I glanced up just in time to see Brax come inside. I

couldn't stop the grin from spreading across my face.

He looked at me, then Todd, cocking a brow my way. I shook my head. I knew Brax's expressions enough to know he didn't like Todd but that he also found it amusing and trusted me enough to know nothing was up.

"Who?" Todd asked just as Brax reached us and sat down, squeezing himself between us. "Dude, a little space?"

"Who the fuck are you?" Brax asked him. Was it bad that my dick twitched a little? Asshole Brax would always be hot as long as I was the one calling him an asshole.

"Todd. I'm friends with Ty. Our dads are close too."

"Oh, what's up, man? I'm Braxton. Ty's boyfriend. My dad is in prison."

Todd looked between the two of us, his shock clear on his face. "Him?"

"Hot, right?" I replied.

"I mean, yeah. I'm shocked, but he's hot. You guys play with others?"

"No," Brax and I answered in unison. Aww, we were so cute.

"Worth a try. I'm off to find someone who's available." Todd bailed.

I nuzzled closer to Brax, tucked my face right into his neck. "Admit it… You were a little jealous."

"I'll admit no such thing."

"But you called me your boyfriend. Like…you said the actual word. It was basically like pissing on my leg to mark your territory."

"You into that? It can totally be arranged," he teased, making me laugh. I was into him. So fucking much.

Beer sloshed into our laps as Ford stumbled. "Shit. Sorry, bro. Beer pong. You're on my team." He grabbed Brax's wrist and tugged him to his feet.

"What the fuck? No," Brax protested.

"Yes. You're Ty's man. That means we have to bond."

"No, it really doesn't." Brax hardly got the words out before Ford dragged him away. He looked at me like, *Help me, please*, but didn't fight it as Ford continued to tug him away. I watched Watty slap him on the back and Collins say something to him. My friends were fucking idiots, but they were also great.

"I knew you guys were fucking." Felix took Brax's

spot beside me. Marshall was gone when I looked over. Bathroom, maybe?

"Yep." I took a sip. "I saw you with Marshall a little bit ago. You trying to make him your hookup for the night?"

"Not for the night...I'm making Marshmallow my teddy bear for good."

"Marshmallow? Teddy bear?" My gut hurt from all the laughter. "That shit's great. I'm totally calling him Marshmallow from now on."

"Fuck no. That's my name for him." His words caught up with me. Holy shit? I'd for sure missed a lot. He wanted Marshall to be his for good? "Speaking of...excuse me while I go get my man."

I swear the crowd basically parted for him when Felix walked over and jumped into Marshall's arms. I hadn't even thought he was paying attention at first, but Marshall caught him and then carried him toward the door.

Awww. How cute. I totally needed to make Brax carry me. And I was already bored without him. This guy had totally screwed with me.

"Boo," I whispered in his ear when I approached. "You should carry me."

"Huh?"

"You're up!" Ford yelled at him.

"Nothing. Go have fun with my friends."

"I hate you."

He totally didn't.

Brax played with the guys for at least an hour. He liked to pretend he wasn't enjoying it, but he was. We drank and hung out, his arm often around me or touching me in different ways. He didn't hide, and that was one of my favorite things about him. Brax might hold himself back and brood sometimes, but when he was in, he was in.

We collapsed in my bed together after three in the morning, and I realized how I'd always considered myself happy before him, but it had nothing on how I felt with Brax in my life.

CHAPTER TWENTY-SEVEN

Brax

HAVING A BOYFRIEND was kinda awesome—at least when it was Ty. All the things that annoyed me about him still did, but they were also cute. When it came to others? It was still frustrating as shit, but when Ty did it, I turned into a goddamned marshmallow. Liking someone was weird and confusing, but I didn't want to stop.

In the back of my head, I reminded myself it was temporary. Hell, most relationships were. How often did people really stick together? Especially people who were as different as me and Ty. But right along with that piece of knowledge was a truth bomb I was still coming to terms with.

I *wanted* it to last.

I wanted Ty in every way I could have him.

I'd turned into a romantic because I wanted to *keep* Ty. I wanted him to keep me even more.

I rolled over and kissed his throat. Friday mornings were my favorite because the house was empty. Ty and I didn't have class, but the rest of his jockholes did. I knew that because I was still staying at Adler every night. I was worried about going home, not only to see what Asher might have done to the place, but because I didn't want him around Ty. What if something went down? What if Asher did something stupid because he was pissed Ty talked shit to him? My brother wasn't violent, not really, but he didn't like to be embarrassed, and he wouldn't be chill with Ty after that last day at the house.

"Sleepy," Ty mumbled in a cute-as-fuck, mumbly voice.

"Really? Because I'm feeling a little bottomy…" There was no doubt in my mind that would wake him up, and I was right. His eyes popped open, his face taken over with his smile.

"I'm awake now. One vers-top reporting for duty."

Laughter tumbled out of my mouth uncontrollably. God, I loved hi—*whoa*. What the fuck? Did I just almost think the *L* word?

"What's wrong? You look like you sucked on something sour."

"Nothing. Just crazy talk."

"But you didn't talk."

"Crazy thought."

"Thought about what?"

"Are you going to fuck me or not, Mr. Vers-Top? I thought you were reporting for duty."

"Yes, you're right. I am. I'll also pretend I don't realize you just changed the subject because you don't want me to know how much you like me." My shock must have shown on my face because he smiled and rolled on top of me. "I know you, Braxton Walker. You can't hide from me. Don't try."

Before I could come up with a response, he lowered his mouth to mine. The kiss started out slow, not urgent but hungry and needy. His tongue slipped into my mouth as I spread my legs for him, my hands landing on his bare ass.

I squeezed him, teased his crease with my finger while Ty basically owned my mouth. We rutted together, dragging our cocks against each other. I had no doubt I could come this way, just by frotting with him, while our mouths moved together.

"You make me crazy, Brax." His lips trailed down my throat. "Why is everything so different with you? Why is it so much better?"

"I don't know, but it is for me too," I admitted.

He gasped like he hadn't expected me to say it, then basically attacked my mouth again like he would die without it.

We grunted and groaned together. I traced his hole, even though he would be taking me instead of the other way around. Ty whimpered, rubbed his cheek against mine before swiping at my earlobe with his tongue.

"That day in Shenanigans, when you did that to me? I think I knew I was a fucking goner right then and there. I've never wanted anyone the way I want you."

"Fuck…you too. Jesus, I can't believe the things you can get me to say. The things you get me to feel."

His kisses moved to my throat, my chest, down my sternum. I reached into the nightstand and grabbed a condom and lube just as he took my achingly hard dick to the back of his throat.

Ty pushed his hand toward me. I pumped lube

into it, spread myself more open for him so he could push a finger inside, while I thrust down his throat. He gagged for me. "My favorite way to shut you up," I teased, but then he added a second finger in my hole, and damned if I didn't let out a deep moan. "Fuck yes. Give me your fingers before I take your cock."

He shuddered, and I knew it was because he was so turned on. I threaded my fingers through his hair, guided him even though he didn't need it, while he sucked me and worked me open. My heels dug into the mattress, which was way more comfortable than mine. I liked being in Ty's bed too much.

I didn't need a third finger, but he gave it to me anyway, and I took it, pumping my hips and fucking his face, my gaze firmly on his the whole time. He was beautiful—beautiful and annoying as shit, but still.

"Come on, Lacrosse, fuck me. Give me your cock before I change my mind and take your ass instead."

"Yes, sir." He pushed up onto his knees.

My dick twitched, a little angry at me. "My cock is missing your mouth."

"It is a great mouth, but Christ, are you ever satisfied? *Fuck me, Ty. Wait, suck my dick, Ty.* I can't do everything at once."

I hoped that for however long we lasted, things never changed between us. That everything would always be this much fun.

He suited up, rolling the condom down his erection. "I can't wait until we can go without these, when I can watch my cum leak out of your hole instead of just pretending."

I'd never gone raw with someone before, but I wanted it with Ty. "I'm negative, but we can still get tested to make sure, and then…"

His eyes lit up. "Yeah?"

"Yeah."

"I've never fucked without a rubber. Never needed that until you."

"You say the sweetest things." It came out playfully, but I meant the words.

I slicked up my hand, jerking myself slowly while Ty slicked up his cock too. He stood, then tugged me to the edge of the bed. "Hands and knees."

"You forgot the magic words."

"Hands and knees so I can dick you down and make you come?"

I smiled. "Exactly."

I did as he said and immediately felt the head of his cock pushing at my rim. Ty was impatient for sex, for me. There was the initial pressure I was familiar with, the initial stretch as he worked his way into my body in the most delicious way.

"Yes, fuck yes. Gimme your cock." I pressed back, and Ty snapped his hips forward, filling me the way I craved, my feelings for him circling my brain and begging to fall from my lips. I had to squeeze my mouth closed not to say them.

His hands held my hips tightly, his blunt nails digging into the skin, and we moved together, each of us meeting the other in the middle as he gave me some really fucking good dick.

"Jack yourself off. I want you to come all over the bed before I fill your ass with my load."

My dick twitched. He was right. That was really fucking hot. My hand tightened around my erection, making the pleasure inside me ratchet up even more. I was sensitive, my satisfaction growing by the second, my cock loving the feel of my hand, and my ass head over fucking heels with the feeling of Ty inside me.

Already, the tingling started at the base of my balls. My body began to tremble, my thighs shaking.

"Fuck me. Give me your load. Fill my ass the way no one ever has."

"Oh shit." Ty's thrusts got messier, more erratic, just as my balls tightened and the hot spurt of cum shot from me, onto my hand and the mattress below me. Ty's dick jerked, grew and throbbed, his hold on me tightening as he cried out and filled the condom with his release. "Shit, that was good." He tugged off the rubber and got rid of it.

"Yeah, I know."

We fell to the bed together, held each other, sweaty and with jizz all over me. I lay on my back, Ty on his side, looking down at me.

"You don't always wear your rings and bracelets, but you do this necklace." He fingered the chain around my neck.

"It was my grandpa's. I was young when he died, but I remember it vividly. He told me I was special…that he was proud of me… He told me it was okay to be sensitive and that in a lot of ways, it was a good thing. I fucking hated that for years—that he'd called me *sensitive*—because it *does* feel like that's a bad thing sometimes. But it is what it is, I guess."

"It's not bad, Brax. It's one of my favorite things

about you. It's why I like you so much. It's what makes me want to do better…to be more." I groaned. "Stop. I'm serious."

He was, and I appreciated it. "I know. I feel comfortable being that way with you." Which was really fucking difficult to admit, but it was true.

"We're gross."

"Super gross," I agreed.

"But kinda cute too."

I grinned. "Yeah, I am."

We laughed, and kissed, and would I ever enjoy anything as much as laughing with Ty and kissing him?

CHAPTER TWENTY-EIGHT

Ty

"WHERE'S YOUR MAN?" Collins asked, the four of us sitting in the courtyard outside Adler House. It was an awesome day—sunny and midsixties, everything I loved about living in San Luco.

"He's at work," I replied, my heart going a little crazy for no apparent reason. It did that a lot when I thought about Brax or talked about Brax, and...yeah, I wasn't dumb enough not to know what that meant. I just hadn't allowed myself to say the words, even in my head. I pretended to be a dumbass because it was easier that way.

"You're like, really fucking into this guy, aren't you?" Watty asked.

For a second, I thought about lying, about playing it cool, but I felt like I might burst out of my skin.

"Yes. God yes. It's ridiculous, really. You guys should make fun of me. I would totally make fun of you if the situation were reversed." My friends laughed. "I'm serious. I think I might…" The words stuck in my throat like I suddenly had the worst case of cotton mouth. "Nope. I can't do it. You have a booger in your nose."

Ford gave me the finger, not falling for my change of subject. "So basically what you're saying is, when we teased you about being in love, it was the truth."

"I believe you said that, not me."

"I believe you didn't argue," Ford countered.

"Yeah, well, that doesn't mean anything." Another round of laughter echoed around us, making even the stoners coming out of Stormer House look over at us like we were crazy. We all knew that meant everything.

"Does he feel the same?" Collins questioned.

I appreciated the fact that they had my back with Brax. It had been rough initially, but since the party and beer pong, they'd been cool.

"First, I didn't confirm feeling anything. You guys are assuming. Second, I don't know. We just talk about how gross we are over each other, which means…yeah? Maybe?"

"Can I just say that I'm straight but that being with a guy sounds awesome? You don't have to admit anything and can just call each other gross?" Ford shoved a handful of chips into his mouth.

"Yeah, but then how do I know if he feels the same?" Shit. I'd asked that question, hadn't I? I turned around to make sure there wasn't another me there.

The picnic table got quiet, all of them looking at me like they couldn't believe I'd asked that either.

"Ha-ha. Just…kidding?"

I tried to stand, but Collins put a hand on my arm. "Nope. You can't get out of this. You said it, so now we're dealing with it. We can do this. We can give relationship advice."

My gaze shifted between my three closest friends. I couldn't say I was convinced. "I'm not sure that you can."

"Tell him you love him when you're fucking," Watty said. "That's what they always do in movies and shit. Then if he doesn't say it back, you can pretend it was in the heat of the moment and…I don't know, that you really meant you love his dick or his ass."

I grabbed one of Ford's chips and threw it at Watty's head. "That was the dumbest thing I've ever heard."

"Is it, though? He has a point," Collins added.

"Shut up."

"Or!" Ford jumped in. "Write him a letter. *Do you love me*, and then draw two boxes, one marked yes and one marked no. I'd give it to him for you if you wanted."

"Fuck yes. Do that!" Watty backslapped him. "Or you can just send me to ask him. I'd take it seriously. I'd be like... *It started over dick, but now that doesn't do the trick. The two of you share so much laughter. Ty wants to be your happily ever after.*" He shoved to his feet and threw his arms in the air. "I am the romance king! That was so badass."

Ford high-fived him, followed by Collins. When he held his hands out for the same from me, I had to give him his props. It actually wasn't too bad. "You just came up with that on the fly?"

Watty sat back down. "Awesome, right?"

"What about Mr. Romance? You can always contact him for an *I love you* plan," Ford suggested. Mr.

Romance was a guy on campus who'd, for a fee, plan a romantic date for anyone who wanted help. People who'd used him raved about him.

"I don't think I need that much help." I could handle this.

"If all else fails, you can just ask him, seriously tell him how you feel," Collins offered.

"Not nearly as fun, but it could work," Ford added.

"I guess I'd support that option too." Watty winked.

I looked down at the table, drew circles on it. "Thanks, guys. For having my back."

"We're your boys. That's what friends are for," Collins said. It was, and I was lucky to have them.

"Now let's get our asses to practice so I can show you up on the field." I stood, and they did the same.

We got ready and headed for lacrosse. Practice was awesome. Coach complimented me more than once. I threw a killer Around-the-World pass that was nothing less than a thing of beauty.

When it was over, I hurried to the locker room, since I had to work tonight. But before I could make my escape, Coach called, "Langley!"

Fuck. I'd been so close. I turned back, my friends going on without me. "Yeah, Coach?"

"Good practice today."

I wanted to remind him that he'd been so worried I couldn't handle my job, school, and lacrosse, but I was making it work. That I was having my best season, and that I was happy, and regardless of how I played, shouldn't that be the most important thing? But I just answered, "Thank you."

I took a quick shower, got dressed, then made my way to Shenanigans. Was it ridiculous that my stomach felt slightly fluttery when I walked inside and Brax looked up at me with a smile? Oh God, it was true. I was so totally fucking in love with this guy, and I *liked* it. I didn't even know it was possible to feel this way.

When Brax frowned, I realized I was standing there staring at him, looking like a dopey motherfucker. I shook my head and walked over. "You miss me?"

"You should have seen how you were looking at me just now. It's clear *you* missed *me*." He leaned in and pressed a kiss to my lips. There were some *awws* in the background because obviously everyone realized we were cute as fuck.

"Shut up and get back to work," Brax told them.

"Why is being brooding and grumpy so hot?"

"Go do your work, dish bitch," Brax teased.

"Our love language is insults," I joked back, then headed to the kitchen. I was a few minutes early, so I took a quick piss and washed my hands. It was almost time to clock in when my cell buzzed.

Seeing Dad's name on the screen, I almost slid it back into my pocket and ignored it, but the hairs on the back of my neck stood on end, something telling me I needed to answer. "I only have a couple of minutes. It's almost time for my shift," I said instead of hello.

"I just wanted to let you know I'll be in town late tonight. I'd like to see you tomorrow."

My spine stiffened, a sinking feeling in my gut. "Why?"

"I have business in Southern California. And do I need a reason to see my son?"

"You know I don't—"

"Your temper tantrum has gone on long enough, Tyson. You're upset with me. I get it. I was wrong, but nothing will change the fact that we're family. I'm still your father whether you want me to be or not."

I opened my mouth, but nothing came out. Why couldn't I find it in me to tell him he wasn't my family anymore? Why, after what he'd done, couldn't I stand up to him more? Why was there a part of me that still wanted to make him proud? Feelings were so fucked up, so confusing and hypocritical, but so damn strong. "We can have lunch. That's it," I found myself saying.

"Okay. We'll eat at the restaurant in my hotel, like we usually do. Meet me at one o'clock. What about this boyfriend of yours? Your mother told me you're seeing someone. I'd like to meet him."

No, he wouldn't. Not really. He would hate Brax. He wouldn't think he was good enough for me. But the truth was, I wanted Brax there. Wanted his support. Wanted my dad to know how much Brax meant to me and that I would never hurt him the way he'd hurt my mom. "I'll see if he's free." And he would be if I asked him to. I had no doubt Brax would find a way to be there if he knew I needed him.

"I'll see you tomorrow, Tyson."

"Yeah, see you tomorrow."

I was in a strange daze as I clocked in and got to work. When I headed back into the main part of the bar, I put on my best smile, cleaned tables, made jokes, and pretended everything was okay.

Brax was watching me, though. In some ways, that was nothing new. We watched each other a lot, probably part of the whole us being gross for each other and me being in love with him.

That definitely wasn't what I should be thinking about… Now, instead of just freaking out about my dad, I was also losing my shit again about being in love with Brax.

A couple of hours later, I approached the counter, and Brax lowered his voice to ask, "Are you good? Something's up."

It was sweet as shit that he'd asked, that he could tell, but also a little unnerving. "Just not feeling great," I lied, but I was scared that if we kept talking, I'd end up saying, *It started over dick, but now that doesn't do the trick. The two of us share so much laughter. I want to be your happily ever after.* Followed by a side of, *That means I love you*, and then adding for good measure, *Also, my dad will be in town tomorrow, so come have lunch with us, please?*

"Lacrosse," he said when I tried to walk away.

There was no doubt in my mind he didn't believe

me. "Later, okay?"

"Yeah, okay," he said, then kissed me again, which made my toes curl.

We kept an eye on each other all night, and I couldn't help wondering if this was what it felt like for everyone. Had my dad ever felt this way about my mom? And if so, how could he have ever wanted someone else instead?

When our shift ended, we walked together toward Liberty Court, where Brax had left his motorcycle. One of the guys in the stoner house was letting him use his parking spot.

"What happened, Ty? Tonight wasn't like you."

No, it wasn't, was it? "Do I have to talk about it?" I asked in my best whining voice.

"Nope. But I'd appreciate it if you did."

"I hate it when you act more grown-up than me."

He grinned. "So you hate me all the time?"

"Basically." We walked for a couple of minutes in silence before I said, "My dad is coming to town tonight. I agreed to have lunch with him tomorrow, and I'm kinda freaking the fuck out about it."

"Shit. Way to drop it on you at the last minute."

"Right? But that's what he does. He caught me off

guard, and hell, I think he knows I won't ignore him in real life." He had more power over me than I wanted to admit. "He wants you to come, by the way."

His voice was huskier when he asked, "Do *you* want me to?"

"Yes." It was true. I wanted Brax there. Somehow I knew that would make it easier.

"Okay, then I'll be there."

The courtyard outside Adler was quiet when we arrived. I motioned toward one of the picnic tables, and Brax followed me over. I sat on top, and he stood between my legs, hooking his finger beneath my chin and tilting my head up so I looked at him. The moon sat high in the sky, shedding light down on us. "I'm sorry. You okay?"

I was right then, at that moment, with him. I nodded, leaned in, brushed his lips with mine. Brax opened up, letting me lick my way inside. He tasted familiar, felt familiar. I wrapped my legs around him. His hand tangled in my hair, and God, why did this feel so good? What made someone *the one* for another person? Because whatever it was, Brax was that for me.

When our lips parted, I dropped my head to his chest. He tickled my nape with the tips of his fingers. "You can do this. You can tell him. You'll feel better when you do." My spine stiffened. I was pretty sure Brax felt it, and while he didn't let go of me, his gentle circles on my nape stopped. "Is that not what you're worried about? *Are you* going to tell him?"

Shame singed my skin, made my gut roll. Why was this so hard? Why did I care what my dad thought? Why did I still want to make him proud? "I don't know. Why does it matter? It's not like you deal with your brother any better." The snippy words tumbled out of my mouth before I could stop them. I wasn't even sure why I'd said it. Embarrassment? All that shame I couldn't tamp down?

Brax pulled away, his lips in a hard line. "What the fuck are you even talking about? All I did was ask a question. What does this have to do with me and Asher?"

"It's how you said it," I doubled down, the whole time my brain telling my mouth to shut up, but it wouldn't listen. "It was judgy." And we both knew that Brax could be that way.

He crossed his arms and shook his head. "Maybe

that's your guilty conscience talking. Don't take your anger for your dad and yourself out on me. I didn't do shit."

The guilty-conscience comment made my pulse spike. "You act like I'm the only one who wants to keep the peace, Brax. Like I'm the only one who stands up for myself but just to a certain point before I accept shit. You do the exact same thing. Hell, you're letting your brother do God knows what in your grandma's house just so you don't have to deal with him."

"I did that for you!" he shouted. And maybe partly he had, but not completely.

"You did it for you too. He walks all over you. You have to lock your bedroom door and can't keep your food in the kitchen. You clean up his messes and learn to sleep through his parties instead of telling him to have some fucking respect for the fact that you're working your goddamned ass off *and* going to school. I'm not the only one who doesn't have the balls to stand up to people he loves, so don't judge me for it."

At some point, I'd pushed off the table but couldn't even say when. We stood a few feet apart, staring at each other, heat between us, missing the playful, sexual tension that had always been between us, even when we thought we didn't get along.

"I'm gonna head out," was all he said.

"Fuck," I cursed quietly. "Brax." I hadn't meant to say any of that, but it didn't make it less true. "I don't want to fight with you."

"I don't either. That's why I'm going. Have a good lunch with your dad."

He didn't look at me as he turned and walked away. And I was a dumbass who just stood there and watched him go…wishing for a do-over, wishing we hadn't fought and that I'd told him I loved him instead.

CHAPTER TWENTY-NINE

Brax

THE HOUSE WAS a disaster when I got home, but Asher wasn't there. Dishes littered the counters. Beer cans, bottles of hard alcohol, and food containers were scattered around the room, some on their sides, leftovers spilled on the floor. "Fuck." I dropped my head back, looked at the ceiling...tried not to think about Ty.

Ty, who'd gotten under my skin.

Ty, whom I wanted to be curled up in bed with.

Still, instead of going back to him, I started to clean up. I wasn't doing it for Asher, but for Grandma. This was her house, and I didn't want it to get fucked up. Which was true...but it also wasn't, because leaving Asher here by himself ever since his fight with Ty wasn't taking care of Grandma's house.

It was giving Asher free rein.

It took me almost two hours to return the place to a semblance of normal. When it was done, I unlocked my door and went into my room. It smelled slightly stale, having only been opened when I came in or out to get something before heading back to Ty's.

I sat on the edge of the mattress, leg bouncing. One of Ty's hoodies lay across the pillows. I wanted to smell it, which was all sorts of fucked up. He had totally taken over my thoughts, my world, and damned if I didn't like that.

But being the stubborn asshole that I was, I didn't head back to his place. Didn't call or text. I tried to sleep but couldn't, and not because of Asher either. For whatever reason, he hadn't come home.

Before dawn, I got up, showered, dressed, and jumped on my bike for a ride. It always helped me clear my head.

I ended up at the beach I'd taken Ty to. I sat in the sand where we'd been, and tried to figure out how we'd gotten from there to where we were now; how I didn't wish it was any other way. Well, I didn't want to fight with him. I'd change that shit but not the rest of it.

Just as pinks and oranges began to color the sky, I took a photo, because of course I did. I was a mopey motherfucker after my first fight with my boyfriend, whom I was never even supposed to like.

I sat out there for a long while. When it wasn't ridiculously early, I went to see my grandma.

"Uh-oh," she said when I stepped into her room.

"Uh-oh, what?" In reality, I wasn't surprised at all she knew something was wrong.

She sighed.

"Nothing's wrong." *Liar, liar, pants on fire.* She cocked a brow at me. Fuck my life. "Fine, something's wrong."

She sat in one of the chairs by the picture window, and I took the one beside her.

"I got in an argument with Ty."

"Oh, Brax." She reached over and grabbed my hand. "What happened?"

I started with the fight with Asher. How Ty had stuck up for me, approached Asher so I could sleep on a night before the test. How after that I'd been staying with him and we'd defined the relationship, before ending with what had happened last night.

She was quiet for a moment, her hold on me

tightening. "You know he's right about a lot of that, don't you?" I closed my eyes, knowing she was going to say that and that she was correct. "How many times have you come in here and made excuses for why Asher doesn't visit? How many times have you taken on his screwups and choices as your own? You did that with your father too."

I let go of her, leaned forward, elbows on my knees and hands in my hair.

"Maybe..." she continued, "that's one of the things you and Ty have in common. You both have big hearts, even though you try to hide them. You love Asher and you love me, so you try to make up for his shortcomings, and you let him walk all over you...and Ty, he's angry with his father, but he wants to make him proud."

"How does following his heart mean he's not making his dad proud?"

"It doesn't, but for whatever reason, Ty's decided that it does. In here." She touched her chest. "When it comes to his father, maybe that's where he sees his worth. That doesn't make it true, but our hearts and minds are good at playing tricks on us sometimes, just like yours did with you, because part of the reason you walked away last night wasn't because of what Ty said, but the fact that you love him, you don't feel worthy of him, and you're afraid that if you meet his dad, he won't approve and Ty will change his mind."

My gaze shot to hers, and I was scared of what she saw when she looked back at me—the truth, the one I hadn't realized until just that second. She was right. I loved Ty. I wanted him to love me too, and if he couldn't even tell his dad he wanted to be a nurse, that he wanted to *help sick people*, how would he ever choose me? How could he ever tell his dad he loved me? Maybe it would end up like it had when people found out about me and Wayne. "I..." Damn. This sucked. I didn't even know what to say.

"He loves you too."

"How do you know?"

"Because I do. I see the way that boy looks at you, and I see the way you look at him. But even more importantly, you're worthy. Anyone would be lucky to have you. You're smart, kind, funny, and adorably grumpy." I couldn't help smiling. "You care about others. You take care of me. If Ty doesn't see that—though I don't think that's the case—if he lets you go, it's his loss. If his dad doesn't approve of you, well, he'll have me to deal with, and I'm a lot tougher than I look."

This time, my smile settled into a chuckle. "You're the strongest person I know."

"Funny, I think the same about you."

"Asher is screwing up. He's partying all the time. He sees Dad. I make excuses for why he doesn't come here when really, it's just him being a jerk." God, I let him chase me out of my own house, our grandma's house, when I couldn't even trust him to take care of it.

Shit was gonna change.

I was gonna change.

"Whatever he does, Asher is responsible for his own decisions, just like your father was, and just like you are right now. I have no doubt you'll set everything right."

I wasn't sure I had the same faith in myself she did, but I sure as shit was gonna try.

CHAPTER THIRTY

Ty

LOVE WAS DUMB.

I'd spent all last night and this morning feeling sad, missing Brax, and okay, maybe I was a little annoyed too. The I-don't-like-you, sexy fighting with Brax was way more fun than the real kind, the one where you loved the other, didn't know if they felt the same, and the two of you walked away mad. This wasn't my favorite part of having a boyfriend, and…did I even still have one? I assumed so. When he left, he said he didn't want to fight with me, not that he didn't want to be with me. I supposed I could message him and find out, but I had lunch with my dad and needed to keep my head on straight.

"I can't believe he bailed on you today," Ford said. I'd spilled my guts to them last night, telling them about Dad and my siblings and wanting to be a nurse. It was as if my fight with Brax had cut me open and I couldn't hold all my truth inside anymore. The guys were cool, stayed up with me most of the night and had only been a little pissed at me for not trusting them enough to tell them all that shit earlier.

"I said some not so great things to him. It's not his fault. We were both being dumbasses." I was pretty sure that came with the territory of being a twenty-one-year-old, but that didn't make it any easier.

"Still, though…and all that shit with your dad. It's heavy." Watty gave me a sad smile.

"Thanks for the reminder." I knew he meant well, but I was already all up in my feels, and talking about it didn't help.

I finished getting ready and headed to the hotel where my dad always stayed when he came to town. I pulled up out front, the valet already there to take my car. Nerves attacked my insides, waging a full-fledged war in my belly. I checked my phone one more time to see if I had a text from Brax, but I didn't. It made my stomach twist even more. Not only did I have my dad to deal with, but I couldn't seem to stop thinking about Brax, wishing last night had gone down better.

After this, I'll go talk to him.

With a deep breath, I walked through the sliding doors and into the upscale hotel. The restaurant was to the right. We'd had plenty of lunches and dinners there over the three years I'd been at FU. I spotted my dad right away. He was wearing slacks and a button-up shirt like he always did, but missing a blazer. I knew he had work afterward, but even if he hadn't, my dad rarely dressed down more than this.

He was typing on his phone. The thing almost never left his hand. He was busy, I got it, but it was sad that I couldn't remember a time when our conversation hadn't been interrupted by a text, email, or call he absolutely had to take.

We looked so much alike…same blond hair, same blue eyes, same slender nose and high cheekbones.

As I approached the table, he immediately frowned. "I thought your friend was joining us."

My dad had no problems with my bisexuality, so I knew that wasn't the reason he'd labeled Brax the way he had, but still, it rubbed me the wrong way. "He's my boyfriend. Remember you called him that yesterday? Something came up." He raised a brow as if he didn't believe me. *Great job, Ty. Maybe next time come up with a story beforehand.*

I pulled out a chair and sat across from him. We stared at each other, each waiting for the other to speak. My dad and I were similar more than just physically. We were both stubborn and liked to be right.

Finally, he said, "I appreciate your coming today."

Oh. I hadn't expected that. I shrugged, unsure how to respond.

"We can't keep going the way we have been. I won't accept this behavior. I know you're angry with me, but I'm still your father. Playing these silly games doesn't change that."

My brows drew together. "Silly games?" I asked, just as the waitress approached. I hadn't even looked at the menu, but at this point, I didn't give a shit what we ordered. I wanted to know what he meant by that.

"I'd like the blackened salmon, rice, and steamed broccoli," Dad ordered, smooth as honey. From the outside, you wouldn't know we'd been talking about something serious.

I was craving a big, fat burger and some fries, but I just asked for the same so we could continue our conversation.

When she walked away, I asked, "What silly games are you talking about?"

"Ignoring my calls or being disrespectful when we speak, that job at the bar. Your grades are slipping. Coach has kept me in the loop with those, and I can't help wondering if any of it has to do with this new boy you've been spending time with."

Brax? He was going to blame this on Brax? My chest tightened. My breathing rushed out in quick, short pants. "Are you kidding me right now? I recently found out I have a twenty-year-old brother, a toddler sister, oh, and my dad left my mom for his baby mama, and you're blaming shit that's not even a real problem on Brax? He's the only thing that's kept me sane!"

"Lower your voice, Tyson," Dad said between tight lips.

"I like my job, Dad. It makes me feel responsible, like I have something that's just mine, ya know? Something I didn't get because of you or Mom. And I'm not talking to you because you hurt me, because you hurt Mom and you took my siblings away from me. Did you know I'm actually jealous of Perry? That

I both envy him and feel bad for him because I had you and he just had money? That I want to meet him but I'm scared because I think he might hate me? I would hate me if I were him."

He flinched, his eyes softening slightly. "Tyson, I—"

"No. Let me do this. I deserve to get this out." We were lucky the restaurant wasn't too busy, the tables around us empty. Even if they weren't, I wouldn't have cared. I needed to say these words. I needed to tell him how I felt. I needed to know he loved me even if I wasn't a mirror image of him. "I spent my whole life wanting to be like you, looking up to you, thinking you were the best man I've ever known, and now, now I see you're just human, like the rest of us. You're flawed, and you make mistakes, and you hurt people. Maybe that shouldn't have come as a surprise to me, but it did.

"And somehow, that truth turned my world upside down, because a part of me still wants you to look at me the way you always have, to make you proud and never disappoint you, while the rest of me is pissed and hurt and so fucking tired of pretending I'm you, that I could be you, or that I want to be you."

I tilted my head down, gaze in my lap. I couldn't look at him, wasn't sure what I would see there and how it might change things. We were both quiet for a moment, the air around us thick and stifling.

"I'm sorry, Tyson. I don't know what I can say other than that. I want what's best for you, and clearly, I haven't always gone about that in the right ways."

"But what about Perry? Don't you want what's best for him too? Why me? Why did I get to be the one you raised? Do you know how terrible I feel about that?"

"It's complicated," he replied softly, with emotion he didn't typically show. "It wasn't just my decision. His mother made it as well. We decided it was what's best and—"

"And now he and I suffer for your decisions?" I ran a hand through my hair. "God, I have so much shit to unpack. Some of it, I didn't even realize it until recently. The rest I've been holding in for years. Did you know I hate tech? That I want nothing to do with computers or Langley Enterprises? Why is it automatically mine and not Perry's? I want to go to nursing school. I want to work with the elderly, and I fought with Brax last night, the guy I'm in love with, because I was angry and embarrassed that I didn't have the balls to tell you. And now I'm afraid I'm going to lose him and—"

"You're not," Brax's soft voice said from behind me. I whipped around in my chair, and he was there, hair styled, wearing slacks and a nice button-up white shirt because he'd wanted to look nice for my dad...because he wanted to make a good impression. "You're not gonna lose me, Lacrosse. I went and did something stupid and fell in love with you too."

My face hurt, my smile was so big, like my head was just going to crack in half because of it. "You did?" I asked, before shaking my head. "I mean, of course you did."

He reached out, cupped my face, brushed his thumb over my cheekbone. "I'm proud of you. You're gonna be the best nurse I know."

"Do you know many others?"

"The ones at the assisted-living facility. Best nurse in California?" He cocked a brow.

"I plan to shoot higher than that."

He rolled his eyes, bent forward, and pressed a

soft kiss to my lips, making every nerve ending inside me spark with electricity. Then he straightened his back, held out his hand to my dad, and said, "Nice to meet you, Mr. Langley. I'm Braxton Walker."

My dad shook it. "You too…and please, call me Montgomery." Dad's voice was terse, wary, but he'd still said it.

Brax pulled out the chair beside me and sat down.

Dad's gaze darted between us. The disapproval was there, the initial judgment when he knew nothing about Brax, but he didn't mention it. Instead, he held my stare. "So…a nurse, huh?"

Brax put his arm around me.

"Yeah," I replied.

"You thought you couldn't tell me that? Why would I be angry with you for wanting to help people?" Dad frowned, the question clear in the wrinkles around his eyes.

I could understand why it sounded silly, but he also couldn't pretend he hadn't put expectations on me. "Because you never gave me a choice. It was always understood I'd be just like you. That I would play lacrosse, go to FU, then take over Langley Enterprises."

He sighed, looked down at the table, before our gazes met again. "I've made a lot of mistakes in my life, son. I have a lot to make up for, but regardless of what I've done, I have always loved you…and your siblings. And if you'll allow me to, I'd like to work on making it up to you."

"All of us?" I wouldn't allow it to be just about me, or hell, even just me and Ainsley.

"That's up to Perry."

Fair enough. "Maybe we can talk some more later? Just me and you?" Because none of it could be fixed with one conversation, but if he was willing to try, I was too.

"I'd like that," Dad replied, before turning to Brax. He cleared his throat, uncomfortable, but asked, "So, tell me a little about yourself."

"He likes computers, Dad. He's majoring in computer science, and he's a whole hell of a lot better at it than me. He's always forcing me to study and do my homework."

Light sparked in Dad's eyes. Just like that, he started to see a different side of Brax. "Oh really?" he asked before launching into a whole conversation about shit I didn't care about, but I liked hearing it simply because it was Brax talking to my dad. Mom already liked him, and now Dad would get to know him too.

We stayed at the restaurant for close to two hours. Dad insisted Brax order food too, and we talked long after we were done eating. For the first time, Dad didn't answer any calls or texts.

When we were done, the three of us walked to the lobby together, and Dad said, "I'm sure the two of you want to spend some time together. I'm not gonna lie, I do need to get some work done, but do you think we could talk some more after your game tomorrow?"

"I'd like that," I answered honestly. We were both trying, both being honest with each other, and because of that, I had hope that we could get to a better place. There was a lot more I had to tell him about my hurt over the years, but we'd landed at a starting place, and for now, that was enough.

"It was very nice to meet you, Brax. I hope the three of us can get together again soon."

"Just have your people call my people," my boyfriend joked.

Dad chuckled. "He has your sense of humor, I

see."

"I'm funnier and he's grumpier."

"He has the second part of that right." Brax took my hand. My dad waved at us, and then we turned around and headed for the door.

CHAPTER THIRTY-ONE

Brax

"GOD, THIS FUCKING collar. How in the hell do people wear this shit?" I let go of Ty's hand the second we stepped outside and immediately started to open the top couple of buttons.

"Dude…you totally dressed up to meet my dad."

"Shut up."

"You also told me you love me."

"I'm also telling you to shut up again." I'd almost swallowed my damn tongue when I'd walked in and heard what he was saying, heard him admit he wanted to be a nurse and that he loved me. He'd had no idea I was there. Ty could have lied, could have focused on the career stuff, could have avoided mentioning me…but he'd *chosen* me. Stood up for me again, wasn't ashamed to be with me like Wayne had been.

As if reading each other's minds, we headed for the beach. The hotel—one of the nicest in San Luco, of course—was close to the ocean, but we didn't head for the water, going instead to a bench on the sidewalk just steps away from the sand.

"I'm sorry about last night, Ty, and hell, about being late today. I knew how big of a deal this was to you. I should have been here from the start."

"Yeah, well, I'm sorry too because I was a dick. I never should have said that stuff about Asher."

I shrugged. "Maybe you shouldn't have. Maybe I shouldn't have said stuff to you either, but the truth is, we were both right. And honestly, it needed to come out. I didn't walk away because of what you said. I walked away because of me."

Ty frowned. "What do you mean?"

Fuck, this was hard. "Do we have to be the kind of boyfriends who talk to each other about important stuff?" I teased.

"I think so."

"Are you sure?"

Ty leaned in and kissed me. Somehow, that helped. "I guess I didn't feel like I deserved you. I thought it was easier to just walk away. I was scared your dad would hate me, or hell, that you'd wake up and realize you can do better."

"Fuck that. You deserve whatever you want, Brax. No one gets me the way you do. There's no one I like sparring verbally with more than you. Even without that, you're the best person I know."

"Can you say that louder? I don't think I heard you."

Ty laughed, and it was perfect and so us.

"I want you, Brax. You challenge me, and I know I do that for you too. We're good together. I mean, dude, I used the *L* word about you, *to my dad*, whom I only had the balls to be honest with because of you."

"God, this is so weird." I rubbed a hand over my face. "I can't believe we're in love with each other."

"Same."

"But I do…love you. I went to see Grandma. She helped wake my dumb ass up. I tried to get here earlier, but I had to buy clothes and get ready, then find your friends and figure out where in the hell you were."

"You did all that for me?" Ty asked playfully.

"I'd do more," I admitted. "Did you look at my Instagram page?"

"What? No." He pulled his phone out.

"I'm a way better boyfriend than you. I checked yours when you posted for me."

"That's because you were jealous and wanted my dick in your mouth."

I chuckled.

He pulled up the photo of the sunrise. The caption read: *Done playing games. I want you.* "I…"

"Not gonna lie, I changed that caption later in the day," I admitted.

"It's still sweet."

"That's because I'm a better boyfriend than you. We've gone over this."

Ty opened up the comments on my post and typed: *I love you.* "Beat that. I just *really* defined our relationship to the whole world. You didn't even tag me."

"No one even knows about that account."

He opened the camera, took a photo of us, and posted it. He typed: *My boyfriend is hot*, then tagged me.

"Fuuuuuck."

"You asked for it."

We laughed together again, and Ty reached over and grabbed my hand.

"Grandma and I are gonna sit down and talk with Asher together. I have a lot I need to tell him, a lot to get off my chest. I'm done letting him walk all over me, and Grandma has some shit she needs to say too."

"Good. You both deserve better than how he treats you."

I shrugged. I didn't have high hopes. I wanted more for him, but I worried Asher was too much like our dad. He would have to get his shit together, though, or get out. That wasn't just my stipulation; it was Grandma's too.

"You realize what we're doing, right?" Ty asked. "We're growing up."

"I've already been grown."

"Yeah, okay. Keep lying to yourself." When I didn't reply, Ty added, "We can't be *too* responsible. Wanna go blow each other in the empty classroom?"

"Fuck yeah. But you're getting on your knees first."

Ty smiled. "As if I'd want anything else."

I'd spent my whole life not letting anyone in, afraid to count on people, and then, as it happened, it was an annoying, cocky jock who broke down my walls and taught me it was okay to love someone. I wouldn't have it any other way.

EPILOGUE

Ty

June

BRAX WAS STILL dead to the world when I slipped out of his bed. Until the end of the school year, we'd stayed at his house a few nights a week and at Adler the rest of the time. It was rare for us to sleep apart, and even though it'd been six months since the hookup that started it all, sometimes I still couldn't believe we were together. That was a good thing, though. We drove each other crazy in every way possible, but in my mind, that was all the more reason we would last. We just *worked*.

I sneaked out of his room, quietly closing the door behind me. Today was a big day. My brother was flying over, and we would meet face-to-face for the first time. We'd spent the last few months texting and sometimes talking on the phone, getting to know each other and trying to make the best of the fucked-up situation we'd been born into. But he was cool. We got along so far. Apparently, we'd both been worrying about a lot of the same issues, both of us feeling guilty for existing and wondering if the other might hate us.

Perry had never been to California, so he was going to spend a week out here, taking in the sights. Then I was flying back with him to spend a month with Mom, and Brax would be heading out for the last five days so he and Mom could meet before we came back to Cali together. Oscar was the fucking man, and we'd found a way to make it work so I would still have my job waiting for me when I returned.

In the meantime, now that the semester had ended, I was staying with Brax until the school year started and I could get another place on campus. My class load would be changing as well. I was officially going for my Bachelor of Science in Nursing and wouldn't graduate next year with Brax and my friends, but I was staying in San Luco with Brax, so that was all I cared about. I figured when he began his career before me, I could start calling him my sugar daddy. I liked to plan ahead.

"'Sup," Asher said when I walked into the kitchen.

"Hey." Things weren't perfect with him, but they were better. Before the big talk, I don't think he'd believed Brax or Matilda would ever force him to get his shit together. He'd thought he could walk all over them, the way their dad had.

He'd left for two months, determined he didn't need them, before coming back and asking to stay. Apparently, things had gone south with their dad. At a visit, he'd tried to get Asher into some things that had finally woken him up to the toxicity and who really cared about him.

It had been Asher who approached Brax and Matilda that time, asking Brax to meet him at the facility. For the first time in years, they'd had a meaningful discussion without Asher blowing it off and getting angry. Maybe seeing Brax and the positive relationships he had in his life, and comparing them to the lack of any substance in his own, had woken Asher up. He'd tried to be who his dad wanted him to be, which was something I was familiar with myself.

Asher was attempting to make changes. He'd gotten a job as a line cook at a chain restaurant, and he and Brax had a schedule worked out when it came to expectations at the house. So far, so good. I was pretty sure Asher still hated me, but I didn't give a fuck. As long as he was good to Brax, that was what mattered.

"You're doing that brother thing or whatever today, right?"

It was pretty cool of him to ask. He really was trying. "Yeah, we're gonna meet him in a little while." I pulled the eggs out of the fridge to scramble some.

"You nervous?"

"Hell yes."

Asher was quiet for a minute before saying, "Yeah, family can be fucked up sometimes." He looked away, and I figured he had to be talking about what happened with their dad.

"You can say that again." I began cracking eggs in the bowl. "You want some?"

"Nah, my ass has to get to work. I wouldn't be up yet if I didn't." He stood and went for the door just as Brax walked down the hallway. "Aw, my little baby brother." Asher wrapped an arm around Brax, trying to get him into a headlock to give him a noogie. He was…a confusing guy, that's for sure. One minute playful and clearly wanting a relationship with Brax, and the next he was up to no good.

"Don't make me kick your ass," Brax told him.

The two of them wrestled around for a minute before laughing and going their separate ways. Asher headed out, and Brax came into the kitchen.

"Look at you, cooking for your man. You're so sweet." He leaned in, licked my ear, then bit it.

"Who said I was making some for you?"

He teasingly fluttered his dark lashes.

"Umm, that shit doesn't work with me. I barter for sexual favors."

Brax laughed. "So fucking romantic."

"You don't want romance."

"You have a point. I just want my idiot boyfriend."

"Sexy idiot to you."

But we did make the eggs together, then ate and washed the dishes side by side. It wasn't something we liked to admit, but we were pretty fucking perfect together.

We showered, got dressed, then took my car to the San Diego airport. "I'm sorry I have to work tonight," Brax said. He went to full-time at Shenanigans during the summer, while I was still part-timing—and not to brag, but I'd gotten to the point where I didn't wear rubber gloves anymore when picking up dirty dishes.

Dad and I had come to an agreement. He was helping with school and I was accepting it, while also keeping my job. *And*, we were doing telehealth therapy together biweekly to work through our shit.

"It's all right," I told Brax. "The three of us will hang out later. Tonight Perry and I can do our own thing, or we can come to the bar and laugh at you while you work."

"That's nice of you."

"That's what boyfriends are for." I waggled my brows. "And we gotta take him to meet Matilda on Sunday." She was absolutely one of my favorite people, not just because of how awesome she was, but because of how completely she loved Brax.

"God, it's so annoying how domestic we are. I don't even recognize myself anymore."

I glanced his way. "Are you complaining?"

He gave me a playfully cocky grin. "No."

We got to the airport early and parked. The first time I met Perry, I didn't want to just pull up and have my brother toss his shit in my ride. He still didn't want anything to do with Dad, and I couldn't blame him. And even though he didn't fault me for anything, I still felt guilty. Hopefully with time that would get better.

I paced in front of baggage claim, nerves beating at my insides.

"Hey," Brax said. He pulled me close, cupped my face, the familiar press of his lips moving against mine. "You're good. It'll be great. I got your back."

"I know. You spent three years trying to get with me. I mean, that right there shows how much you want me."

"What the fuck ever. It's the other way around."

"You were like… *You're so hot, Ty. I wanna bang you, Ty. Will you be my boyfriend forever and ever?*"

"Wait, you're hot?" a voice came from behind Brax. I looked over his shoulder, my heart suddenly slam-dancing against my chest. Standing right there, was my brother. He didn't look like Dad and me. Perry had dark hair and brown eyes, but his smile was similar to my own. "Sorry. I didn't mean to interrupt the lovefest the two of you had going on. Should I come back later?"

"Maybe like ten minutes or so?" I joked.

"I can get my luggage and come back." Perry smiled.

I couldn't say which one of us moved first, but the next thing I knew, we held each other in a tight hug.

"It's good to meet you," he said softly.

"Yeah, you too."

When we parted, his gaze traveled to Brax, and he grinned. "Your boyfriend's hot." He'd seen Brax before, of course, in video calls and photos, but if it had been me, I would have said the same thing.

"I know, right?" I replied.

"Holy shit. There are two of you? I'm so fucked." Brax shook his head, and I knew right then that everything was going to be okay.

Find Riley:

Newsletter

Reader's Group
facebook.com/groups/RileysRebels2.0

Facebook
facebook.com/rileyhartwrites

Twitter
twitter.com/RileyHart5

Goodreads
goodreads.com/author/show/7013384.Riley_Hart

Instagram
instagram.com/rileyhartwrites

BookBub
bookbub.com/profile/riley-hart

Thanks so much for reading Playing Games! If you're curious about Marshall and Felix, you can grab their story, The Dating Disaster.

Want more from me? Grab your copy of Boyfriend Goals!

Meet all the couples of Franklin U!

Brax and Ty's story:
Playing Games

Marshall and Felix's story:
The Dating Disaster

Charlie and Liam's story:
Mr. Romance

Spencer and Cory's story:
Bet You

Chris and Aidan's story:
The Glow Up

Cobey and Vincent's story:
Learning Curve

Alex and Remy's story:
Making Waves

Peyton and Levi's story:
Football Royalty

Series by Riley Hart

Secrets Kept
Briar County
Atlanta Lightning
Blackcreek
Boys In Makeup with Christina Lee
Broken Pieces
Crossroads
Fever Falls with Devon McCormack
Finding
Forbidden Love with Christina Lee
Havenwood
Jared and Kieran
Last Chance
Metropolis with Devon McCormack
Rock Solid Construction
Saint and Lucky
Stumbling Into Love
Wild side

Standalone books:
Boyfriend Goals

Strings Attached
Beautiful & Terrible Things
Love Always
Endless Stretch Of Blue
Looking For Trouble
His Truth

Standalone books with Devon McCormack:
No Good Mitchell
Beautiful Chaos
Weight Of The World
Up For The Challenge

Standalone books with Christina Lee:
Science & Jockstraps
Of Sunlight and Stardust

About the Author

Riley Hart is the girl who wears her heart on her sleeve. Although she primarily focuses on male/male romance, under her various pen names, she's written a little bit of everything. Regardless of the sub-genre, there's always one common theme and that's…romance! No surprise seeing as she's a hopeless romantic herself. Riley's a lover of character-driven plots, flawed characters, and always tries to write stories and characters people can relate to. She believes everyone deserves to see themselves in the books they read. When she's not writing, you'll find her reading, traveling or dreaming about traveling. She has two perfectly sarcastic kids and a husband who still makes her swoon.

Riley Hart is represented by Jane Dystel at Dystel, Goderich & Bourret Literary Management. She's a 2019 Lambda Literary Award Finalist for *Of Sunlight and Stardust*. Under her pen name, her young adult novel, *The History of Us* is an ALA Rainbow Booklist

Recommended Read and *Turn the World Upside Down* is a Florida Authors and Publishers President's Book Award Winner.

Printed in Great Britain
by Amazon